GENTLEMEN DETECTIVES

- An Anthology of Short Stories -

British Library Cataloguing-in-Publication Data
A catalogue record for this book is available from the
British Library

Contents

Contents

GENTLEMEN DETECTIVES

Considering its pervasiveness within modern Western literature, one could be forgiven for thinking that the figure of the gentleman detective is an ancient one; on a par with archetypes such as the doomed hero or the wise fool. In actual fact, the well-bred crime-solver is relatively young, as literary character-types go. Emerging less than two centuries ago, the gentleman detective has undergone quite a trajectory, from intriguing eccentric to staple of crime fiction – one of the most consistently popular (and commercially lucrative) literary genres. The stories contained in this collection chart this trajectory, and speak to how the Western literary tradition has shaped the development of one of its most popular figures.

The first story in the collection is regarded as having invented both the figure of the gentleman detective, and modern detective fiction as a whole – fitting, perhaps, when one considers how much the latter came to be inseparable from the former. Edgar Allen Poe's "The Murders in the Rue Morgue" – first published by *Graham's Magazine* in April of 1841 – centres on a murderous crime, and the solving of that crime by a local Parisian named Monsieur C. Auguste Dupin. Dupin, we are told, is "of an excellent --indeed of an illustrious family," adores literature, shuns popular taste, and possesses "a peculiar analytic ability." He also takes a rather cool, detached approach to what Poe dubbed his "ratiocination." While these character traits might strike us as rather clichéd today – a sort of cut-out Sherlock Holmes – when Poe first created him, Dupin was a new breed.

Ten years after Poe's defining tale, Charles Dickens published his short essay "On Duty With Inspector Field" (1851). Although the

Charles Frederick Field upon whom Dickens based the piece was not strictly speaking a gentleman detective, in the essay he carries a number of characteristics which reveal how much characters like Dupin were beginning to permeate literary depictions of crime and crime-solving: Field exudes calm authority, possesses almost superhuman powers of perception, and has an unwavering sense of right and wrong.

Towards the end of the 1860s, another classic of the gentleman detective genre appeared: *The Moonstone* (1868), by Dickens' close friend Wilkie Collins. *The Moonstone* is widely considered the first true English detective novel in English, and its detective hero, Franklin Blake, wears "a beautiful fawn coloured suit, with gloves and hat to match," and after years of studying abroad carries "foreign airs" which cow various other characters.

A decade after Collins' novel, Anna Katherine Green published *The Leavenworth Case* (1878). A huge success, the novel cemented Green's place as "the mother of the detective novel," and laid out a framework for future writers such as Arthur Conan Doyle and Agatha Christie. Green's most famous creation was Ebenezer Gryce, of the New York Metropolitan Police Force – and it is a short story featuring Gryce (and detailing his origins) that features in this collection.

The 1880s saw the emergence of the famous gentleman detective of all time: Sir Arthur Conan Doyle's Sherlock Holmes. First appearing in *A Study in Scarlet* (1887), Holmes was tremendously popular with readers, and followed Poe's Dupin in cementing various archetypal characteristics of the gentleman detective: Holmes is well bred (his ancestors were "country squires"), he is educated (his speech is replete with references to Shakespeare), he has a taste for high culture (he enjoys classical music and opera), and he is both supremely intelligent and coldly rational.

However, perhaps going some way to explain his lasting appeal –

as recently as 2012, the BBC produced a BAFTA-winning television series titled *Sherlock* – Holmes is far from one-dimensional. He is not simply a cold logician; he is also a bohemian, chain-smoking night-owl with a cocaine habit and a penchant for bare-knuckle boxing. The two stories contained in this collection – "The Adventure of the Red-Headed League" (1891) and "The Adventure of the Speckled Band" (1892) – rank amongst the best Holmes tales outside of the novels. In 1927, writing for the *Strand Magazine*, Doyle selected them as "the best of the Holmes stories." In 1999, in a poll for the *Baker Street Journal*, Sherlockian experts and literary critics from around the globe agreed.

After the appearance of Holmes, the literary floodgates opened, and virtually every author of the day tried their hand at detective fiction. The sixth story in this collection, "The Stranger's Latchkey" (1909), features John Thorndyke. Created by R. Austin Freeman – a towering author in early 20th-century crime fiction, who Raymond Chandler later stated had "no equal in his genre" – Thorndyke is a medical doctor who has shifted to practicing law. However, despite his unusual position as a prototypical forensic scientist, Thorndyke still possesses many of the classic features of the gentleman detective: he is wealthy, cultured, intelligent, and possesses "a great reputation." Although authors were beginning to toy with their characterisations, the gentleman detective still retained those defining characteristics laid down seventy years early by Poe.

Starting in 1911, G. K. Chesterton – one of British literature's great turn of the century authors – turned his attentions to the detective story. In a typically Chesterton spin on the genre, though, his detective was not only highly civilized and deeply intelligent – he was also a Catholic priest. Father Brown is an intriguing counterpoint to Doyle's Sherlock Holmes: where Holmes is an intense, dominating presence, Father Brown is almost comically unobtrusive. Where Holmes is coldly and unrelentingly rational,

Father Brown is inclined towards the intuitive, and his investigative process is rooted in empathising deeply with both the criminal and his victim. "The Sign of the Broken Sword" and "The Hammer of God" are both from Chesterton's debut Father Brown collection, *The Innocence of Father Brown* (1911) – considered by many to be his best.

With 1914 came the first appearance of Ernest Bramah's Max Carrados. Although somewhat forgotten now, in his day Carrados appeared alongside Sherlock Holmes in the *Strand Magazine*, and frequently received the higher billing than his counterpart from Baker Street. In a highly original character twist, Carrados is a blind detective, having lost his sight in a riding accident. The story contained in this collection, "The Coin of Dionysius", details Carrados' origins, as well as those of his sidekick, Mr Carlyle. It is taken from the first Carrados anthology, *Max Carrados* (1914) – later dubbed by George Orwell as the one of "the only detective stories since Poe that are worth re-reading."

The tenth and final story in the collection was written by Edgar Wallace. Wallace was a prolific author, arguably most famous today for being the co-creator of *King Kong*. However, Wallace's best-known long-running character is the crime-fighter J. G. Reeder. Reeder is a tireless and efficient police officer with an uncanny ability to get inside the criminal mind. He also possesses a mean streak, and is willing to bend the rules – in this, he shows the influence of early American hardboiled fiction, with its more grizzled, less cerebral aesthetic. "Sheer Melodrama (The Man from the East)" is taken from *The Mind of Mr. J. G. Reeder* (1925), Wallace's most successful Reeder collection.

Like any literary archetype, then, the gentleman detective has undergone a long and steady evolution. Starting off as a fairly straightforward well-bred Englishman, he has since taken on all manner of characteristics – from a penchant for medical forensics, to a deep involvement with the Catholic faith, to physical blindness. The gentleman detective has even been reborn as a gentlewoman – a year after *The Mind of Mr. J. G. Reeder* (1925) came one of the best-loved detectives of all time: Agatha Christie's Miss Marple.

Today, although popular detectives such as P. D. James' Adam Dalgliesh and Colin Dexter's Inspector Morse are both professional policemen rather than reclusive geniuses, they still carry some of the hallmarks of the archetypal gentleman detective. Dalgliesh's family are gentry, and in his spare time he writes classically styled poetry. Morse, meanwhile, was intelligent enough to win a scholarship to Oxford. Ultimately, one suspects that, as long as the British culture that spawned him is alive and well, in one way or another, the figure of the gentleman detective will persist.

The Murders in the Rue Morgue

Edgar Allan Poe

The Murders in the Rue Morgue

*What song the Syrens sang, or what name Achilles assumed when
he hid himself among women, although puzzling questions, are not
beyond all conjecture.*
--Sir Thomas Browne.

The mental features discoursed of as the analytical, are, in
themselves, but little susceptible of analysis. We appreciate them
only in their effects. We know of them, among other things, that they
are always to their possessor, when inordinately possessed, a source
of the liveliest enjoyment. As the strong man exults in his physical
ability, delighting in such exercises as call his muscles into action,
so glories the analyst in that moral activity which disentangles. He
derives pleasure from even the most trivial occupations bringing
his talent into play. He is fond of enigmas, of conundrums, of
hieroglyphics; exhibiting in his solutions of each a degree of acumen
which appears to the ordinary apprehension præternatural. His
results, brought about by the very soul and essence of method, have,
in truth, the whole air of intuition.

The faculty of re-solution is possibly much invigorated by
mathematical study, and especially by that highest branch of it which,
unjustly, and merely on account of its retrograde operations, has been
called, as if par excellence , analysis. Yet to calculate is not in itself
to analyse. A chess-player, for example, does the one without effort
at the other. It follows that the game of chess, in its effects upon
mental character, is greatly misunderstood. I am not now writing
a treatise, but simply prefacing a somewhat peculiar narrative by
observations very much at random; I will, therefore, take occasion
to assert that the higher powers of the reflective intellect are more

decidedly and more usefully tasked by the unostentatious game of draughts than by a the elaborate frivolity of chess. In this latter, where the pieces have different and bizarre motions, with various and variable values, what is only complex is mistaken (a not unusual error) for what is profound. The attention is here called powerfully into play. If it flag for an instant, an oversight is committed resulting in injury or defeat. The possible moves being not only manifold but involute, the chances of such oversights are multiplied; and in nine cases out of ten it is the more concentrative rather than the more acute player who conquers. In draughts, on the contrary, where the moves are unique and have but little variation, the probabilities of inadvertence are diminished, and the mere attention being left comparatively unemployed, what advantages are obtained by either party are obtained by superior acumen. To be less abstract - Let us suppose a game of draughts where the pieces are reduced to four kings, and where, of course, no oversight is to be expected. It is obvious that here the victory can be decided (the players being at all equal) only by some recherché movement, the result of some strong exertion of the intellect. Deprived of ordinary resources, the analyst throws himself into the spirit of his opponent, identifies himself therewith, and not unfrequently sees thus, at a glance, the sole methods (sometime indeed absurdly simple ones) by which he may seduce into error or hurry into miscalculation.

Whist has long been noted for its influence upon what is termed the calculating power; and men of the highest order of intellect have been known to take an apparently unaccountable delight in it, while eschewing chess as frivolous. Beyond doubt there is nothing of a similar nature so greatly tasking the faculty of analysis. The best chess-player in Christendom may be little more than the best player of chess; but proficiency in whist implies capacity for success in all those more important undertakings where mind struggles with mind. When I say proficiency, I mean that perfection in the game which includes a comprehension of all the sources whence legitimate advantage may be derived. These are not only manifold but multiform, and lie frequently among recesses of thought altogether inaccessible to the ordinary understanding. To observe attentively is to remember distinctly; and, so far, the concentrative chess-player will do very well at whist; while the rules of Hoyle (themselves based upon the mere mechanism of the game) are sufficiently and generally comprehensible. Thus to have a retentive memory, and to proceed by "the book," are points commonly regarded as the sum total of good playing. But it is in matters beyond the limits of mere rule that the skill of the analyst is evinced. He makes, in silence, a host of observations and inferences. So, perhaps, do his companions; and the difference in the extent of the information obtained, lies not so much in the validity of the inference as in the quality of the observation. The necessary knowledge is that of what to observe. Our player confines himself not at all; nor, because the game is the object, does he reject deductions from things external to the game. He examines the countenance of his partner, comparing it carefully with that of each of his opponents. He considers the mode of assorting the cards in each hand; often counting trump by trump, and honor by honor, through the glances bestowed by their holders upon each. He notes every variation of face as the play progresses, gathering a fund of thought from the differences in the expression of certainty, of surprise, of triumph, or of chagrin. From the manner of gathering up a trick he judges whether the person taking it can make another in the suit. He recognises what is played through feint, by the air with which it is thrown upon the table. A casual or inadvertent word; the accidental dropping or turning of a card, with the accompanying anxiety or carelessness in regard to its concealment; the counting of the tricks, with the order of their arrangement; embarrassment, hesitation, eagerness or trepidation - all afford, to his apparently intuitive perception, indications of the true state of affairs. The first two or three rounds having been played, he is in full possession of the contents of each hand, and thenceforward puts down his cards with as absolute a precision of purpose as if the rest of the party had turned outward the faces of their own.

The analytical power should not be confounded with ample ingenuity; for while the analyst is necessarily ingenious, the ingenious man is often remarkably incapable of analysis. The constructive or combining power, by which ingenuity is usually manifested, and to which the phrenologists (I believe erroneously) have assigned a separate organ, supposing it a primitive faculty, has been so frequently seen in those whose intellect bordered otherwise upon idiocy, as to have attracted general observation among writers on morals. Between ingenuity and the analytic ability there exists a difference far greater, indeed, than that between the fancy and the imagination, but of a character very strictly analogous. It will be found, in fact, that the ingenious are always fanciful, and the truly imaginative never otherwise than analytic.

The narrative which follows will appear to the reader somewhat in the light of a commentary upon the propositions just advanced.

Residing in Paris during the spring and part of the summer of 18--, I there became acquainted with a Monsieur C. Auguste Dupin. This young gentleman was of an excellent - indeed of an illustrious family, but, by a variety of untoward events, had been reduced to such poverty that the energy of his character succumbed beneath it, and he ceased to bestir himself in the world, or to care for the retrieval of his fortunes. By courtesy of his creditors, there still remained in his possession a small remnant of his patrimony; and, upon the income arising from this, he managed, by means of a rigorous economy, to procure the necessaries of life, without troubling himself about its superfluities. Books, indeed, were his sole luxuries, and in Paris these are easily obtained.

Our first meeting was at an obscure library in the Rue Montmartre, where the accident of our both being in search of the same very rare and very remarkable volume, brought us into closer communion. We saw each other again and again. I was deeply interested in the little family history which he detailed to me with all that candor which a Frenchman indulges whenever mere self is his theme. I was astonished, too, at the vast extent of his reading; and, above all, I felt my soul enkindled within me by the wild fervor, and the vivid freshness of his imagination. Seeking in Paris the objects I then sought, I felt that the societyof such a man would be to me a treasure beyond price; and this feeling I frankly confided to him. It was at length arranged that we should live together during my stay in the city; and as my worldly circumstances were somewhat less embarrassed than his own, I was permitted to be at the expense of renting, and furnishing in a style which suited the rather fantastic gloom of our common temper, a time-eaten and grotesque mansion, long deserted through superstitions into which we did not inquire, and tottering to its fall in a retired and desolate portion of the Faubourg St. Germain.

Had the routine of our life at this place been known to the world, we should have been regarded as madmen - although, perhaps, as madmen of a harmless nature. Our seclusion was perfect. We admitted no visitors. Indeed the locality of our retirement had been carefully kept a secret from my own former associates; and it had been many years since Dupin had ceased to know or be known in Paris. We existed within ourselves alone.

It was a freak of fancy in my friend (for what else shall I call it?) to be enamored of the Night for her own sake; and into this bizarrerie, as into all his others, I quietly fell; giving myself up to his wild whims with a perfect abandon. The sable divinity would not herself dwell with us always; but we could counterfeit her presence. At the first dawn of the morning we closed all the messy shutters of our old building; lighting a couple of tapers which, strongly perfumed, threw out only the ghastliest and feeblest of rays. By the aid of these we then busied our souls in dreams - reading, writing, or conversing, until warned by the clock of the advent of the true Darkness. Then we sallied forth into the streets arm in arm, continuing the topics of the day, or roaming far and wide until a late hour, seeking, amid the wild lights and shadows of the populous city, that infinity of mental excitement which quiet observation can afford.

At such times I could not help remarking and admiring (although from his rich ideality I had been prepared to expect it) a peculiar analytic ability in Dupin. He seemed, too, to take an eager delight in its exercise - if not exactly in its display - and did not hesitate to confess the pleasure thus derived. He boastedto me, with a low chuckling laugh, that most men, in respect to himself, wore windows in their bosoms, and was wont to follow up such assertions by direct and very startling proofs of his intimate knowledge of my own. His manner at these moments was frigid and abstract; his eyes were vacant in expression; while his voice, usually a rich tenor, rose into a treble which would have sounded petulantly but for the deliberateness and entire distinctness of the enunciation. Observing him in these moods, I often dwelt meditatively upon the old philosophy of the Bi-Part Soul, and amused myself with the fancy of a double Dupin - the creative and the resolvent.

Let it not be supposed, from what I have just said, that I am detailing any mystery, or penning any romance. What I have described in the Frenchman, was merely the result of an excited, or perhaps of a diseased intelligence. But of the character of his remarks at the periods in question an example will best convey the idea.

We were strolling one night down a long dirty street in the vicinity of the Palais Royal. Being both, apparently, occupied with thought, neither of us had spoken a syllable for fifteen minutes at least. All at once Dupin broke forth with these words:

"He is a very little fellow, that's true, and would do better for the

Théâtre des Variétés ."

"There can be no doubt of that," I replied unwittingly, and not at first observing (so much had I been absorbed in reflection) the extraordinary manner in which the speaker had chimed in with my meditations. In an instant afterward I recollected myself, and my astonishment was profound.

"Dupin," said I, gravely, "this is beyond my comprehension. I do not hesitate to say that I am amazed, and can scarcely credit my senses. How was it possible you should know I was thinking of ----- ?" Here I paused, to ascertain beyond a doubt whether he really knew of whom I thought.

-- "of Chantilly," said he, "why do you pause? You were remarking to yourself that his diminutive figure unfitted him for tragedy."

This was precisely what had formed the subject of my reflections. Chantilly was a quondam cobbler of the Rue St. Denis, who, becoming stage-mad, had attempted the rôle of Xerxes, in Crébillon's tragedy so called, and been notoriously Pasquinaded for his pains.

"Tell me, for Heaven's sake," I exclaimed, "the method - if method there is - by which you have been enabled to fathom my soul in this matter." In fact I was even more startled than I would have been willing to express.

"It was the fruiterer," replied my friend, "who brought you to the conclusion that the mender of soles was not of sufficient height for Xerxes et id genus omne ."

"The fruiterer! - you astonish me - I know no fruiterer whomsoever."

"The man who ran up against you as we entered the street - it may have been fifteen minutes ago."

I now remembered that, in fact, a fruiterer, carrying upon his head a large basket of apples, had nearly thrown me down, by accident, as we passed from the Rue C ---- into the thoroughfare where we stood; but what this had to do with Chantilly I could not possibly understand.

There was not a particle of charlâtanerie about Dupin. "I will explain," he said, "and that you may comprehend all clearly, we will first retrace the course of your meditations, from the moment in which I spoke to you until that of the rencontre with the fruiterer in question. The larger links of the chain run thus - Chantilly, Orion, Dr. Nichols, Epicurus, Stereotomy, the street stones, the fruiterer."

There are few persons who have not, at some period of their lives, amused themselves in retracing the steps by which particular conclusions of their own minds have been attained. The occupation is often full of interest and he who attempts it for the first time is astonished by the apparently illimitable distance and incoherence between the starting-point and the goal. What, then, must have been my amazement when I heard the Frenchman speak what he had just spoken, and when I could not help acknowledging that he had spoken the truth. He continued:

"We had been talking of horses, if I remember aright, just before leaving the Rue C ---- . This was the last subject we discussed. As we crossed into this street, a fruiterer, with a large basket upon his head, brushing quickly past us, thrust you upon a pile of paving stones collected at a spot where the causeway is undergoing repair. You stepped upon one of the loose fragments, slipped, slightly strained your ankle, appeared vexed or sulky, muttered a few words, turned to look at the pile, and then proceeded in silence. I was not particularly attentive to what you did; but observation has become with me, of late, a species of necessity.

"You kept your eyes upon the ground - glancing, with a petulant expression, at the holes and ruts in the pavement, (so that I saw you were still thinking of the stones,) until we reached the little alley called Lamartine, which has been paved, by way of experiment, with the overlapping and riveted blocks. Here your countenance brightened up, and, perceiving your lips move, I could not doubt that you murmured the word 'stereotomy,' a term very affectedly applied to this species of pavement. I knew that you could not say to yourself 'stereotomy' without being brought to think of atomies, and thus of the theories of Epicurus; and since, when we discussed this subject not very long ago, I mentioned to you how singularly, yet with how little notice, the vague guesses of that noble Greek had met with confirmation in the late nebular cosmogony, I felt that you could not avoid casting your eyes upward to the great nebula in Orion, and I certainly expected that you would do so. You did look up; and I was now assured that I had correctly followed your steps. But in that bitter tirade upon Chantilly, which appeared in yesterday's ' Musée ,' the satirist, making some disgraceful allusions to the cobbler s change of name upon assuming the buskin, quoted a Latin line about which we have often conversed. I mean the line

Perdidit antiquum litera sonum.

I had told you that this was in reference to Orion, formerly written Urion; and, from certain pungencies connected with this explanation, I was aware that you could not have forgotten it. It was clear, therefore, that you would not fail to combine the two ideas of Orion and Chantilly. That you did combine them I saw by the character of the smile which passed over your lips. You thought of the poor cobbler's immolation. So far, you had been stooping in your gait; but now I saw you draw yourself up to your full height. I was then sure that you reflected upon the diminutive figure of Chantilly. At this point I interrupted your meditations to remark that as, in fact, be was a very little fellow - that Chantilly - he would do better at the Théâtre des Variétés ."

Not long after this, we were looking over an evening edition of the "Gazette des Tribunaux," when the following paragraphs arrested our attention.

"EXTRAORDINARY MURDERS. - This morning, about three o'clock, the inhabitants of the Quartier St. Roch were aroused from sleep by a succession of terrific shrieks, issuing, apparently, from the fourth story of a house in the Rue Morgue, known to be in the sole occupancy of one Madame L'Espanaye, and her daughter Mademoiselle Camille L'Espanaye. After some delay, occasioned by a fruitless attempt to procure admission in the usual manner, the gateway was broken in with a crowbar, and eight or ten of the neighbors entered accompanied by two gendarmes. By this time the cries had ceased; but, as the party rushed up the first flight of stairs, two or more rough voices in angry contention were distinguished and seemed to proceed from the upper part of the house. As the second landing was reached, these sounds, also, had ceased and everything remained perfectly quiet. The party spread themselves and hurried from room to room. Upon arriving at a large back chamber in the fourth story, (the door of which, being found locked, with the key inside, was forced open,) a spectacle presented itself which struck every one present not less with horror than with astonishment.

"The apartment was in the wildest disorder - the furniture broken and thrown about in all directions. There was only one bedstead; and from this the bed had been removed, and thrown into the middle of the floor. On a chair lay a razor, besmeared with blood. On the hearth were two or three long and thick tresses of grey human hair, also dabbled in blood, and seeming to have been pulled out by the roots. Upon the floor were found four Napoleons, an ear-ring of topaz, three large silver spoons, three smaller of métal d'Alger , and two bags, containing nearly four thousand francs in gold. The drawers of a bureau, which stood in one corner were open, and had been, apparently, rifled, although many articles still remained in them. A small iron safe was discovered under the bed (not under the bedstead). It was open, with the key still in the door. It had no contents beyond a few old letters, and other papers of little consequence.

"Of Madame L'Espanaye no traces were here seen; but an unusual quantity of soot being observed in the fire-place, a search was made in the chimney, and (horrible to relate!) the; corpse of the daughter, head downward, was dragged therefrom; it having been thus forced up the narrow aperture for a considerable distance. The body was quite warm. Upon examining it, many excoriations were perceived, no doubt occasioned by the violence with which it had been thrust up and disengaged. Upon the face were many severe scratches, and, upon the throat, dark bruises, and deep indentations of finger nails, as if the deceased had been throttled to death.

"After a thorough investigation of every portion of the house, without farther discovery, the party made its way into a small paved yard in the rear of the building, where lay the corpse of the old lady, with her throat so entirely cut that, upon an attempt to raise her, the head fell off. The body, as well as the head, was fearfully mutilated - the former so much so as scarcely to retain any semblance of humanity.

"To this horrible mystery there is not as yet, we believe, the slightest clew."

The next day's paper had these additional particulars.

"The Tragedy in the Rue Morgue. Many individuals have been examined in relation to this most extraordinary and frightful affair. [The word 'affaire' has not yet, in France, that levity of import which it conveys with us,] "but nothing whatever has transpired to throw light upon it. We give below all the material testimony elicited.

"Pauline Dubourg , laundress, deposes that she has known both the deceased for three years, having washed for them during that period. The old lady and her daughter seemed on good terms - very affectionate towards each other. They were excellent pay. Could not speak in regard to their mode or means of living. Believed that Madame L. told fortunes for a living. Was reputed to have money put by. Never met any persons in the house when she called for the clothes or took them home. Was sure that they had no servant in employ. There appeared to be no furniture in any part of the building except in the fourth story.

"Pierre Moreau, tobacconist, deposes that he has been in the habit of selling small quantities of tobacco and snuff to Madame L'Espanaye for nearly four years. Was born in the neighborhood, and has always resided there. The deceased and her daughter had occupied the house in which the corpses were found, for more than six years. It was formerly occupied by a jeweller, who under-let the upper rooms to various persons. The house was the property of Madame L. She became dissatisfied with the abuse of the premises by her tenant, and moved into them herself, refusing to let any portion. The old lady was childish. Witness had seen the daughter some five or six times during the six years. The two lived an exceedingly retired life - were reputed to have money. Had heard it said among the neighbors that Madame L. told fortunes - did not believe it. Had never seen any person enter the door except the old lady and her daughter, a porter once or twice, and a physician some eight or ten times.

"Many other persons, neighbors, gave evidence to the same effect. No one was spoken of as frequenting the house. It was not known whether there were any living connexions of Madame L. and her daughter. The shutters of the front windows were seldom opened. Those in the rear were always closed, with the exception of the large back room, fourth story. The house was a good house - not very old.

"Isidore Muset, gendarme, deposes that he was called to the house about three o'clock in the morning, and found some twenty or thirty persons at the gateway, endeavoring to gain admittance. Forced it open, at length, with a bayonet - not with a crowbar. Had but little difficulty in getting it open, on account of its being a double or folding gate, and bolted neither at bottom not top. The shrieks were continued until the gate was forced - and then suddenly ceased. They seemed to be screams of some person (or persons) in great agony - were loud and drawn out, not short and quick. Witness led the way up stairs. Upon reaching the first landing, heard two voices in loud and angry contention - the one a gruff voice, the other much shriller - a very strange voice. Could distinguish some words of the former, which was that of a Frenchman. Was positive that it was not a woman's voice. Could distinguish the words ' sacré' and ' diable. ' The shrill voice was that of a foreigner. Could not be sure whether it was the voice of a man or of a woman. Could not make out what was said, but believed the language to be Spanish. The state of the room and of the bodies was described by this witness as we described them yesterday.

"Henri Duval , a neighbor, and by trade a silver-smith, deposes that he was one of the party who first entered the house. Corroborates the testimony of Musèt in general. As soon as they forced an entrance, they reclosed the door, to keep out the crowd, which collected very fast, notwithstanding the lateness of the hour. The shrill voice, this witness thinks, was that of an Italian. Was certain it was not French. Could not be sure that it was a man's voice. It might have been a woman's. Was not acquainted with the Italian language. Could not distinguish the words, but was convinced by the intonation that the speaker was an Italian. Knew Madame L. and her daughter. Had conversed with both frequently. Was sure that the shrill voice was not that of either of the deceased.

"-- Odenheimer, restaurateur. This witness volunteered his testimony. Not speaking French, was examined through an interpreter. Is a native of Amsterdam. Was passing the house at the time of the shrieks. They lasted for several minutes - probably ten. They were long and loud - very awful and distressing. Was one of those who entered the building. Corroborated the previous evidence in every respect but one. Was sure that the shrill voice was that of a man - of a Frenchman. Could not distinguish the words uttered. They were loud and quick - unequal - spoken apparently in fear as well as in anger. The voice was harsh - not so much shrill as harsh. Could not call it a shrill voice. The gruff voice said repeatedly ' sacré ,' 'diable,' and once 'mon Dieu. '

"Jules Mignaud , banker, of the firm of Mignaud et Fils, Rue Deloraine. Is the elder Mignaud. Madame L'Espanaye had some property. Had opened an account with his banking house in the spring of the year - (eight years previously). Made frequent deposits in small sums. Had checked for nothing until the third day before her death, when she took out in person the sum of 4000 francs. This sum was paid in gold, and a clerk went home with the money.

"Adolphe Le Bon , clerk to Mignaud et Fils, deposes that on the day in question, about noon, he accompanied Madame L'Espanaye to her residence with the 4000 francs, put up in two bags. Upon the door being opened, Mademoiselle L. appeared and took from his hands one of the bags, while the old lady relieved him of the other. He then bowed and departed. Did not see any person in the street at the time. It is a bye-street - very lonely.

"William Bird , tailor deposes that he was one of the party who entered the house. Is an Englishman. Has lived in Paris two years. Was one of the first to ascend the stairs. Heard the voices in contention. The gruff voice was that of a Frenchman. Could make out several words, but cannot now remember all. Heard distinctly ' sacré' and ' mon Dieu. ' There was a sound at the moment as if of several persons struggling - a scraping and scuffling sound. The shrill voice was very loud - louder than the gruff one. Is sure that it was not the voice of an Englishman. Appeared to be that of a German. Might have been a woman's voice. Does not understand German.

"Four of the above-named witnesses, being recalled, deposed that the door of the chamber in which was found the body of Mademoiselle L. was locked on the inside when the party reached it. Every thing was perfectly silent - no groans or noises of any kind. Upon forcing the door no person was seen. The windows, both of the back and front room, were down and firmly fastened from within. A door between the two rooms was closed, but not locked. The door leading from the front room into the passage was locked, with the key on the inside. A small room in the front of the house, on the fourth story, at the head of the passage was open, the door being ajar. This room was crowded with old beds, boxes, and so forth. These were carefully removed and searched. There was not an inch of any portion of the house which was not carefully searched. Sweeps were sent up and down the chimneys. The house was a four story one, with garrets (mansardes.) A trap-door on the roof was nailed down very securely - did not appear to have been opened for years. The time elapsing between the hearing of the voices in contention and the breaking open of the room door, was variously stated by the witnesses. Some made it as short as three minutes - some as long as five. The door was opened with difficulty.

"Alfonzo Garcio , undertaker, deposes that he resides in the Rue Morgue. Is a native of Spain. Was one of the party who entered the house. Did not proceed up stairs. Is nervous, and was apprehensive of the consequences of agitation. Heard the voices in contention. The gruff voice was that of a Frenchman. Could not distinguish what was said. The shrill voice was that of an Englishman - is sure of this. Does not understand the English language, but judges by the intonation.

"Alberto Montani , confectioner, deposes that he was among the first to ascend the stairs. Heard the voices in question. The gruff voice was that of a Frenchman. Distinguished several words. The speaker appeared to be expostulating. Could not make out the words of the shrill voice. Spoke quick and unevenly. Thinks it the voice of a Russian. Corroborates the general testimony. Is an Italian. Never conversed with a native of Russia.

"Several witnesses, recalled, here testified that the chimneys of all the rooms on the fourth story were too narrow to admit the passage of a human being. By 'sweeps' were meant cylindrical sweeping brushes, such as are employed by those who clean chimneys. These brushes were passed up and down every flue in the house. There is no back passage by which any one could have descended while the party proceeded up stairs. The body of Mademoiselle L'Espanaye was so firmly wedged in the chimney that it could not be got down until four or five of the party united their strength.

"Paul Dumas , physician, deposes that he was called to view the bodies about day-break. They were both then lying on the sacking of the bedstead in the chamber where Mademoiselle L. was found. The corpse of the young lady was much bruised and excoriated. The fact that it had been thrust up the chimney would sufficiently account for these appearances. The throat was greatly chafed. There were several deep scratches just below the chin, together with a series of livid spots which were evidently the impression of fingers. The face was fearfully discolored, and the eye-balls protruded. The tongue had been partially bitten through. A large bruise was discovered upon the pit of the stomach, produced, apparently, by the pressure of a knee. In the opinion of M. Dumas, Mademoiselle L'Espanaye had been throttled to death by some person or persons unknown. The corpse of the mother was horribly mutilated. All the bones of the right leg and arm were more or less shattered. The left tibia much splintered, as well as all the ribs of the left side. Whole body dreadfully bruised and discolored. It was not possible to say how the injuries had been inflicted. A heavy club of wood, or a broad bar of iron - a chair - any large, heavy, and obtuse weapon would have produced such results, if wielded by the hands of a very powerful man. No woman could have inflicted the blows with any weapon. The head of the deceased, when seen by witness, was entirely separated from the body, and was also greatly shattered. The throat had evidently been cut with some very sharp instrument - probably with a razor.

"Alexandre Etienne , surgeon, was called with M. Dumas to view the bodies. Corroborated the testimony, and the opinions of M. Dumas.

"Nothing farther of importance was elicited, although several other persons were examined. A murder so mysterious, and so perplexing in all its particulars, was never before committed in Paris - if indeed a murder has been committed at all. The police are entirely at fault - an unusual occurrence in affairs of this nature. There is not, however, the shadow of a clew apparent."

The evening edition of the paper stated that the greatest excitement still continued in the Quartier St. Roch - that the premises in question had been carefully re-searched, and fresh examinations of witnesses instituted, but all to no purpose. A postscript, however, mentioned that Adolphe Le Bon had been arrested and imprisoned - although nothing appeared to criminate him, beyond the facts already detailed.

Dupin seemed singularly interested in the progress of this affair -- at least so I judged from his manner, for he made no comments. It was only after the announcement that Le Bon had been imprisoned, that he asked me my opinion respecting the murders.

I could merely agree with all Paris in considering them an insoluble mystery. I saw no means by which it would be possible to trace the murderer.

"We must not judge of the means," said Dupin, "by this shell of an examination. The Parisian police, so much extolled for acumen, are cunning, but no more. There is no method in their proceedings, beyond the method of the moment. They make a vast parade of measures; but, not unfrequently, these are so ill adapted to the objects proposed, as to put us in mind of Monsieur Jourdain's calling for his robe-de-chambre - pour mieux entendre la musique. The results attained by them are not unfrequently surprising, but, for the most part, are brought about by simple diligence and activity. When these qualities are unavailing, their schemes fail. Vidocq, for example, was a good guesser and a persevering man. But, without educated thought, he erred continually by the very intensity of his investigations. He impaired his vision by holding the object too close. He might see, perhaps, one or two points with unusual clearness, but in so doing he, necessarily, lost sight of the matter as a whole. Thus there is such a thing as being too profound. Truth is not always in a well. In fact, as regards the more important knowledge, I do believe that she is invariably superficial. The depth lies in the valleys where we seek her, and not upon the mountain-tops where she is found. The modes and sources of this kind of error are well typified in the contemplation of the heavenly bodies. To look at a star by glances - to view it in a side-long way, by turning toward it the exterior portions of the retina (more susceptible of feeble impressions of light than the interior), is to behold the star distinctly - is to have the best appreciation of its lustre - a lustre which grows dim just in proportion as we turn our vision fully upon it. A greater number of rays actually fall upon the eye in the latter case, but, in the former, there is the more refined capacity for comprehension. By undue profundity we perplex and enfeeble thought; and it is possible to make even Venus herself vanish from the firmanent by a scrutiny too sustained, too concentrated, or too direct.

"As for these murders, let us enter into some examinations for ourselves, before we make up an opinion respecting them. An inquiry will afford us amusement," [I thought this an odd term, so applied, but said nothing] "and, besides, Le Bon once rendered me a service for which I am not ungrateful. We will go and see the premises with our own eyes. I know G----, the Prefect of Police, and shall have no difficulty in obtaining the necessary permission."

The permission was obtained, and we proceeded at once to the Rue Morgue. This is one of those miserable thoroughfares which intervene between the Rue Richelieu and the Rue St. Roch. It was late in the afternoon when we reached it; as this quarter is at a great distance from that in which we resided. The house was readily found; for there were still many persons gazing up at the closed shutters, with an objectless curiosity, from the opposite side of the way. It was an ordinary Parisian house, with a gateway, on one side of which was a glazed watch-box, with a sliding panel in the window, indicating a loge de concierge. Before going in we walked up the street, turned down an alley, and then, again turning, passed in the rear of the building - Dupin, meanwhile examining the whole neighborhood, as well as the house, with a minuteness of attention for which I could see no possible object.

Retracing our steps, we came again to the front of the dwelling, rang, and, having shown our credentials, were admitted by the agents in charge. We went up stairs - into the chamber where the body of Mademoiselle L'Espanaye had been found, and where both the deceased still lay. The disorders of the room had, as usual, been suffered to exist. I saw nothing beyond what had been stated in the "Gazette des Tribunaux." Dupin scrutinized every thing - not excepting the bodies of the victims. We then went into the other rooms, and into the yard; a gendarme accompanying us throughout. The examination occupied us until dark, when we took our departure. On our way home my companion stepped in for a moment at the office of one of the daily papers.

I have said that the whims of my friend were manifold, and that Je les ménagais : - for this phrase there is no English equivalent. It was his humor, now, to decline all conversation on the subject of the murder, until about noon the next day. He then asked me, suddenly, if I had observed any thing peculiar at the scene of the atrocity.

There was something in his manner of emphasizing the word "peculiar," which caused me to shudder, without knowing why.

"No, nothing peculiar," I said; "nothing more, at least, than we both saw stated in the paper."

"The 'Gazette,' " he replied, "has not entered, I fear, into the unusual horror of the thing. But dismiss the idle opinions of this print. It appears to me that this mystery is considered insoluble, for the very reason which should cause it to be regarded as easy of solution - I mean for the outré character of its features. The police are confounded by the seeming absence of motive - not for the murder itself - but for the atrocity of the murder. They are puzzled, too, by the seeming impossibility of reconciling the voices heard in contention, with the facts that no one was discovered up stairs but the assassinated Mademoiselle L'Espanaye, and that there were no means of egress without the notice of the party ascending. The wild disorder of the room; the corpse thrust, with the head downward, up the chimney; the frightful mutilation of the body of the old lady; these considerations, with those just mentioned, and others which I need not mention, have sufficed to paralyze the powers, by putting completely at fault the boasted acumen, of the government agents. They have fallen into the gross but common error of confounding the unusual with the abstruse. But it is by these deviations from the plane of the ordinary, that reason feels its way, if at all, in its search for the true. In investigations such as we are now pursuing, it should not be so much asked 'what has occurred,' as 'what has occurred that has never occurred before.' In fact, the facility with which I shall arrive, or have arrived, at the solution of this mystery, is in the direct ratio of its apparent insolubility in the eyes of the police."

I stared at the speaker in mute astonishment.

"I am now awaiting," continued he, looking toward the door of our apartment - "I am now awaiting a person who, although perhaps not the perpetrator of these butcheries, must have been in some measure implicated in their perpetration. Of the worst portion of the crimes committed, it is probable that he is innocent. I hope that I am right in this supposition; for upon it I build my expectation of reading the entire riddle. I look for the man here - in this room - every moment. It is true that he may not arrive; but the probability is that he will. Should he come, it will be necessary to detain him. Here are pistols; and we both know how to use them when occasion demands their use."

I took the pistols, scarcely knowing what I did, or believing what I heard, while Dupin went on, very much as if in a soliloquy. I have already spoken of his abstract manner at such times. His discourse was addressed to myself; but his voice, although by no means loud, had that intonation which is commonly employed in speaking to some one at a great distance. His eyes, vacant in expression, regarded only the wall.

"That the voices heard in contention," he said, "by the party upon the stairs, were not the voices of the women themselves, was fully proved by the evidence. This relieves us of all doubt upon the question whether the old lady could have first destroyed the daughter and afterward have committed suicide. I speak of this point chiefly for the sake of method; for the strength of Madame L'Espanaye would have been utterly unequal to the task of thrusting her daughter's corpse up the chimney as it was found; and the nature of the wounds upon her own person entirely preclude the idea of self-destruction. Murder, then, has been committed by some third party; and the voices of this third party were those heard in contention. Let me now advert - not to the whole testimony respecting these voices - but to what was peculiar in that testimony. Did you observe any thing peculiar about it?"

I remarked that, while all the witnesses agreed in supposing the gruff voice to be that of a Frenchman, there was much disagreement in regard to the shrill, or, as one individual termed it, the harsh voice.

"That was the evidence itself," said Dupin, "but it was not the peculiarity of the evidence. You have observed nothing distinctive. Yet there was something to be observed. The witnesses, as you remark, agreed about the gruff voice; they were here unanimous. But in regard to the shrill voice, the peculiarity is - not that they disagreed - but that, while an Italian, an Englishman, a Spaniard, a Hollander, and a Frenchman attempted to describe it, each one spoke of it as that of a foreigner . Each is sure that it was not the voice of one of his own countrymen. Each likens it - not to the voice of an individual of any nation with whose language he is conversant - but the converse. The Frenchman supposes it the voice of a Spaniard, and 'might have distinguished some words had he been acquainted with the Spanish. ' The Dutchman maintains it to have been that of a Frenchman; but we find it stated that ' not understanding French this witness was examined through an interpreter. ' The Englishman thinks it the voice of a German, and 'does not understand German. ' The Spaniard 'is sure' that it was that of an Englishman, but 'judges by the intonation' altogether, ' as he has no knowledge of the English. ' The Italian believes it the voice of a Russian, but ' has never conversed with a native of Russia. ' A second Frenchman differs, moreover, with the first, and is positive that the voice was that of an Italian; but, not being cognizant of that tongue , is, like the Spaniard, 'convinced by the intonation.' Now, how strangely unusual must that voice have really been, about which such testimony as this could have been elicited! - in whose tones, even, denizens of the five great divisions of Europe could recognise nothing familiar! You will say that it might have been the voice of an Asiatic - of an African. Neither Asiatics nor Africans abound in Paris; but, without denying the inference, I will now merely call your attention to three points. The voice is termed by one witness 'harsh rather than shrill.' It is represented by two others to have been 'quick and unequal. ' No words - no sounds resembling words - were by any witness mentioned as distinguishable.

"I know not," continued Dupin, "what impression I may have made, so far, upon your own understanding; but I do not hesitate to say that legitimate deductions even from this portion of the testimony - the portion respecting the gruff and shrill voices - are in themselves sufficient to engender a suspicion which should give direction to all farther progress in the investigation of the mystery. I said 'legitimate deductions;' but my meaning is not thus fully expressed. I designed to imply that the deductions are the sole proper ones, and that the suspicion arises inevitably from them as the single result. What the suspicion is, however, I will not say just yet. I merely wish you to bear in mind that, with myself, it was sufficiently forcible to give a definite form - a certain tendency - to my inquiries in the chamber.

"Let us now transport ourselves, in fancy, to this chamber. What shall we first seek here? The means of egress employed by the murderers. It is not too much to say that neither of us believe in præternatural events. Madame and Mademoiselle L'Espanaye were not destroyed by spirits. The doers of the deed were material, and escaped materially. Then how? Fortunately, there is but one mode of reasoning upon the point, and that mode must lead us to a definite decision. - Let us examine, each by each, the possible means of egress. It is clear that the assassins were in the room where Mademoiselle L'Espanaye was found, or at least in the room adjoining, when the party ascended the stairs. It is then only from these two apartments that we have to seek issues. The police have laid bare the floors, the ceilings, and the masonry of the walls, in every direction. No secret issues could have escaped their vigilance. But, not trusting to their eyes, I examined with my own. There were, then, no secret issues. Both doors leading from the rooms into the passage were securely locked, with the keys inside. Let us turn to the chimneys. These, although of ordinary width for some eight or ten feet above the hearths, will not admit, throughout their extent, the body of a large cat. The impossibility of egress, by means already stated, being thus absolute, we are reduced to the windows. Through those of the front room no one could have escaped without notice from the crowd in the street. The murderers must have passed, then, through those of the back room. Now, brought to this conclusion in so unequivocal a manner as we are, it is not our part, as reasoners, to reject it on account of apparent impossibilities. It is only left for us to prove that these apparent 'impossibilities' are, in reality, not such.

"There are two windows in the chamber. One of them is unobstructed by furniture, and is wholly visible. The lower portion of the other is hidden from view by the head of the unwieldy bedstead which is thrust close up against it. The former was found securely fastened from within. It resisted the utmost force of those who endeavored to raise it. A large gimlet-hole had been pierced in its frame to the left, and a very stout nail was found fitted therein, nearly to the head. Upon examining the other window, a similar nail was seen similarly fitted in it; and a vigorous attempt to raise this sash, failed also. The police were now entirely satisfied that egress had not been in these directions. And, therefore, it was thought a matter of supererogation to withdraw the nails and open the windows.

"My own examination was somewhat more particular, and was so for the reason I have just given - because here it was, I knew, that all apparent impossibilities must be proved to be not such in reality.

"I proceeded to think thus - à posteriori . The murderers did escape from one of these windows. This being so, they could not have refastened the sashes from the inside, as they were found fastened; - the consideration which put a stop, through its obviousness, to the scrutiny of the police in this quarter. Yet the sashes were fastened. They must, then, have the power of fastening themselves. There was no escape from this conclusion. I stepped to the unobstructed casement, withdrew the nail with some difficulty and attempted to raise the sash. It resisted all my efforts, as I had anticipated. A concealed spring must, I now know, exist; and this corroboration of my idea convinced me that my premises at least, were correct, however mysterious still appeared the circumstances attending the nails. A careful search soon brought to light the hidden spring. I pressed it, and, satisfied with the discovery, forbore to upraise the sash.

"I now replaced the nail and regarded it attentively. A person passing out through this window might have reclosed it, and the spring would have caught - but the nail could not have been replaced. The conclusion was plain, and again narrowed in the field of my investigations. The assassins must have escaped through the other window. Supposing, then, the springs upon each sash to be the same, as was probable, there must be found a difference between the nails, or at least between the modes of their fixture. Getting upon the sacking of the bedstead, I looked over the head-board minutely at the second casement. Passing my hand down behind the board, I readily discovered and pressed the spring, which was, as I had supposed, identical in character with its neighbor. I now looked at the nail. It was as stout as the other, and apparently fitted in the same manner - driven in nearly up to the head.

"You will say that I was puzzled; but, if you think so, you must have misunderstood the nature of the inductions. To use a sporting phrase, I had not been once 'at fault.' The scent had never for an instant been lost. There was no flaw in any link of the chain. I had traced the secret to its ultimate result, - and that result was the nail. It had, I say, in every respect, the appearance of its fellow in the other window; but this fact was an absolute nullity (conclusive us it might seem to be) when compared with the consideration that here, at this point, terminated the clew. 'There must be something wrong,' I said, 'about the nail.' I touched it; and the head, with about a quarter of an inch of the shank, came off in my fingers. The rest of the shank was in the gimlet-hole where it had been broken off. The fracture was an old one (for its edges were incrusted with rust), and had apparently been accomplished by the blow of a hammer, which had partially imbedded, in the top of the bottom sash, the head portion of the nail. I now carefully replaced this head portion in the indentation whence I had taken it, and the resemblance to a perfect nail was complete - the fissure was invisible. Pressing the spring, I gently raised the sash for a few inches; the head went up with it, remaining firm in its bed. I closed the window, and the semblance of the whole nail was again perfect.

"The riddle, so far, was now unriddled. The assassin had escaped through the window which looked upon the bed. Dropping of its own accord upon his exit (or perhaps purposely closed), it had become fastened by the spring; and it was the retention of this spring which had been mistaken by the police for that of the nail, - farther inquiry being thus considered unnecessary.

"The next question is that of the mode of descent. Upon this point I had been satisfied in my walk with you around the building. About five feet and a half from the casement in question there runs a lightning-rod. From this rod it would have been impossible for any one to reach the window itself, to say nothing of entering it. I observed, however, that the shutters of the fourth story were of the peculiar kind called by Parisian carpenters ferrades - a kind rarely employed at the present day, but frequently seen upon very old mansions at Lyons and Bourdeaux. They are in the form of an ordinary door, (a single, not a folding door) except that the lower half is latticed or worked in open trellis - thus affording an excellent hold for the hands. In the present instance these shutters are fully three feet and a half broad. When we saw them from the rear of the house, they were both about half open - that is to say, they stood off at right angles from the wall. It is probable that the police, as well as myself, examined the back of the tenement; but, if so, in looking at these ferrades in the line of their breadth (as they must have done), they did not perceive this great breadth itself, or, at all events, failed to take it into due consideration. In fact, having once satisfied themselves that no egress could have been made in this quarter, they would naturally bestow here a very cursory examination. It was clear to me, however, that the shutter belonging to the window at the head of the bed, would, if swung fully back to the wall, reach to within two feet of the lightning-rod. It was also evident that, by exertion of a very unusual degree of activity and courage, an entrance into the window, from the rod, might have been thus effected. - By reaching to the distance of two feet and a half (we now suppose the shutter open to its whole extent) a robber might have taken a firm grasp upon the trellis-work. Letting go, then, his hold upon the rod, placing his feet securely against the wall, and springing boldly from it, he might have swung the shutter so as to close it, and, if we imagine the window open at the time, might even have swung himself into the room.

"I wish you to bear especially in mind that I have spoken of a very unusual degree of activity as requisite to success in so hazardous and so difficult a feat. It is my design to show you, first, that the thing might possibly have been accomplished: - but, secondly and chiefly, I wish to impress upon your understanding the very extraordinary - the almost præternatural character of that agility which could have accomplished it.

"You will say, no doubt, using the language of the law, that 'to make out my case,' I should rather undervalue, than insist upon a full estimation of the activity required in this matter. This may be the practice in law, but it is not the usage of reason. My ultimate object is only the truth. My immediate purpose is to lead you to place in juxta-position, that very unusual activity of which I have just spoken with that very peculiar shrill (or harsh) and unequal voice, about whose nationality no two persons could be found to agree, and in whose utterance no syllabification could be detected."

At these words a vague and half-formed conception of the meaning of Dupin flitted over my mind. I seemed to be upon the verge of comprehension without power to comprehend - men, at times, find themselves upon the brink of remembrance without being able, in the end, to remember. My friend went on with his discourse.

"You will see," he said, "that I have shifted the question from the mode of egress to that of ingress. It was my design to convey the idea that both were effected in the same manner, at the same point. Let us now revert to the interior of the room. Let us survey the appearances here. The drawers of the bureau, it is said, had been rifled, although many articles of apparel still remained within them. The conclusion here is absurd. It is a mere guess - a very silly one - and no more. How are we to know that the articles found in the drawers were not all these drawers had originally contained? Madame L'Espanaye and her daughter lived an exceedingly retired life - saw no company - seldom went out - had little use for numerous changes of habiliment. Those found were at least of as good quality as any likely to be possessed by these ladies. If a thief had taken any, why did he not take the best - why did he not take all? In a word, why did he abandon four thousand francs in gold to encumber himself with a bundle of linen? The gold was abandoned. Nearly the whole sum mentioned by Monsieur Mignaud, the banker, was discovered, in bags, upon the floor. I wish you, therefore, to discard from your thoughts the blundering idea of motive, engendered in the brains of the police by that portion of the evidence which speaks of money delivered at the door of the house. Coincidences ten times as remarkable as this (the delivery of the money, and murder committed within three days upon the party receiving it), happen to all of us every hour of our lives, without attracting even momentary notice. Coincidences, in general, are great stumbling-blocks in the way of that class of thinkers who have been educated to know nothing of the theory of probabilities - that theory to which the most glorious objects of human research are indebted for the most glorious of illustration. In the present instance, had the gold been gone, the fact of its delivery three days before would have formed something more than a coincidence. It would have been corroborative of this idea of motive. But, under the real circumstances of the case, if we are to suppose gold the motive of this outrage, we must also imagine the perpetrator so vacillating an idiot as to have abandoned his gold and his motive together.

"Keeping now steadily in mind the points to which I have drawn your attention - that peculiar voice, that unusual agility, and that startling absence of motive in a murder so singularly atrocious as this - let us glance at the butchery itself. Here is a woman strangled to death by manual strength, and thrust up a chimney, head downward. Ordinary assassins employ no such modes of murder as this. Least of all, do they thus dispose of the murdered. In the manner of thrusting the corpse up the chimney, you will admit that there was something excessively outré - something altogether irreconcilable with our common notions of human action, even when we suppose the actors the most depraved of men. Think, too, how great must have been that strength which could have thrust the body up such an aperture so forcibly that the united vigor of several persons was found barely sufficient to drag it down!

"Turn, now, to other indications of the employment of a vigor most marvellous. On the hearth were thick tresses - very thick tresses - of grey human hair. These had been torn out by the roots. You are aware of the great force necessary in tearing thus from the head even twenty or thirty hairs together. You saw the locks in question as well as myself. Their roots (a hideous sight!) were clotted with fragments of the flesh of the scalp - sure token of the prodigious power which had been exerted in uprooting perhaps half a million of hairs at a time. The throat of the old lady was not merely cut, but the head absolutely severed from the body: the instrument was a mere razor. I wish you also to look at the brutal ferocity of these deeds. Of the bruises upon the body of Madame L'Espanaye I do not speak. Monsieur Dumas, and his worthy coadjutor Monsieur Etienne, have pronounced that they were inflicted by some obtuse instrument; and so far these gentlemen are very correct. The obtuse instrument was clearly the stone pavement in the yard, upon which the victim had fallen from the window which looked in upon the bed. This idea, however simple it may now seem, escaped the police for the same reason that the breadth of the shutters escaped them - because, by the affair of the nails, their perceptions had been hermetically sealed against the possibility of the windows having ever been opened at all.

"If now, in addition to all these things, you have properly reflected upon the odd disorder of the chamber, we have gone so far as to combine the ideas of an agility astounding, a strength superhuman, a ferocity brutal, a butchery without motive, a grotesquerie in horror absolutely alien from humanity, and a voice foreign in tone to the ears of men of many nations, and devoid of all distinct or intelligible syllabification. What result, then, has ensued? What impression have I made upon your fancy?"

I felt a creeping of the flesh as Dupin asked me the question. "A madman," I said, "has done this deed - some raving maniac, escaped from a neighboring Maison de Santé. "

"In some respects," he replied, "your idea is not irrelevant. But the voices of madmen, even in their wildest paroxysms, are never found to tally with that peculiar voice heard upon the stairs. Madmen are of some nation, and their language, however incoherent in its words, has always the coherence of syllabification. Besides, the hair of a madman is not such as I now hold in my hand. I disentangled this little tuft from the rigidly clutched fingers of Madame L'Espanaye. Tell me what you can make of it."

"Dupin!" I said, completely unnerved; "this hair is most unusual - this is no human hair."

"I have not asserted that it is," said he; "but, before we decide this point, I wish you to glance at the little sketch I have here traced upon this paper. It is a fac-simile drawing of what has been described in one portion of the testimony as 'dark bruises, and deep indentations of finger nails,' upon the throat of Mademoiselle L'Espanaye, and in another, (by Messrs. Dumas and Etienne,) as a 'series of livid spots, evidently the impression of fingers.'

"You will perceive," continued my friend, spreading out the

paper upon the table before us, "that this drawing gives the idea of a firm and fixed hold. There is no slipping apparent. Each finger has retained - possibly until the death of the victim - the fearful grasp by which it originally imbedded itself. Attempt, now, to place all your fingers, at the same time, in the respective impressions as you see them."

I made the attempt in vain.

"We are possibly not giving this matter a fair trial," he said. "The paper is spread out upon a plane surface; but the human throat is cylindrical. Here is a billet of wood, the circumference of which is about that of the throat. Wrap the drawing around it, and try the experiment again."

I did so; but the difficulty was even more obvious than before. "This," I said, "is the mark of no human hand."

"Read now," replied Dupin, "this passage from Cuvier."

It was a minute anatomical and generally descriptive account of the large fulvous Ourang-Outang of the East Indian Islands. The gigantic stature, the prodigious strength and activity, the wild ferocity, and the imitative propensities of these mammalia are sufficiently well known to all. I understood the full horrors of the murder at once.

"The description of the digits," said I, as I made an end of reading, "is in exact accordance with this drawing. I see that no animal but an Ourang-Outang, of the species here mentioned, could have impressed the indentations as you have traced them. This tuft of tawny hair, too, is identical in character with that of the beast of Cuvier. But I cannot possibly comprehend the particulars of this frightful mystery. Besides, there were two voices heard in contention, and one of them was unquestionably the voice of a Frenchman."

"True; and you will remember an expression attributed almost unanimously, by the evidence, to this voice, - the expression, ' mon Dieu! ' This, under the circumstances, has been justly characterized by one of the witnesses (Montani, the confectioner,) as an expression of remonstrance or expostulation. Upon these two words, therefore, I have mainly built my hopes of a full solution of the riddle. A Frenchman was cognizant of the murder. It is possible - indeed it is far more than probable - that he was innocent of all participation in the bloody transactions which took place. The Ourang-Outang may have escaped from him. He may have traced it to the chamber; but, under the agitating circumstances which ensued, he could never have re-captured it. It is still at large. I will not pursue these guesses - for I have no right to call them more - since the shades of reflection upon which they are based are scarcely of sufficient depth to be appreciable by my own intellect, and since I could not pretend to make them intelligible to the understanding of another. We will call them guesses then, and speak of them as such. If the Frenchman in question is indeed, as I suppose, innocent of this atrocity, this advertisement which I left last night, upon our return home, at the office of 'Le Monde,' (a paper devoted to the shipping interest, and much sought by sailors,) will bring him to our residence."

He handed me a paper, and I read thus:

CAUGHT - In the Bois de Boulogne, early in the morning of the - inst., (the morning of the murder,) a very large, tawny Ourang-Outang of the Bornese species. The owner, (who is ascertained to be a sailor, belonging to a Maltese vessel,) may have the animal again, upon identifying it satisfactorily, and paying a few charges arising from its capture and keeping. Call at No. ---- , Rue ----, Faubourg St. Germain - au troisième.

"How was it possible," I asked, "that you should know the man to be a sailor, and belonging to a Maltese vessel?"

"I do not know it," said Dupin. "I am not sure of it. Here, however, is a small piece of ribbon, which from its form, and from its greasy appearance, has evidently been used in tying the hair in one of those long queues of which sailors are so fond. Moreover, this knot is one which few besides sailors can tie, and is peculiar to the Maltese. I picked the ribbon up at the foot of the lightning-rod. It could not have belonged to either of the deceased. Now if, after all, I am wrong in my induction from this ribbon, that the Frenchman was a sailor belonging to a Maltese vessel, still I can have done no harm in saying what I did in the advertisement. If I am in error, he will merely suppose that I have been misled by some circumstance into which he will not take the trouble to inquire. But if I am right, a great point is gained. Cognizant although innocent of the murder, the Frenchman will naturally hesitate about replying to the advertisement - about demanding the Ourang-Outang. He will reason thus: - 'I am innocent; I am poor; my Ourang-Outang is of great value - to one in my circumstances a fortune of itself - why should I lose it through idle apprehensions of danger? Here it is, within my grasp. It was found in the Bois de Boulogne - at a vast distance from the scene of that butchery. How can it ever be suspected that a brute beast should have done the deed? The police are at fault - they have failed to procure the slightest clew. Should they even trace the animal, it would be impossible to prove me cognizant of the murder, or to implicate me in guilt on account of that cognizance. Above all, I am known. The advertiser designates me as the possessor of the beast. I am not sure to what limit his knowledge may extend. Should I avoid claiming a property of so great value, which it is known that I possess, I will render the animal at least, liable to suspicion. It is not my policy to attract attention either to myself or to the beast. I will answer the advertisement, get the Ourang-Outang, and keep it close until this matter has blown over.' "

At this moment we heard a step upon the stairs.

"Be ready," said Dupin, "with your pistols, but neither use them nor show them until at a signal from myself."

The front door of the house had been left open, and the visiter had entered, without ringing, and advanced several steps upon the staircase. Now, however, he seemed to hesitate. Presently we heard him descending. Dupin was moving quickly to the door, when we again heard him coming up. He did not turn back a second time, but stepped up with decision, and rapped at the door of our chamber.

"Come in," said Dupin, in a cheerful and hearty tone.

A man entered. He was a sailor, evidently, - a tall, stout, and muscular-looking person, with a certain dare-devil expression of countenance, not altogether unprepossessing. His face, greatly sunburnt, was more than half hidden by whisker and mustachio. He had with him a huge oaken cudgel, but appeared to be otherwise unarmed. He bowed awkwardly, and bade us "good evening," in French accents, which, although somewhat Neufchatelish, were still sufficiently indicative of a Parisian origin.

"Sit down, my freind," said Dupin. "I suppose you have called about the Ourang-Outang. Upon my word, I almost envy you the possession of him; a remarkably fine, and no doubt a very valuable animal. How old do you suppose him to be?"

The sailor drew a long breath, with the air of a man relieved of some intolerable burden, and then replied, in an assured tone:

"I have no way of telling - but he can't be more than four or five years old. Have you got him here?"

"Oh no, we had no conveniences for keeping him here. He is at a livery stable in the Rue Dubourg, just by. You can get him in the morning. Of course you are prepared to identify the property?"

"To be sure I am, sir."

"I shall be sorry to part with him," said Dupin.

"I don't mean that you should be at all this trouble for nothing, sir," said the man. "Couldn't expect it. Am very willing to pay a reward for the finding of the animal - that is to say, any thing in reason."

"Well," replied my friend, "that is all very fair, to be sure. Let me think! - what should I have? Oh! I will tell you. My reward shall be this. You shall give me all the information in your power about these murders in the Rue Morgue."

Dupin said the last words in a very low tone, and very quietly. Just as quietly, too, he walked toward the door, locked it and put the key in his pocket. He then drew a pistol from his bosom and placed it, without the least flurry, upon the table.

The sailor's face flushed up as if he were struggling with suffocation. He started to his feet and grasped his cudgel, but the next moment he fell back into his seat, trembling violently, and with the countenance of death itself. He spoke not a word. I pitied him from the bottom of my heart.

"My friend," said Dupin, in a kind tone, "you are alarming yourself unnecessarily - you are indeed. We mean you no harm whatever. I pledge you the honor of a gentleman, and of a Frenchman, that we intend you no injury. I perfectly well know that you are innocent of the atrocities in the Rue Morgue. It will not do, however, to deny that you are in some measure implicated in them. From what I have already said, you must know that I have had means of information about this matter - means of which you could never have dreamed. Now the thing stands thus. You have done nothing which you could have avoided - nothing, certainly, which renders you culpable. You were not even guilty of robbery, when you might have robbed with impunity. You have nothing to conceal. You have no reason for concealment. On the other hand, you are bound by every principle of honor to confess all you know. An innocent man is now imprisoned, charged with that crime of which you can point out the perpetrator."

The sailor had recovered his presence of mind, in a great measure, while Dupin uttered these words; but his original boldness of bearing was all gone.

"So help me God," said he, after a brief pause, "I will tell you all I know about this affair; - but I do not expect you to believe one half I say - I would be a fool indeed if I did. Still, I am innocent, and I will make a clean breast if I die for it."

What he stated was, in substance, this. He had lately made a voyage to the Indian Archipelago. A party, of which he formed one, landed at Borneo, and passed into the interior on an excursion of pleasure. Himself and a companion had captured the Ourang- Outang. This companion dying, the animal fell into his own exclusive possession. After great trouble, occasioned by the intractable ferocity of his captive during the home voyage, he at length succeeded in lodging it safely at his own residence in Paris, where, not to attract toward himself the unpleasant curiosity of his neighbors, he kept it carefully secluded, until such time as it should recover from a wound in the foot, received from a splinter on board ship. His ultimate design was to sell it.

Returning home from some sailors' frolic the night, or rather in the morning of the murder, he found the beast occupying his own bed-room, into which it had broken from a closet adjoining, where it had been, as was thought, securely confined. Razor in hand, and fully lathered, it was sitting before a looking-glass, attempting the operation of shaving, in which it had no doubt previously watched its master through the key-hole of the closet. Terrified at the sight of so dangerous a weapon in the possession of an animal so ferocious, and so well able to use it, the man, for some moments, was at a loss what to do. He had been accustomed, however, to quiet the creature, even in its fiercest moods, by the use of a whip, and to this he now resorted. Upon sight of it, the Ourang-Outang sprang at once through the door of the chamber, down the stairs, and thence, through a window, unfortunately open, into the street.

The Frenchman followed in despair; the ape, razor still in hand, occasionally stopping to look back and gesticulate at its pursuer, until the latter had nearly come up with it. It then again made off. In this manner the chase continued for a long time. The streets were profoundly quiet, as it was nearly three o'clock in the morning. In passing down an alley in the rear of the Rue Morgue, the fugitive's attention was arrested by a light gleaming from the open window of Madame L'Espanaye's chamber, in the fourth story of her house. Rushing to the building, it perceived the lightning rod, clambered up with inconceivable agility, grasped the shutter, which was thrown fully back against the wall, and, by its means, swung itself directly upon the headboard of the bed. The whole feat did not occupy a minute. The shutter was kicked open again by the Ourang-Outang as it entered the room.

The sailor, in the meantime, was both rejoiced and perplexed. He had strong hopes of now recapturing the brute, as it could scarcely escape from the trap into which it had ventured, except by the rod, where it might be intercepted as it came down. On the other hand, there was much cause for anxiety as to what it might do in the house. This latter reflection urged the man still to follow the fugitive. A lightning rod is ascended without difficulty, especially by a sailor; but, when he had arrived as high as the window, which lay far to his left, his career was stopped; the most that he could accomplish was to reach over so as to obtain a glimpse of the interior of the room. At this glimpse he nearly fell from his hold through excess of horror. Now it was that those hideous shrieks arose upon the night, which had startled from slumber the inmates of the Rue Morgue. Madame L'Espanaye and her daughter, habited in their night clothes, had apparently been occupied in arranging some papers in the iron chest already mentioned, which had been wheeled into the middle of the room. It was open, and its contents lay beside it on the floor. The victims must have been sitting with their backs toward the window; and, from the time elapsing between the ingress of the beast and the screams, it seems probable that it was not immediately perceived. The flapping-to of the shutter would naturally have been attributed to the wind.

As the sailor looked in, the gigantic animal had seized Madame L'Espanaye by the hair, (which was loose, as she had been combing it,) and was flourishing the razor about her face, in imitation of the motions of a barber. The daughter lay prostrate and motionless; she had swooned. The screams and struggles of the old lady (during which the hair was torn from her head) had the effect of changing the probably pacific purposes of the Ourang-Outang into those of wrath. With one determined sweep of its muscular arm it nearly severed her head from her body. The sight of blood inflamed its anger into phrenzy. Gnashing its teeth, and flashing fire from its eyes, it flew upon the body of the girl, and imbedded its fearful talons in her throat, retaining its grasp until she expired. Its wandering and wild glances fell at this moment upon the head of the bed, over which the face of its master, rigid with horror, was just discernible. The fury of the beast, who no doubt bore still in mind the dreaded whip, was instantly converted into fear. Conscious of having deserved punishment, it seemed desirous of concealing its bloody deeds, and skipped about the chamber in an agony of nervous agitation; throwing down and breaking the furniture as it moved, and dragging the bed from the bedstead. In conclusion, it seized first the corpse of the daughter, and thrust it up the chimney, as it was found; then that of the old lady, which it immediately hurled through the window headlong.

As the ape approached the casement with its mutilated burden, the sailor shrank aghast to the rod, and, rather gliding than clambering down it, hurried at once home - dreading the consequences of the butchery, and gladly abandoning, in his terror, all solicitude about the fate of the Ourang-Outang. The words heard by the party upon the staircase were the Frenchman's exclamations of horror and affright, commingled with the fiendish jabberings of the brute.

I have scarcely anything to add. The Ourang-Outang must have escaped from the chamber, by the rod, just before the break of the door. It must have closed the window as it passed through it. It was subsequently caught by the owner himself, who obtained for it a very large sum at the Jardin des Plantes. Le Don was instantly released, upon our narration of the circumstances (with some comments from Dupin) at the bureau of the Prefect of Police. This functionary, however well disposed to my friend, could not altogether conceal his chagrin at the turn which affairs had taken, and was fain to indulge in a sarcasm or two, about the propriety of every person minding his own business.

"Let him talk," said Dupin,, who had not thought it necessary to reply. "Let him discourse; it will ease his conscience, I am satisfied with having defeated him in his own castle. Nevertheless, that he failed in the solution of this mystery, is by no means that matter for wonder which he supposes it; for, in truth, our friend the Prefect is somewhat too cunning to be profound. In his wisdom is no stamen. It is all head and no body, like the pictures of the Goddess Laverna, -- or, at best, all head and shoulders, like a codfish. But he is a good creature after all. I like him especially for one master stroke of cant, by which he has attained his reputation for ingenuity. I mean the way he has ' de nier ce qui est, et d'expliquer ce qui n'est pas. ' "

On Duty With
Inspector Field

Charles Dickens

On Duty With Inspector Field

HOW goes the night? Saint Giles's clock is striking nine. The weather is dull and wet, and the long lines of street lamps are blurred, as if we saw them through tears. A damp wind blows and rakes the pieman's fire out, when he opens the door of his little furnace, carrying away an eddy of sparks.

Saint Giles's clock strikes nine. We are punctual. Where is Inspector Field? Assistant Commissioner of Police is already here, enwrapped in oil-skin cloak, and standing in the shadow of Saint Giles's steeple. Detective Sergeant, weary of speaking French all day to foreigners unpacking at the Great Exhibition, is already here. Where is Inspector Field?

Inspector Field is, to-night, the guardian genius of the British Museum. He is bringing his shrewd eye to bear on every corner of its solitary galleries, before he reports 'all right.' Suspicious of the Elgin marbles, and not to be done by cat-faced Egyptian giants with their hands upon their knees, Inspector Field, sagacious, vigilant, lamp in hand, throwing monstrous shadows on the walls and ceilings, passes through the spacious rooms. If a mummy trembled in an atom of its dusty covering, Inspector Field would say, 'Come out of that, Tom Green. I know you!' If the smallest 'Gonoph' about town were crouching at the bottom of a classic bath, Inspector Field would nose him with a finer scent than the ogre's, when adventurous Jack lay trembling in his kitchen copper. But all is quiet, and Inspector Field goes warily on, making little outward show of attending to anything in particular, just recognising the Ichthyosaurus as a familiar acquaintance, and wondering, perhaps, how the detectives did it in the days before the Flood.

Will Inspector Field be long about this work? He may be half-an-hour longer. He sends his compliments by Police Constable, and proposes that we meet at St. Giles's Station House, across the road. Good. It were as well to stand by the fire, there, as in the shadow of Saint Giles's steeple.

Anything doing here to-night? Not much. We are very quiet. A lost boy, extremely calm and small, sitting by the fire, whom we now confide to a constable to take home, for the child says that if you show him Newgate Street, he can show you where he lives - a raving drunken woman in the cells, who has screeched her voice away, and has hardly power enough left to declare, even with the passionate help of her feet and arms, that she is the daughter of a British officer, and, strike her blind and dead, but she'll write a letter to the Queen! but who is soothed with a drink of water - in another cell, a quiet woman with a child at her breast, for begging - in another, her husband in a smock-frock, with a basket of watercresses - in another, a pickpocket - in another, a meek tremulous old pauper man who has been out for a holiday 'and has took but a little drop, but it has overcome him after so many months in the house' - and that's all as yet. Presently, a sensation at the Station House door. Mr. Field, gentlemen!

Inspector Field comes in, wiping his forehead, for he is of a burly figure, and has come fast from the ores and metals of the deep mines of the earth, and from the Parrot Gods of the South Sea Islands, and from the birds and beetles of the tropics, and from the Arts of Greece and Rome, and from the Sculptures of Nineveh, and from the traces of an elder world, when these were not. Is Rogers ready? Rogers is ready, strapped and great-coated, with a flaming eye in the middle of his waist, like a deformed Cyclops. Lead on, Rogers, to Rats' Castle!

How many people may there be in London, who, if we had brought them deviously and blindfold, to this street, fifty paces from the Station House, and within call of Saint Giles's church, would know it for a not remote part of the city in which their lives are passed?

How many, who amidst this compound of sickening smells, these heaps of filth, these tumbling houses, with all their vile contents, animate, and inanimate, slimily overflowing into the black road, would believe that they breathe THIS air? How much Red Tape may there be, that could look round on the faces which now hem us in - for our appearance here has caused a rush from all points to a common centre - the lowering foreheads, the sallow cheeks, the brutal eyes, the matted hair, the infected, vermin-haunted heaps of rags - and say, 'I have thought of this. I have not dismissed the thing. I have neither blustered it away, nor frozen it away, nor tied it up and put it away, nor smoothly said pooh, pooh! to it when it has been shown to me?'

This is not what Rogers wants to know, however. What Rogers wants to know, is, whether you WILL clear the way here, some of you, or whether you won't; because if you don't do it right on end, he'll lock you up! 'What! YOU are there, are you, Bob Miles? You haven't had enough of it yet, haven't you? You want three months more, do you? Come away from that gentleman! What are you creeping round there for?'

'What am I a doing, thinn, Mr. Rogers?' says Bob Miles, appearing, villainous, at the end of a lane of light, made by the lantern.

'I'll let you know pretty quick, if you don't hook it. WILL you hook it?'

A sycophantic murmur rises from the crowd. 'Hook it, Bob, when Mr. Rogers and Mr. Field tells you! Why don't you hook it, when you are told to?'

The most importunate of the voices strikes familiarly on Mr. Rogers's ear. He suddenly turns his lantern on the owner.

'What! YOU are there, are you, Mister Click? You hook it too - come!'

'What for?' says Mr. Click, discomfited.

'You hook it, will you!' says Mr. Rogers with stern emphasis.

Both Click and Miles DO 'hook it,' without another word, or, in plainer English, sneak away.

'Close up there, my men!' says Inspector Field to two constables on duty who have followed. 'Keep together, gentlemen; we are going down here. Heads!'

Saint Giles's church strikes half-past ten. We stoop low, and creep down a precipitous flight of steps into a dark close cellar. There is a fire. There is a long deal table. There are benches. The cellar is full of company, chiefly very young men in various conditions of dirt and raggedness. Some are eating supper. There are no girls or women present. Welcome to Rats' Castle, gentlemen, and to this company of noted thieves!

'Well, my lads! How are you, my lads? What have you been doing to-day? Here's some company come to see you, my lads! - THERE'S a plate of beefsteak, sir, for the supper of a fine young man! And there's a mouth for a steak, sir! Why, I should be too proud of such a mouth as that, if I had it myself! Stand up and show it, sir! Take off your cap. There's a fine young man for a nice little party, sir! An't he?'

Inspector Field is the bustling speaker. Inspector Field's eye is the roving eye that searches every corner of the cellar as he talks. Inspector Field's hand is the well-known hand that has collared half the people here, and motioned their brothers, sisters, fathers, mothers, male and female friends, inexorably to New South Wales. Yet Inspector Field stands in this den, the Sultan of the place. Every thief here cowers before him, like a schoolboy before his schoolmaster. All watch him, all answer when addressed, all laugh at his jokes, all seek to propitiate him. This cellar company alone - to say nothing of the crowd surrounding the entrance from the street above, and making the steps shine with eyes - is strong enough to murder us all, and willing enough to do it; but, let Inspector Field have a mind to pick out one thief here, and take him; let him produce that ghostly truncheon from his pocket, and say, with his business-air, 'My lad, I want you!' and all Rats' Castle shall be stricken with paralysis, and not a finger move against him, as he fits the handcuffs on!

Where's the Earl of Warwick? - Here he is, Mr. Field! Here's the Earl of Warwick, Mr. Field! - O there you are, my Lord. Come for'ard. There's a chest, sir, not to have a clean shirt on. An't it? Take your hat off, my Lord. Why, I should be ashamed if I was you - and an Earl, too - to show myself to a gentleman with my hat on! - The Earl of Warwick laughs and uncovers. All the company laugh. One pickpocket, especially, laughs with great enthusiasm. O what a jolly game it is, when Mr. Field comes down - and don't want nobody!

So, YOU are here, too, are you, you tall, grey, soldierly-looking, grave man, standing by the fire? - Yes, sir. Good evening, Mr. Field! - Let us see. You lived servant to a nobleman once? - Yes, Mr. Field. - And what is it you do now; I forget? - Well, Mr. Field, I job about as well as I can. I left my employment on account of delicate health. The family is still kind to me. Mr. Wix of Piccadilly is also very kind to me when I am hard up. Likewise Mr. Nix of Oxford Street. I get a trifle from them occasionally, and rub on as well as I can, Mr. Field. Mr. Field's eye rolls enjoyingly, for this man is a notorious begging-letter writer. - Good night, my lads! - Good night, Mr. Field, and thank'ee, sir!

Clear the street here, half a thousand of you! Cut it, Mrs. Stalker - none of that - we don't want you! Rogers of the flaming eye, lead on to the tramps' lodging-house!

A dream of baleful faces attends to the door. Now, stand back all of you! In the rear Detective Sergeant plants himself, composedly whistling, with his strong right arm across the narrow passage. Mrs. Stalker, I am something'd that need not be written here, if you won't get yourself into trouble, in about half a minute, if I see that face of yours again!

Saint Giles's church clock, striking eleven, hums through our hand from the dilapidated door of a dark outhouse as we open it, and are stricken back by the pestilent breath that issues from within. Rogers to the front with the light, and let us look!

Ten, twenty, thirty - who can count them! Men, women, children, for the most part naked, heaped upon the floor like maggots in a cheese! Ho! In that dark corner yonder! Does anybody lie there? Me sir, Irish me, a widder, with six children. And yonder? Me sir, Irish me, with me wife and eight poor babes. And to the left there? Me sir, Irish me, along with two more Irish boys as is me friends. And to the right there? Me sir and the Murphy fam'ly, numbering five blessed souls. And what's this, coiling, now, about my foot? Another Irish me, pitifully in want of shaving, whom I have awakened from sleep - and across my other foot lies his wife - and by the shoes of Inspector Field lie their three eldest - and their three youngest are at present squeezed between the open door and the wall. And why is there no one on that little mat before the sullen fire? Because O'Donovan, with his wife and daughter, is not come in from selling Lucifers! Nor on the bit of sacking in the nearest corner? Bad luck! Because that Irish family is late to-night, a-cadging in the streets!

They are all awake now, the children excepted, and most of them sit up, to stare. Wheresoever Mr. Rogers turns the flaming eye, there is a spectral figure rising, unshrouded, from a grave of rags. Who is the landlord here? - I am, Mr. Field! says a bundle of ribs and parchment against the wall, scratching itself. - Will you spend this money fairly, in the morning, to buy coffee for 'em all? - Yes, sir, I will! - O he'll do it, sir, he'll do it fair. He's honest! cry the spectres. And with thanks and Good Night sink into their graves again.

Thus, we make our New Oxford Streets, and our other new streets, never heeding, never asking, where the wretches whom we clear out, crowd. With such scenes at our doors, with all the plagues of Egypt tied up with bits of cobweb in kennels so near our homes, we timorously make our Nuisance Bills and Boards of Health, nonentities, and think to keep away the Wolves of Crime and Filth, by our electioneering ducking to little vestrymen and our gentlemanly handling of Red Tape!

Intelligence of the coffee-money has got abroad. The yard is full, and Rogers of the flaming eye is beleaguered with entreaties to show other Lodging Houses. Mine next! Mine! Mine! Rogers, military, obdurate, stiff-necked, immovable, replies not, but leads away; all falling back before him. Inspector Field follows. Detective Sergeant, with his barrier of arm across the little passage, deliberately waits to close the procession. He sees behind him, without any effort, and exceedingly disturbs one individual far in the rear by coolly calling out, 'It won't do, Mr. Michael! Don't try it!'

After council holden in the street, we enter other lodging-houses, public-houses, many lairs and holes; all noisome and offensive; none so filthy and so crowded as where Irish are. In one, The Ethiopian party are expected home presently - were in Oxford Street when last heard of - shall be fetched, for our delight, within ten minutes. In another, one of the two or three Professors who drew Napoleon Buonaparte and a couple of mackerel, on the pavement and then let the work of art out to a speculator, is refreshing after his labours. In another, the vested interest of the profitable nuisance has been in one family for a hundred years, and the landlord drives in comfortably from the country to his snug little stew in town. In all, Inspector Field is received with warmth. Coiners and smashers droop before him; pickpockets defer to him; the gentle sex (not very gentle here) smile upon him. Half-drunken hags check themselves in the midst of pots of beer, or pints of gin, to drink to Mr. Field, and pressingly to ask the honour of his finishing the draught. One beldame in rusty black has such admiration for him, that she runs a whole street's length to shake him by the hand; tumbling into a heap of mud by the way, and still pressing her attentions when her very form has ceased to be distinguishable through it. Before the power of the law, the power of superior sense - for common thieves are fools beside these men - and the power of a perfect mastery of their character, the garrison of Rats' Castle and the adjacent Fortresses make but a skulking show indeed when reviewed by Inspector Field.

Saint Giles's clock says it will be midnight in half-an-hour, and Inspector Field says we must hurry to the Old Mint in the Borough. The cab-driver is low-spirited, and has a solemn sense of his responsibility. Now, what's your fare, my lad? - O YOU know, Inspector Field, what's the good of asking ME!

Say, Parker, strapped and great-coated, and waiting in dim Borough doorway by appointment, to replace the trusty Rogers whom we left deep in Saint Giles's, are you ready? Ready, Inspector Field, and at a motion of my wrist behold my flaming eye.

This narrow street, sir, is the chief part of the Old Mint, full of low lodging-houses, as you see by the transparent canvas-lamps and blinds, announcing beds for travellers! But it is greatly changed, friend Field, from my former knowledge of it; it is infinitely quieter and more subdued than when I was here last, some seven years ago? O yes! Inspector Haynes, a first-rate man, is on this station now and plays the Devil with them!

Well, my lads! How are you to-night, my lads? Playing cards here, eh? Who wins? - Why, Mr. Field, I, the sulky gentleman with the damp flat side-curls, rubbing my bleared eye with the end of my neckerchief which is like a dirty eel-skin, am losing just at present, but I suppose I must take my pipe out of my mouth, and be submissive to YOU - I hope I see you well, Mr. Field? - Aye, all right, my lad. Deputy, who have you got up-stairs? Be pleased to show the rooms!

Why Deputy, Inspector Field can't say. He only knows that the man who takes care of the beds and lodgers is always called so. Steady, O Deputy, with the flaring candle in the blacking-bottle, for this is a slushy back-yard, and the wooden staircase outside the house creaks and has holes in it.

Again, in these confined intolerable rooms, burrowed out like the holes of rats or the nests of insect-vermin, but fuller of intolerable smells, are crowds of sleepers, each on his foul truckle-bed coiled up beneath a rug. Holloa here! Come! Let us see you! Show your face! Pilot Parker goes from bed to bed and turns their slumbering heads towards us, as a salesman might turn sheep. Some wake up with an execration and a threat. - What! who spoke? O! If it's the accursed glaring eye that fixes me, go where I will, I am helpless. Here! I sit up to be looked at. Is it me you want? Not you, lie down again! and I lie down, with a woful growl.

Whenever the turning lane of light becomes stationary for a moment, some sleeper appears at the end of it, submits himself to be scrutinised, and fades away into the darkness.

There should be strange dreams here, Deputy. They sleep sound enough, says Deputy, taking the candle out of the blacking-bottle, snuffing it with his fingers, throwing the snuff into the bottle, and corking it up with the candle; that's all I know. What is the inscription, Deputy, on all the discoloured sheets? A precaution against loss of linen. Deputy turns down the rug of an unoccupied bed and discloses it. STOP THIEF!

To lie at night, wrapped in the legend of my slinking life; to take the cry that pursues me, waking, to my breast in sleep; to have it staring at me, and clamouring for me, as soon as consciousness returns; to have it for my first-foot on New-Year's day, my Valentine, my Birthday salute, my Christmas greeting, my parting with the old year. STOP THIEF!

And to know that I MUST be stopped, come what will. To know that I am no match for this individual energy and keenness, or this organised and steady system! Come across the street, here, and, entering by a little shop and yard, examine these intricate passages and doors, contrived for escape, flapping and counter- flapping, like the lids of the conjurer's boxes. But what avail they? Who gets in by a nod, and shows their secret working to us? Inspector Field.

Don't forget the old Farm House, Parker! Parker is not the man to forget it. We are going there, now. It is the old Manor-House of these parts, and stood in the country once. Then, perhaps, there was something, which was not the beastly street, to see from the shattered low fronts of the overhanging wooden houses we are passing under - shut up now, pasted over with bills about the literature and drama of the Mint, and mouldering away. This long paved yard was a paddock or a garden once, or a court in front of the Farm House. Perchance, with a dovecot in the centre, and fowls peeking about - with fair elm trees, then, where discoloured chimney-stacks and gables are now - noisy, then, with rooks which have yielded to a different sort of rookery. It's likelier than not, Inspector Field thinks, as we turn into the common kitchen, which is in the yard, and many paces from the house.

Well, my lads and lasses, how are you all? Where's Blackey, who has stood near London Bridge these five-and-twenty years, with a painted skin to represent disease? - Here he is, Mr. Field! - How are you, Blackey? - Jolly, sa! Not playing the fiddle to-night, Blackey? - Not a night, sa! A sharp, smiling youth, the wit of the kitchen, interposes. He an't musical to-night, sir. I've been giving him a moral lecture; I've been a talking to him about his latter end, you see. A good many of these are my pupils, sir. This here young man (smoothing down the hair of one near him, reading a Sunday paper) is a pupil of mine. I'm a teaching of him to read, sir. He's a promising cove, sir. He's a smith, he is, and gets his living by the sweat of the brow, sir. So do I, myself, sir. This young woman is my sister, Mr. Field. SHE'S getting on very well too. I've a deal of trouble with 'em, sir, but I'm richly rewarded, now I see 'em all a doing so well, and growing up so creditable. That's a great comfort, that is, an't it, sir? - In the midst of the kitchen (the whole kitchen is in ecstasies with this impromptu 'chaff') sits a young, modest, gentle-looking creature, with a beautiful child in her lap. She seems to belong to the company, but is so strangely unlike it. She has such a pretty, quiet face and voice, and is so proud to hear the child admired - thinks you would hardly believe that he is only nine months old! Is she as bad as the rest, I wonder? Inspectorial experience does not engender a belief contrariwise, but prompts the answer, Not a ha'porth of difference!

There is a piano going in the old Farm House as we approach. It stops. Landlady appears. Has no objections, Mr. Field, to gentlemen being brought, but wishes it were at earlier hours, the lodgers complaining of ill-conwenience. Inspector Field is polite and soothing - knows his woman and the sex. Deputy (a girl in this case) shows the way up a heavy, broad old staircase, kept very clean, into clean rooms where many sleepers are, and where painted panels of an older time look strangely on the truckle beds. The sight of whitewash and the smell of soap - two things we seem by this time to have parted from in infancy - make the old Farm House a phenomenon, and connect themselves with the so curiously misplaced picture of the pretty mother and child long after we have left it, - long after we have left, besides, the neighbouring nook with something of a rustic flavour in it yet, where once, beneath a low wooden colonnade still standing as of yore, the eminent Jack Sheppard condescended to regale himself, and where, now, two old bachelor brothers in broad hats (who are whispered in the Mint to have made a compact long ago that if either should ever marry, he must forfeit his share of the joint property) still keep a sequestered tavern, and sit o' nights smoking pipes in the bar, among ancient bottles and glasses, as our eyes behold them.

How goes the night now? Saint George of Southwark answers with twelve blows upon his bell. Parker, good night, for Williams is already waiting over in the region of Ratcliffe Highway, to show the houses where the sailors dance.

I should like to know where Inspector Field was born. In Ratcliffe Highway, I would have answered with confidence, but for his being equally at home wherever we go. HE does not trouble his head as I do, about the river at night. HE does not care for its creeping, black and silent, on our right there, rushing through sluice-gates, lapping at piles and posts and iron rings, hiding strange things in its mud, running away with suicides and accidentally drowned bodies faster than midnight funeral should, and acquiring such various experience between its cradle and its grave. It has no mystery for HIM. Is there not the Thames Police!

Accordingly, Williams leads the way. We are a little late, for some of the houses are already closing. No matter. You show us plenty. All the landlords know Inspector Field. All pass him, freely and good-humouredly, wheresoever he wants to go. So thoroughly are all these houses open to him and our local guide, that, granting that sailors must be entertained in their own way - as I suppose they must, and have a right to be - I hardly know how such places could be better regulated. Not that I call the company very select, or the dancing very graceful - even so graceful as that of the German Sugar Bakers, whose assembly, by the Minories, we stopped to visit - but there is watchful maintenance of order in every house, and swift expulsion where need is. Even in the midst of drunkenness, both of the lethargic kind and the lively, there is sharp landlord supervision, and pockets are in less peril than out of doors. These houses show, singularly, how much of the picturesque and romantic there truly is in the sailor, requiring to be especially addressed. All the songs (sung in a hailstorm of halfpence, which are pitched at the singer without the least tenderness for the time or tune - mostly from great rolls of copper carried for the purpose - and which he occasionally dodges like shot as they fly near his head) are of the sentimental sea sort. All the rooms are decorated with nautical subjects. Wrecks, engagements, ships on fire, ships passing lighthouses on iron-bound coasts, ships blowing up, ships going down, ships running ashore, men lying out upon the main-yard in a gale of wind, sailors and ships in every variety of peril, constitute the illustrations of fact. Nothing can be done in the fanciful way, without a thumping boy upon a scaly dolphin.

How goes the night now? Past one. Black and Green are waiting in Whitechapel to unveil the mysteries of Wentworth Street. Williams, the best of friends must part. Adieu!

Are not Black and Green ready at the appointed place? O yes! They glide out of shadow as we stop. Imperturbable Black opens the cab- door; Imperturbable Green takes a mental note of the driver. Both Green and Black then open each his flaming eye, and marshal us the way that we are going.

The lodging-house we want is hidden in a maze of streets and courts. It is fast shut. We knock at the door, and stand hushed looking up for a light at one or other of the begrimed old lattice windows in its ugly front, when another constable comes up - supposes that we want 'to see the school.' Detective Sergeant meanwhile has got over a rail, opened a gate, dropped down an area, overcome some other little obstacles, and tapped at a window. Now returns. The landlord will send a deputy immediately.

Deputy is heard to stumble out of bed. Deputy lights a candle, draws back a bolt or two, and appears at the door. Deputy is a shivering shirt and trousers by no means clean, a yawning face, a shock head much confused externally and internally. We want to look for some one. You may go up with the light, and take 'em all, if you like, says Deputy, resigning it, and sitting down upon a bench in the kitchen with his ten fingers sleepily twisting in his hair.

Halloa here! Now then! Show yourselves. That'll do. It's not you. Don't disturb yourself any more! So on, through a labyrinth of airless rooms, each man responding, like a wild beast, to the keeper who has tamed him, and who goes into his cage. What, you haven't found him, then? says Deputy, when we came down. A woman mysteriously sitting up all night in the dark by the smouldering ashes of the kitchen fire, says it's only tramps and cadgers here; it's gonophs over the way. A man mysteriously walking about the kitchen all night in the dark, bids her hold her tongue. We come out. Deputy fastens the door and goes to bed again.

Black and Green, you know Bark, lodging-house keeper and receiver of stolen goods? - O yes, Inspector Field. - Go to Bark's next.

Bark sleeps in an inner wooden hutch, near his street door. As we parley on the step with Bark's Deputy, Bark growls in his bed. We enter, and Bark flies out of bed. Bark is a red villain and a wrathful, with a sanguine throat that looks very much as if it were expressly made for hanging, as he stretches it out, in pale defiance, over the half-door of his hutch. Bark's parts of speech are of an awful sort - principally adjectives. I won't, says Bark, have no adjective police and adjective strangers in my adjective premises! I won't, by adjective and substantive! Give me my trousers, and I'll send the whole adjective police to adjective and substantive! Give me, says Bark, my adjective trousers! I'll put an adjective knife in the whole bileing of 'em. I'll punch their adjective heads. I'll rip up their adjective substantives. Give me my adjective trousers! says Bark, and I'll spile the bileing of 'em!

Now, Bark, what's the use of this? Here's Black and Green, Detective Sergeant, and Inspector Field. You know we will come in. - I know you won't! says Bark. Somebody give me my adjective trousers! Bark's trousers seem difficult to find. He calls for them as Hercules might for his club. Give me my adjective trousers! says Bark, and I'll spile the bileing of 'em!

Inspector Field holds that it's all one whether Bark likes the visit or don't like it. He, Inspector Field, is an Inspector of the Detective Police, Detective Sergeant IS Detective Sergeant, Black and Green are constables in uniform. Don't you be a fool, Bark, or you know it will be the worse for you. - I don't care, says Bark. Give me my adjective trousers!

At two o'clock in the morning, we descend into Bark's low kitchen, leaving Bark to foam at the mouth above, and Imperturbable Black and Green to look at him. Bark's kitchen is crammed full of thieves, holding a CONVERSAZIONE there by lamp-light. It is by far the most dangerous assembly we have seen yet. Stimulated by the ravings of Bark, above, their looks are sullen, but not a man speaks. We ascend again. Bark has got his trousers, and is in a state of madness in the passage with his back against a door that shuts off the upper staircase. We observe, in other respects, a ferocious individuality in Bark. Instead of 'STOP THIEF!' on his linen, he prints 'STOLEN FROM Bark's!'

Now, Bark, we are going up-stairs! - No, you ain't! - YOU refuse admission to the Police, do you, Bark? - Yes, I do! I refuse it to all the adjective police, and to all the adjective substantives. If the adjective coves in the kitchen was men, they'd come up now, and do for you! Shut me that there door! says Bark, and suddenly we are enclosed in the passage. They'd come up and do for you! cries Bark, and waits. Not a sound in the kitchen! They'd come up and do for you! cries Bark again, and waits. Not a sound in the kitchen! We are shut up, half-a-dozen of us, in Bark's house in the innermost recesses of the worst part of London, in the dead of the night - the house is crammed with notorious robbers and ruffians - and not a man stirs. No, Bark. They know the weight of the law, and they know Inspector Field and Co. too well.

We leave bully Bark to subside at leisure out of his passion and his trousers, and, I dare say, to be inconveniently reminded of this little brush before long. Black and Green do ordinary duty here, and look serious.

As to White, who waits on Holborn Hill to show the courts that are eaten out of Rotten Gray's Inn, Lane, where other lodging-houses are, and where (in one blind alley) the Thieves' Kitchen and Seminary for the teaching of the art to children is, the night has so worn away, being now

almost at odds with morning, which is which,

that they are quiet, and no light shines through the chinks in the shutters. As undistinctive Death will come here, one day, sleep comes now. The wicked cease from troubling sometimes, even in this life.

The Staircase at the Hearts Delight

Anna Katharine Green

(Mrs. Charles Rohlfs)

The Staircase at the Hearts Delight

AS TOLD BY MR. GRYCE.

"In the spring of 1840, the attention of the New York police was attracted by the many cases of well-known men found drowned in the various waters surrounding the lower portion of our great city. Among these may be mentioned the name of Elwood Henderson, the noted tea merchant, whose remains were washed ashore at Redhook Point; and of Christopher Bigelow, who was picked up off Governor's Island after having been in the water for five days, and of another well-known millionaire whose name I cannot now recall, but who, I remember, was seen to walk towards the East River one March evening, and was not met with again till the 5th of April, when his body floated into one of the docks near Peck Slip.

"As it seemed highly improbable that there should have been a concerted action among so many wealthy and distinguished men to end their lives within a few weeks of each other, and all by the same method of drowning, we soon became suspicious that a more serious verdict than that of suicide should have been rendered in the case of Henderson, Bigelow and the other gentleman I have mentioned. Yet one fact, common to all these cases, pointed so conclusively to deliberate intention on the part of the sufferers that we hesitated to take action.

"This was, that upon the body of each of the above-mentioned persons there were found, not only valuables in the shape of money and jewelry, but papers and memoranda of a nature calculated to fix the identity of the drowned man, in case the water should rob him of his personal characteristics. Consequently, we could not ascribe these deaths to a desire for plunder on the part of some unknown person.

"I was a young man in those days, and full of ambition. So, though I said nothing, I did not let this matter drop when the others did, but kept my mind persistently upon it and waited, with odd results as you will hear, for another victim to be reported at police headquarters.

"Meantime I sought to discover some bond or connection between the several men who had been found drowned, which would serve to explain their similar fate. But all my efforts in this direction were fruitless. There was no bond between them, and the matter remained for a while an unsolved mystery.

"Suddenly one morning a clew was placed, not in my hands, but in those of a superior official who at that time exerted a great influence over the whole force. He was sitting in his private room, when there was ushered into his presence a young man of a dissipated but not unprepossessing appearance, who, after a pause of marked embarrassment, entered upon the following story:

"I don't know whether or no, I should offer an excuse for the communication I am about to make; but the matter I have to relate is simply this: Being hard up last night (for though a rich man's son I often lack money), I went to a certain pawn-shop in the Bowery where I had been told I could raise money on my prospects. This place—you may see it sometime, so I will not enlarge upon it—did not strike me favorably; but, being very anxious for a certain definite sum of money, I wrote my name in a book which was brought to me from some unknown quarter, and proceeded to follow the young woman who attended me into what she was pleased to call her good master's private office. He may have been a good master, but he was anything but a good man, In short, sir, when he found out who I was, and how much I needed money, he suggested that I should make an appointment with my father at a place he called Judah's in Grand Street, where, said he, 'your little affair will be arranged, and you made a rich man within thirty days. That is,' he slyly added, 'unless your father has already made a will, disinheriting you.'

"I was shocked, sir, shocked beyond all my powers of concealment, not so much at his words, which I hardly understood, as at his looks, which had a world of evil suggestion in them; so I raised my fist and would have knocked him down, only that I found two young fellows at my elbows, who held me quiet for five minutes, while the old fellow talked to me. He asked me if I came to him on a fool's errand or really to get money; and when I admitted that I had cherished hopes of obtaining a clear two thousand dollars from him, he coolly replied that he knew of but one way in which I could hope to get such an amount, and that if I was too squeamish to adopt it, I had made a mistake in coming to his shop, which was no missionary institution, etc., etc. Not wishing to irritate him, for there was menace in his eye, I asked, with a certain weak show of being sorry for my former heat, whereabouts in Grand Street I should find this Judah. The retort was quick, 'Judah is not his name,' said he, 'and Grand Street is not where you are to go to find him. I threw out a bait to see if you would snap at it, but I find you timid, and therefore advise you to drop the matter entirely.' I was quite willing to do so, and answered him to this effect; whereupon, with a side glance I did not understand but which made me more or less uneasy in regard to his intentions towards me, he motioned to the men who held my arms to let go their hold, which they at once did.

"'We have your signature,' growled the old man as I went out. 'If you peach on us or trouble us in any way we will show it to your father and that will put an end to all your hopes of future fortune.' Then raising his voice he shouted to the girl in the outer office, 'Let the young man see what he has signed.' She smiled and again brought forward the book in which I had so recklessly placed my name, and there at the top of the page I read these words: 'For moneys received, I agree to notify Levi Solomon, within the month, of the death of my father, that he may recover from me, without loss of time, the sum of ten thousand dollars from the amount I am bound to receive as my father's heir.' The sight of these lines knocked me hollow. But I am less of a coward morally than physically, and I determined to acquaint my father at once with what I had done, and get his advice as to whether or not I should inform the police of my adventure. He heard me with more consideration than I expected, but insisted that I should immediately make known to you my experience in this Bowery pawnbroker's shop.

"The officer, highly interested, took down the young man's statement in writing, and, after getting a more accurate description of the Jew's house, allowed his visitor to go.

"Fortunately for me I was in the building at the time, and was able to respond when a man was called up to investigate this matter. Thinking that I saw a connection between it and the various mysterious deaths of which I have previously spoken, I entered into the affair with much spirit. But, wishing to be sure that my possibly unwarranted conclusions were correct, I took pains to inquire, before proceeding upon my errand, into the character of the heirs who had inherited the property of Elwood Henderson and Christopher Bigelow, and found that in each case there was one among the rest who was well known for his profligacy and reckless expenditure. It was a significant discovery, and increased, if possible, my interest in running down this nefarious trafficker in the lives of wealthy men.

"Knowing that I could hope for no success in my character of detective, I made an arrangement with the father of the young gentleman before alluded to, by which I was to enter the pawn-shop as an emissary of the latter. I accordingly appeared there, one dull November afternoon, in the garb of a certain western sporting man, who, for a consideration, allowed me the temporary use of his name and credentials.

"Entering beneath the three golden balls, with, the swagger and general air of ownership I thought most likely to impose upon the self-satisfied female who presided over the desk, I asked to see her boss.

"'On your own business?' she queried, glancing with suspicion at my short coat, which was rather more showy than elegant.

"'No,' I returned, 'not on my own business, but on that of a young gent——'

"'Anyone whose name is written here?' she interposed, reaching towards me the famous book, over the top of which, however, she was careful to lay her arm.

"I glanced down the page she had opened and instantly detected that of the young gentleman on whose behalf I was supposed to be there, and nodded 'Yes,' with all the assurance of which I was capable.

"'Very well, then,' said she, 'come!' and she ushered me without much ado into a den of discomfort where sat a man, with a great beard and such heavy overhanging eyebrows that I could hardly detect the twinkle of his eyes, keen and incisive as they were.

"Smiling upon him, but not in the same way I had upon the girl, I glanced behind me at the open door, and above me at the partitions, which failed to reach the ceiling. Then I shook my head and drew a step nearer.

"'I have come,' I insinuatingly whispered, 'on behalf of a certain party who left this place in a huff a day or so ago, but who since then has had time to think the matter over, and has sent me with an apology which he hopes'—here I put on a diabolical smile, copied, I declare to you, from the one I saw at that moment on his own lips—'you will accept.'

"The old wretch regarded me for full two minutes in a way to unmask me had I possessed less confidence in my disguise and in my ability to support it.

"'And what is this young gentleman's name?' he finally asked.

"For reply, I handed him a slip of paper. He took it and read the few lines written on it, after which he began to rub his palms together with a snaky unction eminently in keeping with the stray glints of light that now and then found their way through his' bushy eyebrows.

"'And so the young gentleman had not the courage to come again himself?' he softly suggested, with just the suspicion of an ironical laugh. 'Thought, perhaps, I would exact too much commission; or make him pay too roundly for his impertinent assurance.'

"I shrugged my shoulders, but vouchsafed no immediate reply, and he saw that he had to open the business himself. He did it warily and with many an incisive question which would have tripped me up if I had not been very much on my guard; but it all ended, as such matters usually do, in mutual understanding, and a promise that if the young gentleman was willing to sign a certain paper, which, by the way, was not shown me, he would in exchange give him an address which, if made proper use of, would lead to my patron finding himself an independent man within a very few days.

"As this address was the thing above all others which I most desired, I professed myself satisfied with the arrangement, and proceeded to hunt up my patron, as he was called. Informing him of the result of my visit, I asked if his interest in ferreting out these criminals was strong enough to lead him to sign the vile document which the Jew would probably have in readiness for him on the morrow; and being told it was, we separated for that day, with the understanding that we were to meet the next morning at the spot chosen by the Jew for the completion of his nefarious bargain.

"Being certain that I was being followed in all my movements by the agents of this adept in villainy, I took care, upon leaving Mr. L——, to repair to the hotel of the sporting man I was personifying. Making myself square with the proprietor, I took up my quarters in the room of my sporting friend, and, the better to deceive any spy who might be lurking about, I received his letters and sent out his telegrams, which, if they did not create confusion in the affairs of

'The Plunger,' must at least have occasioned him no little work the next day.

"Promptly at ten o'clock on the following morning I met my patron at the place of rendezvous appointed by the old Jew; and when I tell you that this was no other than the old cemetery of which a portion is still to be seen off Chatham Square, you will understand the uncanny nature of this whole adventure, and the lurking sense there was in it of brooding death and horror. The scene, which in these days is disturbed by elevated railroad trains and the flapping of long lines of parti-colored clothes strung high up across the quiet tombstones, was at that time one of peaceful rest, in the midst of a quarter devoted to everything for which that rest is the fitting and desirable end; and as we paused among the mossy stones, we found it hard to realize that in a few minutes there would be standing beside us the concentrated essence of all that was evil and despicable in human nature.

"He arrived with a smile on his countenance that completed his ugliness, and would have frightened any honest man from his side at once. Merely glancing my way, he shuffled up to my companion, and leading him aside, drew out a paper which he laid on a flat tombstone with a gesture significant of his desire that the other should affix to it the required signature.

"Meantime I stood guard, and while attempting to whistle a light air, was carelessly taking in the surroundings, and conjecturing, as best I might, the reasons which had induced the old ghoul to make use of this spot for his diabolical business, and had about decided that it was because he was a ghoul, and thus felt at home among the symbols of mortality, when I caught sight of two or three young fellows, who were lounging on the other side of the fence.

"These were so evidently accomplices that I wondered if the two sly boys I had engaged to stand by me through this affair had spotted them, and would know enough to follow them back to their haunts.

"A few minutes later, the old rascal came sneaking towards me, with a gleam of satisfaction in his half-closed eyes.

"'You are not wanted any longer,' he grunted. 'The young gentleman told me to say that he could look out for himself now.'

"'The young gentleman had better pay me the round fifty he promised me,' I grumbled in return, with that sudden change from indifference to menace which I thought best calculated to further my plans; and shouldering the miserable wretch aside, I stepped up to my companion, who was still lingering in a state of hesitation among the gravestones.

"'Quick! Tell me the number and street which he has given you! 'I whispered, in a tone strangely in contrast with the angry and reproachful air I had assumed.

"He was about to answer, when the old fellow came sidling up behind us. Instantly the young man before me rose to the occasion, and putting on an air of conciliation said in a soothing tone:

"'There, there, don't bluster. Do one thing more for me, and I will add another fifty to those I promised you. Conjure up an anonymous letter—you know how—and send it to my father, saying that if he wants to know where his son loses his hundreds, he must go to the place on the dock, opposite 5 South Street, some night shortly after nine. It would not work with most men, but it will with my father, and when he has been in and out of that place, and I succeed to the fortune he will leave me, then I will remember you, and——'

"'Say, too,' a sinister voice here added in my ear, 'that if he wishes to effect an entrance into the gambling den which his son haunts, he must take the precaution of tying a bit of blue ribbon in his button-hole. It is a signal meaning business, and must not be forgotten,' chuckled the old fellow, evidently deceived at last into thinking I was really one of his own kind.

"I answered by a wink, and taking care to attempt no further communication with my patron, I left the two, as soon as possible, and went back to the hotel, where I dropped 'the sport,' and assumed a character and dress which enabled me to make my way undetected to the house of my young patron, where for two days I lay low, waiting for a suitable time in which to make my final attempt to penetrate this mystery.

"I knew that for the adventure I was now contemplating considerable courage was required. But I did not hesitate. The time had come for me to show my mettle. In the few communications I was enabled to hold with my superiors I told them of my progress and arranged with them my plan of work. As we all agreed that I was about to encounter no common villainy, these plans naturally partook of finesse, as you will see if you will follow my narrative to the end.

"Early in the evening of a cool November night I sallied forth into the streets, dressed in the habiliments and wearing the guise of the wealthy old gentleman whose secret guest I had been for the last few days. As he was old and portly, and I young and spare, this disguise had cost me no little thought and labor. But assisted as I was by the darkness, I had but little fear of betraying myself to any chance spy who might be upon the watch, especially as Mr. L—— had a peculiar walk, which, in my short stay with him, I had learned to imitate perfectly. In the lapel of my overcoat I had tied a tag of blue ribbon, and, though for all I knew this was a signal devoting me to a secret and mysterious death, I walked along in a buoyant condition of mind, attributable, no doubt, to the excitement of the venture and to my desire to test my powers, even at the risk of my life.

"It was nine o'clock when I reached South Street. It was no new region to me, nor was I ignorant of the specified drinking den on the dock to which I had been directed. I remembered it as a bright spot in a mass of ship-prows and bow-rigging, and was possessed, besides, of a vague consciousness that there was something odd in connection with it which had aroused my curiosity sufficiently in the past for me to have once formed the resolution of seeing it again under circumstances which would allow me to give, it some attention. But I never thought that the circumstances would involve my own life, impossible as it is for a detective to reckon upon the future or to foresee the events into which he will be hurried by the next crime which may be reported at police headquarters.

"There were but few persons in the street when I crossed to The Heart's Delight,—so named from the heart-shaped opening in the framework of the door, through which shone a light, inviting enough to one chilled by the keen November air and oppressed by the desolate appearance of the almost deserted street. But amongst those persons I thought I recognized more than one familiar form, and felt reassured as to the watch which had been set upon the house. The night was dark and the river especially so, but in the gloomy space beyond the dock I detected a shadow blacker than the rest, which I took for the police-boat they had promised to have in readiness in case I needed rescue from the water-side. Otherwise the surroundings were as usual, and saving the gruff singing of some drunken sailor coming from a narrow side street near by, no sound disturbed the somewhat lugubrious silence of this weird and forsaken spot.

"Pausing an instant before entering, I glanced up at the building, which was about three stories high, and endeavored to see what there was about it which had once arrested my attention, and came to the conclusion that it was its exceptional situation on the dock, and the ghostly effect of the hoisting-beam projecting from the upper story like a gibbet. And yet this beam was common to many a warehouse in the vicinity, though in none of them were there any such signs of life as proceeded from the curious mixture of sail loft, boat shop and drinking saloon, now before me. Could it be that the ban of criminality was upon the house, and that I had been conscious of this without being able to realize the cause of my interest?

"Not stopping to solve my sensations further, I tried the door, and, finding it yield easily to my touch, turned the knob and entered. For a moment I was blinded by the smoky glare of the heated atmosphere into which I stepped, but presently I was able to distinguish the vague outlines of an oyster bar in the distance, and the motionless figures of some half dozen men, whose movements had been arrested by my sudden entrance. For an instant this picture remained; then the drinking and card-playing were resumed, and I stood, as it were, alone on the sanded floor near the door. Improving the opportunity for a closer inspection of the place, I was struck by its picturesqueness. It had evidently been once used as a ship chandlery, and on the walls, which were but partly plastered, there still hung old bits of marlin, rusty rings and such other evidences of former traffic as did not interfere with the present more lucrative business.

"Below were the two bars, one at the right of the door, and the other at the lower end of the room near a window, through whose small, square panes I caught a glimpse of the colored lights of a couple of ferry boats, passing each other in midstream.

"At a table near me sat two men, grumbling at each other over a game of cards. They were large and powerful figures in the contracted space of this long and narrow room, and my heart gave a bound of joy as I recognized on them certain marks by which I was to know friend from foe in this possible den of thieves and murderers.

"Two sailors at the bar were bona fide habitués of the place, and so I judged to be the one or two other specimens of water-side character whose backs I could faintly discern in one of the dim corners. Meantime a man was approaching me.

"Let me see if I can describe him. He was about thirty, and had the complexion and figure of a consumptive, but his eye shone with the yellow glare of a beast of prey, and in the cadaverous hollows of his ashen cheeks and amid the lines about his thin drawn lips there lay for all his conciliatory smile, an expression so cold and yet so ferocious that I spotted him at once as the man to whose genius we were indebted for the new scheme of murder which I was jeopardizing my life to understand. But I allowed none of the repugnance with which he inspired me to appear in my manner, and, greeting him with half a nod, waited for him to speak. His voice had that smooth quality which betrays the hypocrite.

"'Has the gentleman an appointment here?' he asked, letting his glance fall for the merest instant on the lapel of my coat.

"I returned a decided affirmative. Or rather, I went on, with a meaning look he evidently comprehended, 'my son has, and I have made up my mind to know just what deviltry he is up to these days. You see I can make it worth your while to give me the opportunity.'

"'O, I see,' he assented with a glance at the pocketbook I had just drawn out. 'You want a private room from which you can watch the young scapegrace. I understand, I understand. But the private rooms are above. Gentlemen are not comfortable here.'

"'I should say not,' I murmured, and drew from the pocketbook a bill which I slid quietly into his hand. 'Now take me where I shall be safe,' I suggested, 'and yet in full sight of the room where the young gentlemen play. I wish to catch him at his tricks. Afterwards——'

"'All will be well,' he finished smoothly, with another glance at my blue ribbon. 'You see I do not ask you the young gentleman's name. I take your money and leave all the rest to you. Only don't make a scandal, I pray, for my house has the name of being quiet.'

"'Yes,' thought I, 'too quiet!' and for an instant felt my spirits fail me. But it was only for an instant. I had friends about me and a pistol at half cock in the pocket of my overcoat. Why should I fear any surprise, prepared as I was for every emergency?

"'I will show you up in a moment,' said he; and left me to put up a heavy board-shutter over the window opening on the river. Was this a signal or a precaution? I glanced towards my two friends playing cards, took another note of their broad shoulders and brawny arms, and prepared to follow my host, who now stood bowing at the other end of the room, before a covered staircase which was manifestly the sole means of reaching the floor above.

"The staircase was quite a feature in the room. It ran from back to front, and was boarded all the way up to the ceiling. On these boards hung a few useless bits of chain, wire and knotted ends of tarred ropes, which swung to and fro as the sharp November blast struck the building, giving out a weird and strangely muffled sound. Why did this sound, so easily to be accounted for, ring in my ears like a note of warning? I understand now, but I did not then, full of expectation as I was for developments out of the ordinary.

"Crossing the room, I entered upon the staircase, in the wake of my companion. Though the two men at cards did not look up as I passed them, I noticed that they were alert and ready for any signal I might choose to give them. But I was not ready to give one yet. I must see danger before I summoned help, and there was no token of danger yet.

"When we were about half-way up the stairs the faint light which had illuminated us from below suddenly vanished, and we found ourselves in total darkness. The door at the foot had been closed by a careful hand, and I felt, rather than heard, the stealthy pushing of a bolt across it.

"My first impulse was to forsake my guide and rush back, but I subdued the unworthy impulse and stood quite still, while my companion exclaiming, 'Damn that fellow! What does he mean by shutting the door before we're half-way up!' struck a match and lit a gas jet in the room above, which poured a flood of light upon the staircase. Drawing my hand from the pocket in which I had put my revolver, I hastened after him into the small landing at the top of the stairs. An open door was before me, in which he stood bowing, with the half-burnt match in his hand. 'This is the place, sir,' he announced, motioning me in.

"I entered and he remained by the door, while I passed quickly about the room, which was bare of every article of furniture save a solitary table and chair. There was not even a window in it, with the exception of one small light situated so high up in the corner made by the jutting-up staircase that I wondered at its use, and was only relieved of extreme apprehension at the prison-like appearance of the place by the gleam of light which came through this dusty pane, showing that I was not entirely removed from the presence of my foes if I was from that of my friends.

"'Ah, you have spied the window,' remarked my host, advancing toward me with a countenance he vainly endeavored to make reassuring and friendly. 'That is your post of observation, sir,' he whispered, with a great show of mystery. 'By mounting on the table you can peer into the room where my young friends sit securely at play.'

"As it was not part of my scheme to show any special mistrust, I merely smiled a little grimly, and cast a glance at the table on which stood a bottle of brandy and one glass.

"'Very good brandy,' he whispered, 'Not such stuff as we give those fellows down-stairs.'

"I shrugged my shoulders and he slowly backed towards the door.

"'The young men you bid me watch are very quiet,' I suggested, with a careless wave of my hand towards the room he had mentioned.

"'Oh, there is no one there yet. They begin to straggle in about ten o'clock.'

"'Ah,' was my quiet rejoinder, 'I am likely, then, to have use for your brandy.'

"He smiled again and made a swift motion towards the door.

"'If you want anything,' said he, 'just step to the foot of the staircase and let me know. The whole establishment is at your service.' And with one final grin that remains in my mind as the most threatening and diabolical I have ever witnessed, he laid his hand on the knob of the door and slid quickly out.

"It was done with such an air of final farewell, that I felt my apprehensions take a positive form. Rushing towards the door through which he had just vanished, I listened and heard, as I thought, his stealthy feet descend the stair. But when I sought to follow, I found myself for the second time overwhelmed by darkness. The gas jet, which had hitherto burned with great brightness in the small room, had been turned off from below, and beyond the faint glimmer which found its way through the small window of which I have spoken, not a ray of light now disturbed the heavy gloom of this gruesome apartment.

"I had thought of every contingency but this, and for a few minutes my spirits were dashed. But I soon recovered some remnants of self-possession, and began feeling for the knob I could no longer see. Finding it after a few futile attempts, I was relieved to discover that this door at least was not locked; and, opening it with a careful hand, I listened intently, but could hear nothing save the smothered sound of men talking in the room below.

"Should I signal for my companions? No, for the secret was not yet mine as to how men passed from this room into the watery grave which was the evident goal for all wearers of the blue ribbon.

"Stepping back into the middle of the room, I carefully pondered my situation, but could get no further than the fact that I was somehow, and in some way, in mortal peril. Would it come in the form of a bullet, or a deadly thrust from an unseen knife? I did not think so. For, to say nothing of the darkness, there was one reassuring fact which recurred constantly to my mind in connection with the murders I was endeavoring to trace to this den of iniquity.

"None of the gentlemen who had been found drowned had shown any marks of violence on their bodies, so it was not attack I was to fear, but some mysterious, underhanded treachery which would rob me of consciousness and make the precipitation of my body into the water both safe and easy. Perhaps it was in the bottle of brandy that the peril lay; perhaps—but why speculate further! I would watch till midnight and then, if nothing happened, signal my companions to raid the house.

"Meantime a peep into the next room might help me towards solving the mystery. Setting the bottle and glass aside, I dragged the table across the floor, placed it under the lighted window, mounted, and was about to peer through, when the light in that apartment was put out also. Angry and overwhelmed, I leapt down, and, stretching out my hands till they touched the wainscoting, I followed the wall around till I came to the knob of the door, which I frantically clutched. But I did not turn it immediately, I was too anxious to catch these villains at work. Would I be conscious of the harm they meditated against me, or would I imperceptibly yield to some influence of which I was not yet conscious, and drop to the floor before I could draw my revolver or put to my mouth the whistle upon which I depended for assistance and safety? It was hard to tell, but I determined to cling to my first intention a little longer, and so stood waiting and counting the minutes, while wondering if the captain of the police boat was not getting impatient, and whether I had not more to fear from the anxiety of my friends than the cupidity of my foes.

"You see I had anticipated communicating with the men in this boat by certain signals and tokens which had been arranged between us. But the lack of windows in the room had made all such arrangements futile, so I knew as little of their actions as they of my sufferings; all of which did not tend to add to the cheerfulness of my position.

"I, however, held out for a half-hour, listening, waiting and watching in a darkness which, like that of Egypt, could be felt, and when the suspense grew intolerable I struck a match and let its blue flame flicker for a moment over the face of my watch. But the matches soon gave out and with them my patience, if not my courage, and I determined to end the suspense by knocking at the door beneath.

"This resolution taken, I pulled open the door before me and stepped out. Though I could see nothing, I remembered the narrow landing at the top of the stairs, and, stretching out my arms, I felt for the boarding on either hand, guilding myself by it, and began to descend, when something rising, as it were, out of the cavernous darkness before me made me halt and draw back in mingled dread and horror.

"But the impression, strong as it was, was only momentary, and, resolved to be done with the matter, I precipitated myself downward, when suddenly, at about the middle of the staircase, my feet slipped and I slid forward, plunging and reaching out with hands whose frenzied grasp found nothing to cling to, down a steep inclined plane—or what to my bewildered senses appeared such,—till I struck a yielding surface and passed with one sickening plunge into the icy waters of the river which in another moment had closed dark and benumbing above my head.

"It was all so rapid I did not think of uttering a cry. But happily for me the splash I made told the story, and I was rescued before I could sink a second time.

"It was a full half hour before I had sufficiently recovered from the shock to relate my story. But when once I had made it known, you can imagine the gusto with which the police prepared to enter the house and confound the obliging host with a sight of my dripping garments and accusing face. And indeed in all my professional experience I have never beheld a more sudden merging of the bully into a coward than was to be seen in this slick villain's face, when I was suddenly pulled from the crowd and placed before him, with the old man's wig gone from my head, and the tag of blue ribbon still clinging to my wet coat.

"His game was up, and he saw it; and Ebenezer Gryce's career had begun.

"Like all destructive things the device by which I had been run into the river was simple enough when understood. In the first place it had been constructed to serve the purpose of a stairway and chute. The latter was in plain sight when it was used by the sailmakers to run the finished sails into the waiting yawls below. At the time of my adventure, and for some time before, the possibilities of the place had been discovered by mine host, who had ingeniously put a partition up the entire stairway, dividing the steps from the smooth runway. At the upper part of the runway he had built a few steps, wherewith to lure the unwary far enough down to insure a fatal descent. To make sure of his game he had likewise ceiled the upper room all around, including the enclosure of the stairs. The door to the chute and the door to the stairs were side by side, and being made of the same boards as the wainscoting, were scarcely visible when closed, while the single knob that was used, being transferable from one to the other, naturally gave the impression that there was but one door. When this adroit villain called my attention to the little window around the corner, he no doubt removed the knob from the stairs' door and quickly placed it in the one opening upon the chute. Another door, connecting the two similar landings without, explains how he got from the chute staircase into which he passed, on leaving me, to the one communicating with the room below.

"The mystery was solved, and my footing on the force secured; but to this day—and I am an old man now—I have not forgotten the horror of the moment when my feet slipped from under me, and I felt myself sliding downward, without hope of rescue, into a pit of heaving waters, where so many men of conspicuous virtue had already ended their valuable lives.

"Myriad thoughts flashed through my brain in that brief interval, and among them the whole method of operating this death-trap, together with every detail of evidence that would secure the conviction of the entire gang."

The Adventure of the Red-Headed League

Sir Arthur Conan Doyle

The Adventure of the Red-Headed League

I had called upon my friend, Mr. Sherlock Holmes, one day in the autumn of last year and found him in deep conversation with a very stout, florid-faced, elderly gentleman with fiery red hair. With an apology for my intrusion, I was about to withdraw when Holmes pulled me abruptly into the room and closed the door behind me.

"You could not possibly have come at a better time, my dear Watson," he said cordially.

"I was afraid that you were engaged."

"So I am. Very much so."

"Then I can wait in the next room."

"Not at all. This gentleman, Mr. Wilson, has been my partner and helper in many of my most successful cases, and I have no doubt that he will be of the utmost use to me in yours also."

The stout gentleman half rose from his chair and gave a bob of greeting, with a quick little questioning glance from his small fat-encircled eyes.

"Try the settee," said Holmes, relapsing into his armchair and putting his fingertips together, as was his custom when in judicial moods. "I know, my dear Watson, that you share my love of all that is bizarre and outside the conventions and humdrum routine of everyday life. You have shown your relish for it by the enthusiasm which has prompted you to chronicle, and, if you will excuse my saying so, somewhat to embellish so many of my own little adventures."

"Your cases have indeed been of the greatest interest to me," I observed.

"You will remember that I remarked the other day, just before we went into the very simple problem presented by Miss Mary

Sutherland, that for strange effects and extraordinary combinations we must go to life itself, which is always far more daring than any effort of the imagination."

"A proposition which I took the liberty of doubting."

"You did, Doctor, but none the less you must come round to my view, for otherwise I shall keep on piling fact upon fact on you until your reason breaks down under them and acknowledges me to be right. Now, Mr. Jabez Wilson here has been good enough to call upon me this morning, and to begin a narrative which promises to be one of the most singular which I have listened to for some time. You have heard me remark that the strangest and most unique things are very often connected not with the larger but with the smaller crimes, and occasionally, indeed, where there is room for doubt whether any positive crime has been committed. As far as I have heard, it is impossible for me to say whether the present case is an instance of crime or not, but the course of events is certainly among the most singular that I have ever listened to. Perhaps, Mr. Wilson, you would have the great kindness to recommence your narrative. I ask you not merely because my friend Dr. Watson has not heard the opening part but also because the peculiar nature of the story makes me anxious to have every possible detail from your lips. As a rule, when I have heard some slight indication of the course of events, I am able to guide myself by the thousands of other similar cases which occur to my memory. In the present instance I am forced to admit that the facts are, to the best of my belief, unique."

The portly client puffed out his chest with an appearance of some little pride and pulled a dirty and wrinkled newspaper from the inside pocket of his greatcoat. As he glanced down the advertisement column, with his head thrust forward and the paper flattened out upon his knee, I took a good look at the man and endeavoured, after the fashion of my companion, to read the indications which might be presented by his dress or appearance.

I did not gain very much, however, by my inspection. Our visitor bore every mark of being an average commonplace British tradesman, obese, pompous, and slow. He wore rather baggy grey shepherd's check trousers, a not over-clean black frock-coat, unbuttoned in the front, and a drab waistcoat with a heavy brassy Albert chain, and a square pierced bit of metal dangling down as an ornament. A frayed top-hat and a faded brown overcoat with a wrinkled velvet collar lay upon a chair beside him. Altogether, look as I would, there was nothing remarkable about the man save his blazing red head, and the expression of extreme chagrin and discontent upon his features.

Sherlock Holmes' quick eye took in my occupation, and he shook his head with a smile as he noticed my questioning glances. "Beyond the obvious facts that he has at some time done manual labour, that he takes snuff, that he is a Freemason, that he has been in China, and that he has done a considerable amount of writing lately, I can deduce nothing else."

Mr. Jabez Wilson started up in his chair, with his forefinger upon the paper, but his eyes upon my companion.

"How, in the name of good-fortune, did you know all that, Mr. Holmes?" he asked. "How did you know, for example, that I did manual labour. It's as true as gospel, for I began as a ship's carpenter."

"Your hands, my dear sir. Your right hand is quite a size larger than your left. You have worked with it, and the muscles are more developed."

"Well, the snuff, then, and the Freemasonry?"

"I won't insult your intelligence by telling you how I read that, especially as, rather against the strict rules of your order, you use an arc-and-compass breastpin."

"Ah, of course, I forgot that. But the writing?"

"What else can be indicated by that right cuff so very shiny for five inches, and the left one with the smooth patch near the elbow where you rest it upon the desk?"

"Well, but China?"

"The fish that you have tattooed immediately above your right wrist could only have been done in China. I have made a small study of tattoo marks and have even contributed to the literature of the subject. That trick of staining the fishes' scales of a delicate pink is quite peculiar to China. When, in addition, I see a Chinese coin hanging from your watch-chain, the matter becomes even more simple."

Mr. Jabez Wilson laughed heavily. "Well, I never!" said he. "I thought at first that you had done something clever, but I see that there was nothing in it after all."

"I begin to think, Watson," said Holmes, "that I make a mistake in explaining. '*Omne ignotum pro magnifico*,' you know, and my poor little reputation, such as it is, will suffer shipwreck if I am so candid. Can you not find the advertisement, Mr. Wilson?"

"Yes, I have got it now," he answered with his thick red finger planted halfway down the column. "Here it is. This is what began it all. You just read it for yourself, sir."

I took the paper from him and read as follows:

"TO THE RED-HEADED LEAGUE: On account of the bequest of the late Ezekiah Hopkins, of Lebanon, Pennsylvania, U. S. A., there is now another vacancy open which entitles a member of the League to a salary of £4 a week for purely nominal services. All red-headed men who are sound in body and mind and above the age of twenty-one years, are eligible. Apply in person on Monday, at eleven o'clock, to Duncan Ross, at the offices of the League, 7 Pope's Court, Fleet Street."

"What on earth does this mean?" I ejaculated after I had twice read over the extraordinary announcement.

Holmes chuckled and wriggled in his chair, as was his habit when in high spirits. "It is a little off the beaten track, isn't it?" said he.

"And now, Mr. Wilson, off you go at scratch and tell us all about yourself, your household, and the effect which this advertisement had upon your fortunes. You will first make a note, Doctor, of the paper and the date."

"It is *The Morning Chronicle* of April 27, 1890. Just two months ago."

"Very good. Now, Mr. Wilson?"

"Well, it is just as I have been telling you, Mr. Sherlock Holmes," said Jabez Wilson, mopping his forehead; "I have a small pawnbroker's business at Coburg Square, near the City. It's not a very large affair, and of late years it has not done more than just give me a living. I used to be able to keep two assistants, but now I only keep one; and I would have a job to pay him but that he is willing to come for half wages so as to learn the business."

"What is the name of this obliging youth?" asked Sherlock Holmes.

"His name is Vincent Spaulding, and he's not such a youth, either. It's hard to say his age. I should not wish a smarter assistant, Mr. Holmes; and I know very well that he could better himself and earn twice what I am able to give him. But, after all, if he is satisfied, why should I put ideas in his head?"

"Why, indeed? You seem most fortunate in having an employé who comes under the full market price. It is not a common experience among employers in this age. I don't know that your assistant is not as remarkable as your advertisement."

"Oh, he has his faults, too," said Mr. Wilson. "Never was such a fellow for photography. Snapping away with a camera when he ought to be improving his mind, and then diving down into the cellar like a rabbit into its hole to develop his pictures. That is his main fault, but on the whole he's a good worker. There's no vice in him."

"He is still with you, I presume?"

"Yes, sir. He and a girl of fourteen, who does a bit of simple cooking and keeps the place clean—that's all I have in the house, for I am a widower and never had any family. We live very quietly, sir, the three of us; and we keep a roof over our heads and pay our debts, if we do nothing more.

"The first thing that put us out was that advertisement. Spaulding, he came down into the office just this day eight weeks, with this very paper in his hand, and he says:

" 'I wish to the Lord, Mr. Wilson, that I was a red-headed man.'

" 'Why that?' I asks.

" 'Why,' says he, 'here's another vacancy on the League of the Red-headed Men. It's worth quite a little fortune to any man who gets it, and I understand that there are more vacancies than there are men, so that the trustees are at their wits' end what to do with the money. If my hair would only change colour, here's a nice little crib all ready for me to step into.'

" 'Why, what is it, then?' I asked. You see, Mr. Holmes, I am a very stay-at-home man, and as my business came to me instead of my having to go to it, I was often weeks on end without putting my foot over the door-mat. In that way I didn't know much of what was going on outside, and I was always glad of a bit of news.

" 'Have you never heard of the League of the Red-headed Men?' he asked with his eyes open.

" 'Never.'

" 'Why, I wonder at that, for you are eligible yourself for one of the vacancies.'

" 'And what are they worth?' I asked.

" 'Oh, merely a couple of hundred a year, but the work is slight, and it need not interfere very much with one's other occupations.'

"Well, you can easily think that that made me prick up my ears, for the business has not been over good for some years, and an extra couple of hundred would have been very handy.

" 'Tell me all about it,' said I.

" 'Well,' said he, showing me the advertisement, 'you can see for yourself that the League has a vacancy, and there is the address where you should apply for particulars. As far as I can make out, the League was founded by an American millionaire, Ezekiah Hopkins, who was very peculiar in his ways. He was himself red-headed, and he had a great sympathy for all red-headed men; so, when he died, it was found that he had left his enormous fortune in the hands of trustees, with instructions to apply the interest to the providing of easy berths to men whose hair is of that colour. From all I hear it is splendid pay and very little to do.'

" 'But,' said I, 'there would be millions of red-headed men who would apply.'

" 'Not so many as you might think,' he answered. 'You see it is really confined to Londoners, and to grown men. This American had started from London when he was young, and he wanted to do the old town a good turn. Then, again, I have heard it is no use your applying if your hair is light red, or dark red, or anything but real bright, blazing, fiery red. Now, if you cared to apply, Mr. Wilson, you would just walk in; but perhaps it would hardly be worth your while to put yourself out of the way for the sake of a few hundred pounds.'

"Now, it is a fact, gentlemen, as you may see for yourselves, that my hair is of a very full and rich tint, so that it seemed to me that if there was to be any competition in the matter I stood as good a chance as any man that I had ever met. Vincent Spaulding seemed to know so much about it that I thought he might prove useful, so I just ordered him to put up the shutters for the day and to come right away with me. He was very willing to have a holiday, so we shut the business up and started off for the address that was given us in the advertisement.

"I never hope to see such a sight as that again, Mr. Holmes. From north, south, east, and west every man who had a shade of red in his hair had tramped into the city to answer the advertisement. Fleet

Street was choked with red-headed folk, and Pope's Court looked like a coster's orange barrow. I should not have thought there were so many in the whole country as were brought together by that single advertisement. Every shade of colour they were—straw, lemon, orange, brick, Irish-setter, liver, clay; but, as Spaulding said, there were not many who had the real vivid flame-coloured tint. When I saw how many were waiting, I would have given it up in despair; but Spaulding would not hear of it. How he did it I could not imagine, but he pushed and pulled and butted until he got me through the crowd, and right up to the steps which led to the office. There was a double stream upon the stair, some going up in hope, and some coming back dejected; but we wedged in as well as we could and soon found ourselves in the office."

"Your experience has been a most entertaining one," remarked Holmes as his client paused and refreshed his memory with a huge pinch of snuff. "Pray continue your very interesting statement."

"There was nothing in the office but a couple of wooden chairs and a deal table, behind which sat a small man with a head that was even redder than mine. He said a few words to each candidate as he came up, and then he always managed to find some fault in them which would disqualify them. Getting a vacancy did not seem to be such a very easy matter, after all. However, when our turn came the little man was much more favourable to me than to any of the others, and he closed the door as we entered, so that he might have a private word with us.

" 'This is Mr. Jabez Wilson,' said my assistant, 'and he is willing to fill a vacancy in the League.'

" 'And he is admirably suited for it,' the other answered. 'He has every requirement. I cannot recall when I have seen anything so fine.' He took a step backward, cocked his head on one side, and gazed at my hair until I felt quite bashful. Then suddenly he plunged forward, wrung my hand, and congratulated me warmly on my success.

" 'It would be injustice to hesitate,' said he. 'You will, however, I am sure, excuse me for taking an obvious precaution.' With that he seized my hair in both his hands, and tugged until I yelled with the pain. 'There is water in your eyes,' said he as he released me. 'I perceive that all is as it should be. But we have to be careful, for we have twice been deceived by wigs and once by paint. I could tell you tales of cobbler's wax which would disgust you with human nature.' He stepped over to the window and shouted through it at the top of his voice that the vacancy was filled. A groan of disappointment came up from below, and the folk all trooped away in different directions until there was not a red-head to be seen except my own and that of the manager.

" 'My name,' said he, 'is Mr. Duncan Ross, and I am myself one of the pensioners upon the fund left by our noble benefactor. Are you a married man, Mr. Wilson? Have you a family?'

"I answered that I had not.

"His face fell immediately.

" 'Dear me!' he said gravely, 'that is very serious indeed! I am sorry to hear you say that. The fund was, of course, for the propagation and spread of the red-heads as well as for their maintenance. It is exceedingly unfortunate that you should be a bachelor.'

"My face lengthened at this, Mr. Holmes, for I thought that I was not to have the vacancy after all; but after thinking it over for a few minutes he said that it would be all right.

" 'In the case of another,' said he, 'the objection might be fatal, but we must stretch a point in favour of a man with such a head of hair as yours. When shall you be able to enter upon your new duties?'

" 'Well, it is a little awkward, for I have a business already,' said I.

" 'Oh, never mind about that, Mr. Wilson!' said Vincent Spaulding. 'I should be able to look after that for you.'

" 'What would be the hours?' I asked.

" 'Ten to two.'

"Now a pawnbroker's business is mostly done of an evening, Mr. Holmes, especially Thursday and Friday evening, which is just before pay-day; so it would suit me very well to earn a little in the mornings. Besides, I knew that my assistant was a good man, and that he would see to anything that turned up.

" 'That would suit me very well,' said I. 'And the pay?'

" 'Is £4 a week.'

" 'And the work?'

" 'Is purely nominal.'

" 'What do you call purely nominal?'

" 'Well, you have to be in the office, or at least in the building, the whole time. If you leave, you forfeit your whole position forever. The will is very clear upon that point. You don't comply with the conditions if you budge from the office during that time.'

" 'It's only four hours a day, and I should not think of leaving,' said I.

" 'No excuse will avail,' said Mr. Duncan Ross; 'neither sickness nor business nor anything else. There you must stay, or you lose your billet.'

" 'And the work?'

" 'Is to copy out the *Encyclopaedia Britannica*. There is the first volume of it in that press. You must find your own ink, pens, and blotting-paper, but we provide this table and chair. Will you be ready to-morrow?'

" 'Certainly,' I answered.

" 'Then, good-bye, Mr. Jabez Wilson, and let me congratulate you once more on the important position which you have been fortunate enough to gain.' He bowed me out of the room and I went home with my assistant, hardly knowing what to say or do, I was so pleased at my own good fortune.

"Well, I thought over the matter all day, and by evening I was in low spirits again; for I had quite persuaded myself that the whole affair must be some great hoax or fraud, though what its object might be I could not imagine. It seemed altogether past belief that anyone could make such a will, or that they would pay such a sum for doing anything so simple as copying out the *Encyclopaedia Britannica*. Vincent Spaulding did what he could to cheer me up, but by bedtime I had reasoned myself out of the whole thing. However, in the morning I determined to have a look at it anyhow, so I bought a penny bottle of ink, and with a quill-pen, and seven sheets of foolscap paper, I started off for Pope's Court.

"Well, to my surprise and delight, everything was as right as possible. The table was set out ready for me, and Mr. Duncan Ross was there to see that I got fairly to work. He started me off upon the letter A, and then he left me; but he would drop in from time to time to see that all was right with me. At two o'clock he bade me good-day, complimented me upon the amount that I had written, and locked the door of the office after me.

"This went on day after day, Mr. Holmes, and on Saturday the manager came in and planked down four golden sovereigns for my week's work. It was the same next week, and the same the week after. Every morning I was there at ten, and every afternoon I left at two. By degrees Mr. Duncan Ross took to coming in only once of a morning, and then, after a time, he did not come in at all. Still, of course, I never dared to leave the room for an instant, for I was not sure when he might come, and the billet was such a good one, and suited me so well, that I would not risk the loss of it.

"Eight weeks passed away like this, and I had written about Abbots and Archery and Armour and Architecture and Attica, and hoped with diligence that I might get on to the B's before very long. It cost me something in foolscap, and I had pretty nearly filled a shelf with my writings. And then suddenly the whole business came to an end."

"To an end?"

"Yes, sir. And no later than this morning. I went to my work as usual at ten o'clock, but the door was shut and locked, with a little square of cardboard hammered on to the middle of the panel with a tack. Here it is, and you can read for yourself."

He held up a piece of white cardboard about the size of a sheet of note-paper. It read in this fashion:

THE RED-HEADED LEAGUE

IS

DISSOLVED.

October 9, 1890.

Sherlock Holmes and I surveyed this curt announcement and the rueful face behind it, until the comical side of the affair so completely overtopped every other consideration that we both burst out into a roar of laughter.

"I cannot see that there is anything very funny," cried our client, flushing up to the roots of his flaming head. "If you can do nothing better than laugh at me, I can go elsewhere."

"No, no," cried Holmes, shoving him back into the chair from which he had half risen. "I really wouldn't miss your case for the world. It is most refreshingly unusual. But there is, if you will excuse my saying so, something just a little funny about it. Pray what steps did you take when you found the card upon the door?"

"I was staggered, sir. I did not know what to do. Then I called at the offices round, but none of them seemed to know anything about it. Finally, I went to the landlord, who is an accountant living on the ground floor, and I asked him if he could tell me what had become of the Red-headed League. He said that he had never heard of any such body. Then I asked him who Mr. Duncan Ross was. He answered that the name was new to him.

" 'Well,' said I, 'the gentleman at No. 4.'

" 'What, the red-headed man?'

" 'Yes.'

" 'Oh,' said he, 'his name was William Morris. He was a solicitor and was using my room as a temporary convenience until his new premises were ready. He moved out yesterday.'

" 'Where could I find him?'

" 'Oh, at his new offices. He did tell me the address. Yes, 17 King Edward Street, near St. Paul's.'

"I started off, Mr. Holmes, but when I got to that address it was a manufactory of artificial knee-caps, and no one in it had ever heard of either Mr. William Morris or Mr. Duncan Ross."

"And what did you do then?" asked Holmes.

"I went home to Saxe-Coburg Square, and I took the advice of my assistant. But he could not help me in any way. He could only say that if I waited I should hear by post. But that was not quite good enough, Mr. Holmes. I did not wish to lose such a place without a struggle, so, as I had heard that you were good enough to give advice to poor folk who were in need of it, I came right away to you."

"And you did very wisely," said Holmes. "Your case is an exceedingly remarkable one, and I shall be happy to look into it. From what you have told me I think that it is possible that graver issues hang from it than might at first sight appear."

"Grave enough!" said Mr. Jabez Wilson. "Why, I have lost four pound a week."

"As far as you are personally concerned," remarked Holmes, "I do not see that you have any grievance against this extraordinary league. On the contrary, you are, as I understand, richer by some £30, to say nothing of the minute knowledge which you have gained on every subject which comes under the letter A. You have lost nothing by them."

"No, sir. But I want to find out about them, and who they are, and what their object was in playing this prank—if it was a prank—upon me. It was a pretty expensive joke for them, for it cost them two and thirty pounds."

"We shall endeavour to clear up these points for you. And, first, one or two questions, Mr. Wilson. This assistant of yours who first called your attention to the advertisement—how long had he been with you?"

"About a month then."

"How did he come?"

"In answer to an advertisement."

"Was he the only applicant?"

"No, I had a dozen."

"Why did you pick him?"

"Because he was handy and would come cheap."

"At half wages, in fact."

"Yes."

"What is he like, this Vincent Spaulding?"

"Small, stout-built, very quick in his ways, no hair on his face, though he's not short of thirty. Has a white splash of acid upon his forehead."

Holmes sat up in his chair in considerable excitement. "I thought as much," said he. "Have you ever observed that his ears are pierced for earrings?"

"Yes, sir. He told me that a gipsy had done it for him when he was a lad."

"Hum!" said Holmes, sinking back in deep thought. "He is still with you?"

"Oh, yes, sir; I have only just left him."

"And has your business been attended to in your absence?"

"Nothing to complain of, sir. There's never very much to do of a morning."

"That will do, Mr. Wilson. I shall be happy to give you an opinion upon the subject in the course of a day or two. To-day is Saturday, and I hope that by Monday we may come to a conclusion."

"Well, Watson," said Holmes when our visitor had left us, "what do you make of it all?"

"I make nothing of it," I answered frankly. "It is a most mysterious business."

"As a rule," said Holmes, "the more bizarre a thing is the less mysterious it proves to be. It is your commonplace, featureless crimes which are really puzzling, just as a commonplace face is the most difficult to identify. But I must be prompt over this matter."

"What are you going to do, then?" I asked.

"To smoke," he answered. "It is quite a three pipe problem, and I beg that you won't speak to me for fifty minutes." He curled himself up in his chair, with his thin knees drawn up to his hawk-like nose, and there he sat with his eyes closed and his black clay pipe thrusting out like the bill of some strange bird. I had come to the conclusion that he had dropped asleep, and indeed was nodding myself, when he suddenly sprang out of his chair with the gesture of a man who has made up his mind and put his pipe down upon the mantelpiece.

"Sarasate plays at the St. James's Hall this afternoon," he remarked. "What do you think, Watson? Could your patients spare you for a few hours?"

"I have nothing to do to-day. My practice is never very absorbing."

"Then put on your hat and come. I am going through the City first, and we can have some lunch on the way. I observe that there is a good deal of German music on the programme, which is rather more to my taste than Italian or French. It is introspective, and I want to introspect. Come along!"

We travelled by the Underground as far as Aldersgate; and a

short walk took us to Saxe-Coburg Square, the scene of the singular story which we had listened to in the morning. It was a poky, little, shabby-genteel place, where four lines of dingy two-storied brick houses looked out into a small railed-in enclosure, where a lawn of weedy grass and a few clumps of faded laurel bushes made a hard fight against a smoke-laden and uncongenial atmosphere. Three gilt balls and a brown board with "JABEZ WILSON" in white letters, upon a corner house, announced the place where our red-headed client carried on his business. Sherlock Holmes stopped in front of it with his head on one side and looked it all over, with his eyes shining brightly between puckered lids. Then he walked slowly up the street, and then down again to the corner, still looking keenly at the houses. Finally he returned to the pawnbroker's, and, having thumped vigorously upon the pavement with his stick two or three times, he went up to the door and knocked. It was instantly opened by a bright-looking, clean-shaven young fellow, who asked him to step in.

"Thank you," said Holmes, "I only wished to ask you how you would go from here to the Strand."

"Third right, fourth left," answered the assistant promptly, closing the door.

"Smart fellow, that," observed Holmes as we walked away. "He is, in my judgment, the fourth smartest man in London, and for daring I am not sure that he has not a claim to be third. I have known something of him before."

"Evidently," said I, "Mr. Wilson's assistant counts for a good deal in this mystery of the Red-headed League. I am sure that you inquired your way merely in order that you might see him."

"Not him."

"What then?"

"The knees of his trousers."

"And what did you see?"

"What I expected to see."

"Why did you beat the pavement?"

"My dear doctor, this is a time for observation, not for talk. We are spies in an enemy's country. We know something of Saxe-Coburg Square. Let us now explore the parts which lie behind it."

The road in which we found ourselves as we turned round the corner from the retired Saxe-Coburg Square presented as great a contrast to it as the front of a picture does to the back. It was one of the main arteries which conveyed the traffic of the City to the north and west. The roadway was blocked with the immense stream of commerce flowing in a double tide inward and outward, while the footpaths were black with the hurrying swarm of pedestrians. It was difficult to realise as we looked at the line of fine shops and stately business premises that they really abutted on the other side upon the faded and stagnant square which we had just quitted.

"Let me see," said Holmes, standing at the corner and glancing along the line, "I should like just to remember the order of the houses here. It is a hobby of mine to have an exact knowledge of London. There is Mortimer's, the tobacconist, the little newspaper shop, the Coburg branch of the City and Suburban Bank, the Vegetarian Restaurant, and McFarlane's carriage-building depot. That carries us right on to the other block. And now, Doctor, we've done our work, so it's time we had some play. A sandwich and a cup of coffee, and then off to violin-land, where all is sweetness and delicacy and harmony, and there are no red-headed clients to vex us with their conundrums."

My friend was an enthusiastic musician, being himself not only a very capable performer but a composer of no ordinary merit. All the afternoon he sat in the stalls wrapped in the most perfect happiness, gently waving his long, thin fingers in time to the music, while his gently smiling face and his languid, dreamy eyes were as unlike those of Holmes the sleuth-hound, Holmes the relentless, keen-witted, ready-handed criminal agent, as it was possible to conceive. In his singular character the dual nature alternately asserted itself, and his extreme exactness and astuteness represented, as I have often thought, the reaction against the poetic and contemplative mood which occasionally predominated in him. The swing of his nature took him from extreme languor to devouring energy; and, as I knew well, he was never so truly formidable as when, for days on end, he had been lounging in his armchair amid his improvisations and his black-letter editions. Then it was that the lust of the chase would suddenly come upon him, and that his brilliant reasoning power would rise to the level of intuition, until those who were unacquainted with his methods would look askance at him as on a man whose knowledge was not that of other mortals. When I saw him that afternoon so enwrapped in the music at St. James's Hall I felt that an evil time might be coming upon those whom he had set himself to hunt down.

"You want to go home, no doubt, Doctor," he remarked as we emerged.

"Yes, it would be as well."

"And I have some business to do which will take some hours. This business at Coburg Square is serious."

"Why serious?"

"A considerable crime is in contemplation. I have every reason to believe that we shall be in time to stop it. But to-day being Saturday rather complicates matters. I shall want your help to-night."

"At what time?"

"Ten will be early enough."

"I shall be at Baker Street at ten."

"Very well. And, I say, Doctor, there may be some little danger, so kindly put your army revolver in your pocket." He waved his hand, turned on his heel, and disappeared in an instant among the crowd.

I trust that I am not more dense than my neighbours, but I was always oppressed with a sense of my own stupidity in my dealings with Sherlock Holmes. Here I had heard what he had heard, I had seen what he had seen, and yet from his words it was evident that he saw clearly not only what had happened but what was about to happen, while to me the whole business was still confused and grotesque. As I drove home to my house in Kensington I thought over it all, from the extraordinary story of the red-headed copier of the *Encyclopaedia* down to the visit to Saxe-Coburg Square, and the ominous words with which he had parted from me. What was this nocturnal expedition, and why should I go armed? Where were we going, and what were we to do? I had the hint from Holmes that this smooth-faced pawnbroker's assistant was a formidable man—a man who might play a deep game. I tried to puzzle it out, but gave it up in despair and set the matter aside until night should bring an explanation.

It was a quarter-past nine when I started from home and made my way across the Park, and so through Oxford Street to Baker Street. Two hansoms were standing at the door, and as I entered the passage I heard the sound of voices from above. On entering his room, I found Holmes in animated conversation with two men, one of whom I recognised as Peter Jones, the official police agent, while the other was a long, thin, sad-faced man, with a very shiny hat and oppressively respectable frock-coat.

"Ha! Our party is complete," said Holmes, buttoning up his pea-jacket and taking his heavy hunting crop from the rack. "Watson, I think you know Mr. Jones, of Scotland Yard? Let me introduce you to Mr. Merryweather, who is to be our companion in to-night's adventure."

"We're hunting in couples again, Doctor, you see," said Jones in his consequential way. "Our friend here is a wonderful man for starting a chase. All he wants is an old dog to help him to do the running down."

"I hope a wild goose may not prove to be the end of our chase," observed Mr. Merryweather gloomily.

"You may place considerable confidence in Mr. Holmes, sir," said the police agent loftily. "He has his own little methods, which are, if he won't mind my saying so, just a little too theoretical and fantastic, but he has the makings of a detective in him. It is not too much to say that once or twice, as in that business of the Sholto murder and the Agra treasure, he has been more nearly correct than the official force."

"Oh, if you say so, Mr. Jones, it is all right," said the stranger with deference. "Still, I confess that I miss my rubber. It is the first Saturday night for seven-and-twenty years that I have not had my rubber."

"I think you will find," said Sherlock Holmes, "that you will play for a higher stake to-night than you have ever done yet, and that the play will be more exciting. For you, Mr. Merryweather, the stake will be some £30,000; and for you, Jones, it will be the man upon whom you wish to lay your hands."

"John Clay, the murderer, thief, smasher, and forger. He's a young man, Mr. Merryweather, but he is at the head of his profession, and I would rather have my bracelets on him than on any criminal in London. He's a remarkable man, is young John Clay. His grandfather was a royal duke, and he himself has been to Eton and Oxford. His brain is as cunning as his fingers, and though we meet signs of him at every turn, we never know where to find the man himself. He'll crack a crib in Scotland one week, and be raising money to build an orphanage in Cornwall the next. I've been on his track for years and have never set eyes on him yet."

"I hope that I may have the pleasure of introducing you to-night. I've had one or two little turns also with Mr. John Clay, and I agree with you that he is at the head of his profession. It is past ten, however, and quite time that we started. If you two will take the first hansom, Watson and I will follow in the second."

Sherlock Holmes was not very communicative during the long drive and lay back in the cab humming the tunes which he had heard in the afternoon. We rattled through an endless labyrinth of gas-lit streets until we emerged into Farrington Street.

"We are close there now," my friend remarked. "This fellow Merryweather is a bank director, and personally interested in the matter. I thought it as well to have Jones with us also. He is not a bad fellow, though an absolute imbecile in his profession. He has one positive virtue. He is as brave as a bulldog and as tenacious as a lobster if he gets his claws upon anyone. Here we are, and they are waiting for us."

We had reached the same crowded thoroughfare in which we had found ourselves in the morning. Our cabs were dismissed, and, following the guidance of Mr. Merryweather, we passed down a narrow passage and through a side door, which he opened for us. Within there was a small corridor, which ended in a very massive iron gate. This also was opened, and led down a flight of winding stone steps, which terminated at another formidable gate. Mr. Merryweather stopped to light a lantern, and then conducted us down a dark, earth-smelling passage, and so, after opening a third door, into a huge vault or cellar, which was piled all round with crates and massive boxes.

"You are not very vulnerable from above," Holmes remarked as he held up the lantern and gazed about him.

"Nor from below," said Mr. Merryweather, striking his stick upon the flags which lined the floor. "Why, dear me, it sounds quite hollow!" he remarked, looking up in surprise.

"I must really ask you to be a little more quiet!" said Holmes severely. "You have already imperilled the whole success of our expedition. Might I beg that you would have the goodness to sit down upon one of those boxes, and not to interfere?"

The solemn Mr. Merryweather perched himself upon a crate, with a very injured expression upon his face, while Holmes fell upon his knees upon the floor and, with the lantern and a magnifying lens, began to examine minutely the cracks between the stones. A few seconds sufficed to satisfy him, for he sprang to his feet again and put his glass in his pocket.

"We have at least an hour before us," he remarked, "for they can hardly take any steps until the good pawnbroker is safely in bed. Then they will not lose a minute, for the sooner they do their work the longer time they will have for their escape. We are at present, Doctor—as no doubt you have divined—in the cellar of the City branch of one of the principal London banks. Mr. Merryweather is the chairman of directors, and he will explain to you that there are reasons why the more daring criminals of London should take a considerable interest in this cellar at present."

"It is our French gold," whispered the director. "We have had several warnings that an attempt might be made upon it."

"Your French gold?"

"Yes. We had occasion some months ago to strengthen our resources and borrowed for that purpose 30,000 napoleons from the Bank of France. It has become known that we have never had occasion to unpack the money, and that it is still lying in our cellar. The crate upon which I sit contains 2,000 napoleons packed between layers of lead foil. Our reserve of bullion is much larger at present than is usually kept in a single branch office, and the directors have had misgivings upon the subject."

"Which were very well justified," observed Holmes. "And now it is time that we arranged our little plans. I expect that within an hour matters will come to a head. In the meantime Mr. Merryweather, we must put the screen over that dark lantern."

"And sit in the dark?"

"I am afraid so. I had brought a pack of cards in my pocket, and

I thought that, as we were a *partie carrée*, you might have your rubber after all. But I see that the enemy's preparations have gone so far that we cannot risk the presence of a light. And, first of all, we must choose our positions. These are daring men, and though we shall take them at a disadvantage, they may do us some harm unless we are careful. I shall stand behind this crate, and do you conceal yourselves behind those. Then, when I flash a light upon them, close in swiftly. If they fire, Watson, have no compunction about shooting them down."

I placed my revolver, cocked, upon the top of the wooden case behind which I crouched. Holmes shot the slide across the front of his lantern and left us in pitch darkness—such an absolute darkness as I have never before experienced. The smell of hot metal remained to assure us that the light was still there, ready to flash out at a moment's notice. To me, with my nerves worked up to a pitch of expectancy, there was something depressing and subduing in the sudden gloom, and in the cold dank air of the vault.

"They have but one retreat," whispered Holmes. "That is back through the house into Saxe-Coburg Square. I hope that you have done what I asked you, Jones?"

"I have an inspector and two officers waiting at the front door."

"Then we have stopped all the holes. And now we must be silent and wait."

What a time it seemed! From comparing notes afterwards it was but an hour and a quarter, yet it appeared to me that the night must have almost gone, and the dawn be breaking above us. My limbs were weary and stiff, for I feared to change my position; yet my nerves were worked up to the highest pitch of tension, and my hearing was so acute that I could not only hear the gentle breathing of my companions, but I could distinguish the deeper, heavier in-breath of the bulky Jones from the thin, sighing note of the bank director. From my position I could look over the case in the direction of the floor. Suddenly my eyes caught the glint of a light.

At first it was but a lurid spark upon the stone pavement. Then it lengthened out until it became a yellow line, and then, without any warning or sound, a gash seemed to open and a hand appeared, a white, almost womanly hand, which felt about in the centre of the little area of light. For a minute or more the hand, with its writhing fingers, protruded out of the floor. Then it was withdrawn as suddenly as it appeared, and all was dark again save the single lurid spark which marked a chink between the stones.

Its disappearance, however, was but momentary. With a rending, tearing sound, one of the broad, white stones turned over upon its side and left a square, gaping hole, through which streamed the light of a lantern. Over the edge there peeped a clean-cut, boyish face, which looked keenly about it, and then, with a hand on either side of the aperture, drew itself shoulder-high and waist-high, until one knee rested upon the edge. In another instant he stood at the side of the hole and was hauling after him a companion, lithe and small like himself, with a pale face and a shock of very red hair.

"It's all clear," he whispered. "Have you the chisel and the bags? Great Scott! Jump, Archie, jump, and I'll swing for it!"

Sherlock Holmes had sprung out and seized the intruder by the collar. The other dived down the hole, and I heard the sound of rending cloth as Jones clutched at his skirts. The light flashed upon the barrel of a revolver, but Holmes' hunting crop came down on the man's wrist, and the pistol clinked upon the stone floor.

"It's no use, John Clay," said Holmes blandly. "You have no chance at all."

"So I see," the other answered with the utmost coolness. "I fancy that my pal is all right, though I see you have got his coat-tails."

"There are three men waiting for him at the door," said Holmes.

"Oh, indeed! You seem to have done the thing very completely. I must compliment you."

"And I you," Holmes answered. "Your red-headed idea was very new and effective."

"You'll see your pal again presently," said Jones. "He's quicker at climbing down holes than I am. Just hold out while I fix the derbies."

"I beg that you will not touch me with your filthy hands," remarked our prisoner as the handcuffs clattered upon his wrists. "You may not be aware that I have royal blood in my veins. Have the goodness, also, when you address me always to say 'sir' and 'please.' "

"All right," said Jones with a stare and a snigger. "Well, would you please, sir, march upstairs, where we can get a cab to carry your Highness to the police-station?"

"That is better," said John Clay serenely. He made a sweeping bow to the three of us and walked quietly off in the custody of the detective.

"Really, Mr. Holmes," said Mr. Merryweather as we followed them from the cellar, "I do not know how the bank can thank you or repay you. There is no doubt that you have detected and defeated in the most complete manner one of the most determined attempts at bank robbery that have ever come within my experience."

"I have had one or two little scores of my own to settle with Mr. John Clay," said Holmes. "I have been at some small expense over this matter, which I shall expect the bank to refund, but beyond that I am amply repaid by having had an experience which is in many ways unique, and by hearing the very remarkable narrative of the Red-headed League."

"You see, Watson," he explained in the early hours of the morning as we sat over a glass of whisky and soda in Baker Street, "it was perfectly obvious from the first that the only possible object of this rather fantastic business of the advertisement of the League, and the copying of the *Encyclopaedia*, must be to get this not over-bright pawnbroker out of the way for a number of hours every day. It was a curious way of managing it, but, really, it would be difficult to suggest a better. The method was no doubt suggested to Clay's ingenious mind by the colour of his accomplice's hair. The £4 a week was a lure which must draw him, and what was it to them, who were playing for thousands? They put in the advertisement, one rogue has the temporary office, the other rogue incites the man to apply for it, and together they manage to secure his absence every morning in the week. From the time that I heard of the assistant having come for half wages, it was obvious to me that he had some strong motive for securing the situation."

"But how could you guess what the motive was?"

"Had there been women in the house, I should have suspected a mere vulgar intrigue. That, however, was out of the question. The man's business was a small one, and there was nothing in his house which could account for such elaborate preparations, and such an expenditure as they were at. It must, then, be something out of the house. What could it be? I thought of the assistant's fondness for photography, and his trick of vanishing into the cellar. The cellar! There was the end of this tangled clue. Then I made inquiries as to this mysterious assistant and found that I had to deal with one of the coolest and most daring criminals in London. He was doing something in the cellar—something which took many hours a day for months on end. What could it be, once more? I could think of nothing save that he was running a tunnel to some other building.

"So far I had got when we went to visit the scene of action. I surprised you by beating upon the pavement with my stick. I was ascertaining whether the cellar stretched out in front or behind. It was not in front. Then I rang the bell, and, as I hoped, the assistant answered it. We have had some skirmishes, but we had never set eyes upon each other before. I hardly looked at his face. His knees were what I wished to see. You must yourself have remarked how worn, wrinkled, and stained they were. They spoke of those hours of burrowing. The only remaining point was what they were burrowing for. I walked round the corner, saw the City and Suburban Bank abutted on our friend's premises, and felt that I had solved my problem. When you drove home after the concert I called upon Scotland Yard and upon the chairman of the bank directors, with the result that you have seen."

"And how could you tell that they would make their attempt to-night?" I asked.

"Well, when they closed their League offices that was a sign that they cared no longer about Mr. Jabez Wilson's presence—in other words, that they had completed their tunnel. But it was essential that they should use it soon, as it might be discovered, or the bullion might be removed. Saturday would suit them better than any other day, as it would give them two days for their escape. For all these reasons I expected them to come to-night."

"You reasoned it out beautifully," I exclaimed in unfeigned admiration. "It is so long a chain, and yet every link rings true."

"It saved me from ennui," he answered, yawning. "Alas! I already feel it closing in upon me. My life is spent in one long effort to escape from the commonplaces of existence. These little problems help me to do so."

"And you are a benefactor of the race," said I.

He shrugged his shoulders. "Well, perhaps, after all, it is of some little use," he remarked. " '*L'homme c'est rien—l'oeuvre c'est tout,*' as Gustave Flaubert wrote to George Sand."

The Adventure of the Speckled Band

Sir Arthur Conan Doyle

The Adventure of the Speckled Band

On glancing over my notes of the seventy odd cases in which I have during the last eight years studied the methods of my friend Sherlock Holmes, I find many tragic, some comic, a large number merely strange, but none commonplace; for, working as he did rather for the love of his art than for the acquirement of wealth, he refused to associate himself with any investigation which did not tend towards the unusual, and even the fantastic. Of all these varied cases, however, I cannot recall any which presented more singular features than that which was associated with the well-known Surrey family of the Roylotts of Stoke Moran. The events in question occurred in the early days of my association with Holmes, when we were sharing rooms as bachelors in Baker Street. It is possible that I might have placed them upon record before, but a promise of secrecy was made at the time, from which I have only been freed during the last month by the untimely death of the lady to whom the pledge was given. It is perhaps as well that the facts should now come to light, for I have reasons to know that there are widespread rumours as to the death of Dr. Grimesby Roylott which tend to make the matter even more terrible than the truth.

It was early in April in the year '83 that I woke one morning to find Sherlock Holmes standing, fully dressed, by the side of my bed. He was a late riser, as a rule, and as the clock on the mantelpiece showed me that it was only a quarter-past seven, I blinked up at him in some surprise, and perhaps just a little resentment, for I was myself regular in my habits.

"Very sorry to knock you up, Watson," said he, "but it's the common lot this morning. Mrs. Hudson has been knocked up, she retorted upon me, and I on you."

"What is it, then—a fire?"

"No; a client. It seems that a young lady has arrived in a considerable state of excitement, who insists upon seeing me. She is waiting now in the sitting-room. Now, when young ladies wander about the metropolis at this hour of the morning, and knock sleepy people up out of their beds, I presume that it is something very pressing which they have to communicate. Should it prove to be an interesting case, you would, I am sure, wish to follow it from the outset. I thought, at any rate, that I should call you and give you the chance."

"My dear fellow, I would not miss it for anything."

I had no keener pleasure than in following Holmes in his professional investigations, and in admiring the rapid deductions, as swift as intuitions, and yet always founded on a logical basis with which he unravelled the problems which were submitted to him. I rapidly threw on my clothes and was ready in a few minutes to accompany my friend down to the sitting-room. A lady dressed in black and heavily veiled, who had been sitting in the window, rose as we entered.

"Good-morning, madam," said Holmes cheerily. "My name is Sherlock Holmes. This is my intimate friend and associate, Dr. Watson, before whom you can speak as freely as before myself. Ha! I am glad to see that Mrs. Hudson has had the good sense to light the fire. Pray draw up to it, and I shall order you a cup of hot coffee, for I observe that you are shivering."

"It is not cold which makes me shiver," said the woman in a low voice, changing her seat as requested.

"What, then?"

"It is fear, Mr. Holmes. It is terror." She raised her veil as she spoke, and we could see that she was indeed in a pitiable state of agitation, her face all drawn and grey, with restless frightened eyes, like those of some hunted animal. Her features and figure were those of a woman of thirty, but her hair was shot with premature grey, and her expression was weary and haggard. Sherlock Holmes ran her over with one of his quick, all-comprehensive glances.

"You must not fear," said he soothingly, bending forward and patting her forearm. "We shall soon set matters right, I have no doubt. You have come in by train this morning, I see."

"You know me, then?"

"No, but I observe the second half of a return ticket in the palm of your left glove. You must have started early, and yet you had a good drive in a dog-cart, along heavy roads, before you reached the station."

The lady gave a violent start and stared in bewilderment at my companion.

"There is no mystery, my dear madam," said he, smiling. "The left arm of your jacket is spattered with mud in no less than seven places. The marks are perfectly fresh. There is no vehicle save a dog-cart which throws up mud in that way, and then only when you sit on the left-hand side of the driver."

"Whatever your reasons may be, you are perfectly correct," said she. "I started from home before six, reached Leatherhead at twenty past, and came in by the first train to Waterloo. Sir, I can stand this strain no longer; I shall go mad if it continues. I have no one to turn to—none, save only one, who cares for me, and he, poor fellow, can be of little aid. I have heard of you, Mr. Holmes; I have heard of you from Mrs. Farintosh, whom you helped in the hour of her sore need. It was from her that I had your address. Oh, sir, do you not think that you could help me, too, and at least throw a little light through the dense darkness which surrounds me? At present it is out of my power to reward you for your services, but in a month or six weeks I shall be married, with the control of my own income, and then at least you shall not find me ungrateful."

Holmes turned to his desk and, unlocking it, drew out a small case-book, which he consulted.

"Farintosh," said he. "Ah yes, I recall the case; it was concerned with an opal tiara. I think it was before your time, Watson. I can only say, madam, that I shall be happy to devote the same care to your case as I did to that of your friend. As to reward, my profession is its own reward; but you are at liberty to defray whatever expenses I may be put to, at the time which suits you best. And now I beg that you will lay before us everything that may help us in forming an opinion upon the matter."

"Alas!" replied our visitor, "the very horror of my situation lies in the fact that my fears are so vague, and my suspicions depend so entirely upon small points, which might seem trivial to another, that even he to whom of all others I have a right to look for help and advice looks upon all that I tell him about it as the fancies of a nervous woman. He does not say so, but I can read it from his soothing answers and averted eyes. But I have heard, Mr. Holmes, that you can see deeply into the manifold wickedness of the human heart. You may advise me how to walk amid the dangers which encompass me."

"I am all attention, madam."

"My name is Helen Stoner, and I am living with my stepfather, who is the last survivor of one of the oldest Saxon families in England, the Roylotts of Stoke Moran, on the western border of Surrey."

Holmes nodded his head. "The name is familiar to me," said he.

"The family was at one time among the richest in England, and the estates extended over the borders into Berkshire in the north, and Hampshire in the west. In the last century, however, four successive heirs were of a dissolute and wasteful disposition, and the family ruin was eventually completed by a gambler in the days of the Regency. Nothing was left save a few acres of ground, and the two-hundred-year-old house, which is itself crushed under a heavy mortgage. The last squire dragged out his existence there, living the horrible life of an aristocratic pauper; but his only son, my stepfather, seeing that he must adapt himself to the new conditions, obtained an advance from a relative, which enabled him to take a medical degree and went out to Calcutta, where, by his professional skill and his force of character, he established a large practice. In a fit of anger, however, caused by some robberies which had been perpetrated in the house, he beat his native butler to death and narrowly escaped a capital sentence. As it was, he suffered a long term of imprisonment and afterwards returned to England a morose and disappointed man.

"When Dr. Roylott was in India he married my mother, Mrs. Stoner, the young widow of Major-General Stoner, of the Bengal Artillery. My sister Julia and I were twins, and we were only two years old at the time of my mother's re-marriage. She had a considerable sum of money—not less than £1000 a year—and this she bequeathed to Dr. Roylott entirely while we resided with him, with a provision that a certain annual sum should be allowed to each of us in the event of our marriage. Shortly after our return to England my mother died— she was killed eight years ago in a railway accident near Crewe. Dr. Roylott then abandoned his attempts to establish himself in practice in London and took us to live with him in the old ancestral house at Stoke Moran. The money which my mother had left was enough for all our wants, and there seemed to be no obstacle to our happiness.

"But a terrible change came over our stepfather about this time. Instead of making friends and exchanging visits with our neighbours, who had at first been overjoyed to see a Roylott of Stoke Moran back in the old family seat, he shut himself up in his house and seldom came out save to indulge in ferocious quarrels with whoever might cross his path. Violence of temper approaching to mania has been hereditary in the men of the family, and in my stepfather's case it had, I believe, been intensified by his long residence in the tropics. A series of disgraceful brawls took place, two of which ended in the police-court, until at last he became the terror of the village, and the folks would fly at his approach, for he is a man of immense strength, and absolutely uncontrollable in his anger.

"Last week he hurled the local blacksmith over a parapet into a stream, and it was only by paying over all the money which I could gather together that I was able to avert another public exposure. He had no friends at all save the wandering gipsies, and he would give these vagabonds leave to encamp upon the few acres of bramble-covered land which represent the family estate, and would accept in return the hospitality of their tents, wandering away with them sometimes for weeks on end. He has a passion also for Indian animals, which are sent over to him by a correspondent, and he has at this moment a cheetah and a baboon, which wander freely over his grounds and are feared by the villagers almost as much as their master.

"You can imagine from what I say that my poor sister Julia and I had no great pleasure in our lives. No servant would stay with us, and for a long time we did all the work of the house. She was but thirty at the time of her death, and yet her hair had already begun to whiten, even as mine has."

"Your sister is dead, then?"

"She died just two years ago, and it is of her death that I wish to speak to you. You can understand that, living the life which I have described, we were little likely to see anyone of our own age and position. We had, however, an aunt, my mother's maiden sister, Miss Honoria Westphail, who lives near Harrow, and we were occasionally allowed to pay short visits at this lady's house. Julia went there at Christmas two years ago, and met there a half-pay major of marines, to whom she became engaged. My stepfather learned of the engagement when my sister returned and offered no objection to the marriage; but within a fortnight of the day which had been fixed for the wedding, the terrible event occurred which has deprived me of my only companion."

Sherlock Holmes had been leaning back in his chair with his eyes closed and his head sunk in a cushion, but he half opened his lids now and glanced across at his visitor.

"Pray be precise as to details," said he.

"It is easy for me to be so, for every event of that dreadful time is seared into my memory. The manor-house is, as I have already said, very old, and only one wing is now inhabited. The bedrooms in this wing are on the ground floor, the sitting-rooms being in the central block of the buildings. Of these bedrooms the first is Dr. Roylott's, the second my sister's, and the third my own. There is no communication between them, but they all open out into the same corridor. Do I make myself plain?"

"Perfectly so."

"The windows of the three rooms open out upon the lawn. That fatal night Dr. Roylott had gone to his room early, though we knew that he had not retired to rest, for my sister was troubled by the smell of the strong Indian cigars which it was his custom to smoke. She left her room, therefore, and came into mine, where she sat for some time, chatting about her approaching wedding. At eleven o'clock she rose to leave me, but she paused at the door and looked back.

" 'Tell me, Helen,' said she, 'have you ever heard anyone whistle in the dead of the night?'

" 'Never,' said I.

" 'I suppose that you could not possibly whistle, yourself, in your sleep?'

" 'Certainly not. But why?'

" 'Because during the last few nights I have always, about three in the morning, heard a low, clear whistle. I am a light sleeper, and it has awakened me. I cannot tell where it came from—perhaps from the next room, perhaps from the lawn. I thought that I would just ask you whether you had heard it.'

" 'No, I have not. It must be those wretched gipsies in the plantation.'

" 'Very likely. And yet if it were on the lawn, I wonder that you did not hear it also.'

" 'Ah, but I sleep more heavily than you.'

" 'Well, it is of no great consequence, at any rate.' She smiled back at me, closed my door, and a few moments later I heard her key turn in the lock."

"Indeed," said Holmes. "Was it your custom always to lock yourselves in at night?"

"Always."

"And why?"

"I think that I mentioned to you that the doctor kept a cheetah and a baboon. We had no feeling of security unless our doors were locked."

"Quite so. Pray proceed with your statement."

"I could not sleep that night. A vague feeling of impending misfortune impressed me. My sister and I, you will recollect, were twins, and you know how subtle are the links which bind two souls which are so closely allied. It was a wild night. The wind was howling outside, and the rain was beating and splashing against the windows. Suddenly, amid all the hubbub of the gale, there burst forth the wild scream of a terrified woman. I knew that it was my sister's voice. I sprang from my bed, wrapped a shawl round me, and rushed into the corridor. As I opened my door I seemed to hear a low whistle, such as my sister described, and a few moments later a clanging sound, as if a mass of metal had fallen. As I ran down the passage, my sister's door was unlocked, and revolved slowly upon its hinges. I stared at it horror-stricken, not knowing what was about to issue from it. By the light of the corridor-lamp I saw my sister appear at the opening, her face blanched with terror, her hands groping for help, her whole figure swaying to and fro like that of a drunkard. I ran to her and threw my arms round her, but at that moment her knees seemed to give way and she fell to the ground. She writhed as one who is in terrible pain, and her limbs were dreadfully convulsed. At first I thought that she had not recognised me, but as I bent over her she suddenly shrieked out in a voice which I shall never forget, 'Oh, my God! Helen! It was the band! The speckled band!' There was something else which she would fain have said, and she stabbed with her finger into the air in the direction of the doctor's room, but a fresh convulsion seized her and choked her words. I rushed out, calling loudly for my stepfather, and I met him hastening from his room in his dressing-gown. When he reached my sister's side she was unconscious, and though he poured brandy down her throat and sent for medical aid from the village, all efforts were in vain, for she slowly sank and died without having recovered her consciousness. Such was the dreadful end of my beloved sister."

"One moment," said Holmes, "are you sure about this whistle and metallic sound? Could you swear to it?"

"That was what the county coroner asked me at the inquiry. It is my strong impression that I heard it, and yet, among the crash of the gale and the creaking of an old house, I may possibly have been deceived."

"Was your sister dressed?"

"No, she was in her night-dress. In her right hand was found the charred stump of a match, and in her left a match-box."

"Showing that she had struck a light and looked about her when the alarm took place. That is important. And what conclusions did the coroner come to?"

"He investigated the case with great care, for Dr. Roylott's conduct had long been notorious in the county, but he was unable to find any satisfactory cause of death. My evidence showed that the door had been fastened upon the inner side, and the windows were blocked by old-fashioned shutters with broad iron bars, which were secured every night. The walls were carefully sounded, and were shown to be quite solid all round, and the flooring was also thoroughly examined, with the same result. The chimney is wide, but is barred up by four large staples. It is certain, therefore, that my sister was quite alone when she met her end. Besides, there were no marks of any violence upon her."

"How about poison?"

"The doctors examined her for it, but without success."

"What do you think that this unfortunate lady died of, then?"

"It is my belief that she died of pure fear and nervous shock, though what it was that frightened her I cannot imagine."

"Were there gipsies in the plantation at the time?"

"Yes, there are nearly always some there."

"Ah, and what did you gather from this allusion to a band—a speckled band?"

"Sometimes I have thought that it was merely the wild talk of delirium, sometimes that it may have referred to some band of people, perhaps to these very gipsies in the plantation. I do not know whether the spotted handkerchiefs which so many of them wear over their heads might have suggested the strange adjective which she used."

Holmes shook his head like a man who is far from being satisfied.

"These are very deep waters," said he; "pray go on with your narrative."

"Two years have passed since then, and my life has been until lately lonelier than ever. A month ago, however, a dear friend, whom I have known for many years, has done me the honour to ask my hand in marriage. His name is Armitage—Percy Armitage—the second son of Mr. Armitage, of Crane Water, near Reading. My stepfather has offered no opposition to the match, and we are to be married in the course of the spring. Two days ago some repairs were started in the west wing of the building, and my bedroom wall has been pierced, so that I have had to move into the chamber in which my sister died, and to sleep in the very bed in which she slept.

Imagine, then, my thrill of terror when last night, as I lay awake, thinking over her terrible fate, I suddenly heard in the silence of the night the low whistle which had been the herald of her own death. I sprang up and lit the lamp, but nothing was to be seen in the room. I was too shaken to go to bed again, however, so I dressed, and as soon as it was daylight I slipped down, got a dog-cart at the Crown Inn, which is opposite, and drove to Leatherhead, from whence I have come on this morning with the one object of seeing you and asking your advice."

"You have done wisely," said my friend. "But have you told me all?"

"Yes, all."

"Miss Roylott, you have not. You are screening your stepfather."

"Why, what do you mean?"

For answer Holmes pushed back the frill of black lace which fringed the hand that lay upon our visitor's knee. Five little livid spots, the marks of four fingers and a thumb, were printed upon the white wrist.

"You have been cruelly used," said Holmes.

The lady coloured deeply and covered over her injured wrist. "He is a hard man," she said, "and perhaps he hardly knows his own strength."

There was a long silence, during which Holmes leaned his chin upon his hands and stared into the crackling fire.

"This is a very deep business," he said at last. "There are a thousand details which I should desire to know before I decide upon our course of action. Yet we have not a moment to lose. If we were to come to Stoke Moran to-day, would it be possible for us to see over these rooms without the knowledge of your stepfather?"

"As it happens, he spoke of coming into town to-day upon some most important business. It is probable that he will be away all day, and that there would be nothing to disturb you. We have a housekeeper now, but she is old and foolish, and I could easily get her out of the way."

"Excellent. You are not averse to this trip, Watson?"

"By no means."

"Then we shall both come. What are you going to do yourself?"

"I have one or two things which I would wish to do now that I am in town. But I shall return by the twelve o'clock train, so as to be there in time for your coming."

"And you may expect us early in the afternoon. I have myself some small business matters to attend to. Will you not wait and breakfast?"

"No, I must go. My heart is lightened already since I have confided my trouble to you. I shall look forward to seeing you again this afternoon." She dropped her thick black veil over her face and glided from the room.

"And what do you think of it all, Watson?" asked Sherlock Holmes, leaning back in his chair.

"It seems to me to be a most dark and sinister business."

"Dark enough and sinister enough."

"Yet if the lady is correct in saying that the flooring and walls are sound, and that the door, window, and chimney are impassable, then her sister must have been undoubtedly alone when she met her mysterious end."

"What becomes, then, of these nocturnal whistles, and what of the very peculiar words of the dying woman?"

"I cannot think."

"When you combine the ideas of whistles at night, the presence of a band of gipsies who are on intimate terms with this old doctor, the fact that we have every reason to believe that the doctor has an interest in preventing his stepdaughter's marriage, the dying allusion to a band, and, finally, the fact that Miss Helen Stoner heard a metallic clang, which might have been caused by one of those metal bars that secured the shutters falling back into its place, I think that there is good ground to think that the mystery may be cleared along those lines."

"But what, then, did the gipsies do?"

"I cannot imagine."

"I see many objections to any such theory."

"And so do I. It is precisely for that reason that we are going to Stoke Moran this day. I want to see whether the objections are fatal, or if they may be explained away. But what in the name of the devil!"

The ejaculation had been drawn from my companion by the fact that our door had been suddenly dashed open, and that a huge man had framed himself in the aperture. His costume was a peculiar mixture of the professional and of the agricultural, having a black top-hat, a long frock-coat, and a pair of high gaiters, with a hunting-crop swinging in his hand. So tall was he that his hat actually brushed the cross bar of the doorway, and his breadth seemed to span it across from side to side. A large face, seared with a thousand wrinkles, burned yellow with the sun, and marked with every evil passion, was turned from one to the other of us, while his deep-set, bile-shot eyes, and his high, thin, fleshless nose, gave him somewhat the resemblance to a fierce old bird of prey.

"Which of you is Holmes?" asked this apparition.

"My name, sir; but you have the advantage of me," said my companion quietly.

"I am Dr. Grimesby Roylott, of Stoke Moran."

"Indeed, Doctor," said Holmes blandly. "Pray take a seat."

"I will do nothing of the kind. My stepdaughter has been here. I have traced her. What has she been saying to you?"

"It is a little cold for the time of the year," said Holmes.

"What has she been saying to you?" screamed the old man furiously.

"But I have heard that the crocuses promise well," continued my companion imperturbably.

"Ha! You put me off, do you?" said our new visitor, taking a step forward and shaking his hunting-crop. "I know you, you scoundrel! I have heard of you before. You are Holmes, the meddler."

My friend smiled.

"Holmes, the busybody!"

His smile broadened.

"Holmes, the Scotland Yard Jack-in-office!"

Holmes chuckled heartily. "Your conversation is most entertaining," said he. "When you go out close the door, for there is a decided draught."

"I will go when I have said my say. Don't you dare to meddle with my affairs. I know that Miss Stoner has been here. I traced her! I am a dangerous man to fall foul of! See here." He stepped swiftly forward, seized the poker, and bent it into a curve with his huge brown hands.

"See that you keep yourself out of my grip," he snarled, and hurling the twisted poker into the fireplace he strode out of the room.

"He seems a very amiable person," said Holmes, laughing. "I am not quite so bulky, but if he had remained I might have shown him that my grip was not much more feeble than his own." As he spoke he picked up the steel poker and, with a sudden effort, straightened it out again.

"Fancy his having the insolence to confound me with the official detective force! This incident gives zest to our investigation, however, and I only trust that our little friend will not suffer from her imprudence in allowing this brute to trace her. And now, Watson, we shall order breakfast, and afterwards I shall walk down to Doctors' Commons, where I hope to get some data which may help us in this matter."

It was nearly one o'clock when Sherlock Holmes returned from his excursion. He held in his hand a sheet of blue paper, scrawled

.over with notes and figures.

"I have seen the will of the deceased wife," said he. "To determine its exact meaning I have been obliged to work out the present prices of the investments with which it is concerned. The total income, which at the time of the wife's death was little short of £1100, is now, through the fall in agricultural prices, not more than £750. Each daughter can claim an income of £250, in case of marriage. It is evident, therefore, that if both girls had married, this beauty would have had a mere pittance, while even one of them would cripple him to a very serious extent. My morning's work has not been wasted, since it has proved that he has the very strongest motives for standing in the way of anything of the sort. And now, Watson, this is too serious for dawdling, especially as the old man is aware that we are interesting ourselves in his affairs; so if you are ready, we shall call a cab and drive to Waterloo. I should be very much obliged if you would slip your revolver into your pocket. An Eley's No. 2 is an excellent argument with gentlemen who can twist steel pokers into knots. That and a tooth-brush are, I think, all that we need."

At Waterloo we were fortunate in catching a train for Leatherhead, where we hired a trap at the station inn and drove for four or five miles through the lovely Surrey lanes. It was a perfect day, with a bright sun and a few fleecy clouds in the heavens. The trees and wayside hedges were just throwing out their first green shoots, and the air was full of the pleasant smell of the moist earth. To me at least there was a strange contrast between the sweet promise of the spring and this sinister quest upon which we were engaged. My companion sat in the front of the trap, his arms folded, his hat pulled down over his eyes, and his chin sunk upon his breast, buried in the deepest thought. Suddenly, however, he started, tapped me on the shoulder, and pointed over the meadows.

"Look there!" said he.

A heavily timbered park stretched up in a gentle slope, thickening into a grove at the highest point. From amid the branches there jutted out the grey gables and high roof-tree of a very old mansion.

"Stoke Moran?" said he.

"Yes, sir, that be the house of Dr. Grimesby Roylott," remarked the driver.

"There is some building going on there," said Holmes; "that is where we are going."

"There's the village," said the driver, pointing to a cluster of roofs some distance to the left; "but if you want to get to the house, you'll find it shorter to get over this stile, and so by the foot-path over the fields. There it is, where the lady is walking."

"And the lady, I fancy, is Miss Stoner," observed Holmes, shading his eyes. "Yes, I think we had better do as you suggest."

We got off, paid our fare, and the trap rattled back on its way to Leatherhead.

"I thought it as well," said Holmes as we climbed the stile, "that this fellow should think we had come here as architects, or on some definite business. It may stop his gossip. Good-afternoon, Miss Stoner. You see that we have been as good as our word."

Our client of the morning had hurried forward to meet us with a face which spoke her joy. "I have been waiting so eagerly for you," she cried, shaking hands with us warmly. "All has turned out splendidly. Dr. Roylott has gone to town, and it is unlikely that he will be back before evening."

"We have had the pleasure of making the doctor's acquaintance," said Holmes, and in a few words he sketched out what had occurred. Miss Stoner turned white to the lips as she listened.

"Good heavens!" she cried, "he has followed me, then."

"So it appears."

"He is so cunning that I never know when I am safe from him. What will he say when he returns?"

"He must guard himself, for he may find that there is someone more cunning than himself upon his track. You must lock yourself up from him to-night. If he is violent, we shall take you away to your aunt's at Harrow. Now, we must make the best use of our time, so kindly take us at once to the rooms which we are to examine."

The building was of grey, lichen-blotched stone, with a high central portion and two curving wings, like the claws of a crab, thrown out on each side. In one of these wings the windows were broken and blocked with wooden boards, while the roof was partly caved in, a picture of ruin. The central portion was in little better repair, but the right-hand block was comparatively modern, and the blinds in the windows, with the blue smoke curling up from the chimneys, showed that this was where the family resided. Some scaffolding had been erected against the end wall, and the stone-work had been broken into, but there were no signs of any workmen at the moment of our visit. Holmes walked slowly up and down the ill-trimmed lawn and examined with deep attention the outsides of the windows.

"This, I take it, belongs to the room in which you used to sleep, the centre one to your sister's, and the one next to the main building to Dr. Roylott's chamber?"

"Exactly so. But I am now sleeping in the middle one."

"Pending the alterations, as I understand. By the way, there does not seem to be any very pressing need for repairs at that end wall."

"There were none. I believe that it was an excuse to move me from my room."

"Ah! that is suggestive. Now, on the other side of this narrow wing runs the corridor from which these three rooms open. There are windows in it, of course?"

"Yes, but very small ones. Too narrow for anyone to pass through."

"As you both locked your doors at night, your rooms were unapproachable from that side. Now, would you have the kindness to go into your room and bar your shutters?"

Miss Stoner did so, and Holmes, after a careful examination

through the open window, endeavoured in every way to force the shutter open, but without success. There was no slit through which a knife could be passed to raise the bar. Then with his lens he tested the hinges, but they were of solid iron, built firmly into the massive masonry. "Hum!" said he, scratching his chin in some perplexity, "my theory certainly presents some difficulties. No one could pass these shutters if they were bolted. Well, we shall see if the inside throws any light upon the matter."

A small side door led into the whitewashed corridor from which the three bedrooms opened. Holmes refused to examine the third chamber, so we passed at once to the second, that in which Miss Stoner was now sleeping, and in which her sister had met with her fate. It was a homely little room, with a low ceiling and a gaping fireplace, after the fashion of old country-houses. A brown chest of drawers stood in one corner, a narrow white-counterpaned bed in another, and a dressing-table on the left-hand side of the window. These articles, with two small wicker-work chairs, made up all the furniture in the room save for a square of Wilton carpet in the centre. The boards round and the panelling of the walls were of brown, worm-eaten oak, so old and discoloured that it may have dated from the original building of the house. Holmes drew one of the chairs into a corner and sat silent, while his eyes travelled round and round and up and down, taking in every detail of the apartment.

"Where does that bell communicate with?" he asked at last pointing to a thick bell-rope which hung down beside the bed, the tassel actually lying upon the pillow.

"It goes to the housekeeper's room."

"It looks newer than the other things?"

"Yes, it was only put there a couple of years ago."

"Your sister asked for it, I suppose?"

"No, I never heard of her using it. We used always to get what we wanted for ourselves."

"Indeed, it seemed unnecessary to put so nice a bell-pull there. You will excuse me for a few minutes while I satisfy myself as to this floor." He threw himself down upon his face with his lens in his hand and crawled swiftly backward and forward, examining minutely the cracks between the boards. Then he did the same with the wood-work with which the chamber was panelled. Finally he walked over to the bed and spent some time in staring at it and in running his eye up and down the wall. Finally he took the bell-rope in his hand and gave it a brisk tug.

"Why, it's a dummy," said he.

"Won't it ring?"

"No, it is not even attached to a wire. This is very interesting. You can see now that it is fastened to a hook just above where the little opening for the ventilator is."

"How very absurd! I never noticed that before."

"Very strange!" muttered Holmes, pulling at the rope. "There are one or two very singular points about this room. For example, what a fool a builder must be to open a ventilator into another room, when, with the same trouble, he might have communicated with the outside air!"

"That is also quite modern," said the lady.

"Done about the same time as the bell-rope?" remarked Holmes.

"Yes, there were several little changes carried out about that time."

"They seem to have been of a most interesting character—dummy bell-ropes, and ventilators which do not ventilate. With your permission, Miss Stoner, we shall now carry our researches into the inner apartment."

Dr. Grimesby Roylott's chamber was larger than that of his step-daughter, but was as plainly furnished. A camp-bed, a small wooden shelf full of books, mostly of a technical character, an armchair beside the bed, a plain wooden chair against the wall, a round table, and a large iron safe were the principal things which met the eye.

Holmes walked slowly round and examined each and all of them with the keenest interest.

"What's in here?" he asked, tapping the safe.

"My stepfather's business papers."

"Oh! you have seen inside, then?"

"Only once, some years ago. I remember that it was full of papers."

"There isn't a cat in it, for example?"

"No. What a strange idea!"

"Well, look at this!" He took up a small saucer of milk which stood on the top of it.

"No; we don't keep a cat. But there is a cheetah and a baboon."

"Ah, yes, of course! Well, a cheetah is just a big cat, and yet a saucer of milk does not go very far in satisfying its wants, I daresay. There is one point which I should wish to determine." He squatted down in front of the wooden chair and examined the seat of it with the greatest attention.

"Thank you. That is quite settled," said he, rising and putting his lens in his pocket. "Hullo! Here is something interesting!"

The object which had caught his eye was a small dog lash hung on one corner of the bed. The lash, however, was curled upon itself and tied so as to make a loop of whipcord.

"What do you make of that, Watson?"

"It's a common enough lash. But I don't know why it should be tied."

"That is not quite so common, is it? Ah, me! it's a wicked world, and when a clever man turns his brains to crime it is the worst of all. I think that I have seen enough now, Miss Stoner, and with your permission we shall walk out upon the lawn."

I had never seen my friend's face so grim or his brow so dark as it was when we turned from the scene of this investigation. We had walked several times up and down the lawn, neither Miss Stoner nor myself liking to break in upon his thoughts before he roused himself from his reverie.

"It is very essential, Miss Stoner," said he, "that you should absolutely follow my advice in every respect."

"I shall most certainly do so."

"The matter is too serious for any hesitation. Your life may depend upon your compliance."

"I assure you that I am in your hands."

"In the first place, both my friend and I must spend the night in your room."

Both Miss Stoner and I gazed at him in astonishment.

"Yes, it must be so. Let me explain. I believe that that is the village inn over there?"

"Yes, that is the Crown."

"Very good. Your windows would be visible from there?"

"Certainly."

"You must confine yourself to your room, on pretence of a headache, when your stepfather comes back. Then when you hear him retire for the night, you must open the shutters of your window, undo the hasp, put your lamp there as a signal to us, and then withdraw quietly with everything which you are likely to want into the room which you used to occupy. I have no doubt that, in spite of the repairs, you could manage there for one night."

"Oh, yes, easily."

"The rest you will leave in our hands."

"But what will you do?"

"We shall spend the night in your room, and we shall investigate the cause of this noise which has disturbed you."

"I believe, Mr. Holmes, that you have already made up your mind," said Miss Stoner, laying her hand upon my companion's sleeve.

"Perhaps I have."

"Then, for pity's sake, tell me what was the cause of my sister's death."

"I should prefer to have clearer proofs before I speak."

"You can at least tell me whether my own thought is correct, and if she died from some sudden fright."

"No, I do not think so. I think that there was probably some more tangible cause. And now, Miss Stoner, we must leave you for if Dr. Roylott returned and saw us our journey would be in vain. Good-bye, and be brave, for if you will do what I have told you, you may rest assured that we shall soon drive away the dangers that threaten you."

Sherlock Holmes and I had no difficulty in engaging a bedroom and sitting-room at the Crown Inn. They were on the upper floor, and from our window we could command a view of the avenue gate, and of the inhabited wing of Stoke Moran Manor House. At dusk we saw Dr. Grimesby Roylott drive past, his huge form looming up beside the little figure of the lad who drove him. The boy had some slight difficulty in undoing the heavy iron gates, and we heard the hoarse roar of the doctor's voice and saw the fury with which he shook his clinched fists at him. The trap drove on, and a few minutes later we saw a sudden light spring up among the trees as the lamp was lit in one of the sitting-rooms.

"Do you know, Watson," said Holmes as we sat together in the gathering darkness, "I have really some scruples as to taking you to-night. There is a distinct element of danger."

"Can I be of assistance?"

"Your presence might be invaluable."

"Then I shall certainly come."

"It is very kind of you."

"You speak of danger. You have evidently seen more in these rooms than was visible to me."

"No, but I fancy that I may have deduced a little more. I imagine that you saw all that I did."

"I saw nothing remarkable save the bell-rope, and what purpose that could answer I confess is more than I can imagine."

"You saw the ventilator, too?"

"Yes, but I do not think that it is such a very unusual thing to have a small opening between two rooms. It was so small that a rat could hardly pass through."

"I knew that we should find a ventilator before ever we came to Stoke Moran."

"My dear Holmes!"

"Oh, yes, I did. You remember in her statement she said that her sister could smell Dr. Roylott's cigar. Now, of course that suggested at once that there must be a communication between the two rooms. It could only be a small one, or it would have been remarked upon at the coroner's inquiry. I deduced a ventilator."

"But what harm can there be in that?"

"Well, there is at least a curious coincidence of dates. A ventilator is made, a cord is hung, and a lady who sleeps in the bed dies. Does not that strike you?"

"I cannot as yet see any connection."

"Did you observe anything very peculiar about that bed?"

"No."

"It was clamped to the floor. Did you ever see a bed fastened like that before?"

"I cannot say that I have."

"The lady could not move her bed. It must always be in the same relative position to the ventilator and to the rope—or so we may call it, since it was clearly never meant for a bell-pull."

"Holmes," I cried, "I seem to see dimly what you are hinting at. We are only just in time to prevent some subtle and horrible crime."

"Subtle enough and horrible enough. When a doctor does go wrong he is the first of criminals. He has nerve and he has knowledge. Palmer and Pritchard were among the heads of their profession. This man strikes even deeper, but I think, Watson, that we shall be able to strike deeper still. But we shall have horrors enough before the night is over; for goodness' sake let us have a quiet pipe and turn our minds for a few hours to something more cheerful."

About nine o'clock the light among the trees was extinguished, and all was dark in the direction of the Manor House. Two hours passed slowly away, and then, suddenly, just at the stroke of eleven, a single bright light shone out right in front of us.

"That is our signal," said Holmes, springing to his feet; "it comes from the middle window."

As we passed out he exchanged a few words with the landlord, explaining that we were going on a late visit to an acquaintance, and that it was possible that we might spend the night there. A moment later we were out on the dark road, a chill wind blowing in our faces, and one yellow light twinkling in front of us through the gloom to guide us on our sombre errand.

There was little difficulty in entering the grounds, for unrepaired breaches gaped in the old park wall. Making our way among the trees, we reached the lawn, crossed it, and were about to enter through the window when out from a clump of laurel bushes there darted what seemed to be a hideous and distorted child, who threw itself upon the grass with writhing limbs and then ran swiftly across the lawn into the darkness.

"My God!" I whispered; "did you see it?"

Holmes was for the moment as startled as I. His hand closed like a vice upon my wrist in his agitation. Then he broke into a low laugh and put his lips to my ear.

"It is a nice household," he murmured. "That is the baboon."

I had forgotten the strange pets which the doctor affected. There was a cheetah, too; perhaps we might find it upon our shoulders at any moment. I confess that I felt easier in my mind when, after following Holmes' example and slipping off my shoes, I found myself inside the bedroom. My companion noiselessly closed the shutters, moved the lamp onto the table, and cast his eyes round the room. All was as we had seen it in the daytime. Then creeping up to me and making a trumpet of his hand, he whispered into my ear again so gently that it was all that I could do to distinguish the words:

"The least sound would be fatal to our plans."

I nodded to show that I had heard.

"We must sit without light. He would see it through the ventilator."

I nodded again.

"Do not go asleep; your very life may depend upon it. Have your pistol ready in case we should need it. I will sit on the side of the bed, and you in that chair."

I took out my revolver and laid it on the corner of the table.

Holmes had brought up a long thin cane, and this he placed upon the bed beside him. By it he laid the box of matches and the stump of a candle. Then he turned down the lamp, and we were left in darkness.

How shall I ever forget that dreadful vigil? I could not hear a sound, not even the drawing of a breath, and yet I knew that my companion sat open-eyed, within a few feet of me, in the same state of nervous tension in which I was myself. The shutters cut off the least ray of light, and we waited in absolute darkness.

From outside came the occasional cry of a night-bird, and once at our very window a long drawn catlike whine, which told us that the cheetah was indeed at liberty. Far away we could hear the deep tones of the parish clock, which boomed out every quarter of an hour. How long they seemed, those quarters! Twelve struck, and one and two and three, and still we sat waiting silently for whatever might befall.

Suddenly there was the momentary gleam of a light up in the direction of the ventilator, which vanished immediately, but was succeeded by a strong smell of burning oil and heated metal. Someone in the next room had lit a dark-lantern. I heard a gentle sound of movement, and then all was silent once more, though the smell grew stronger. For half an hour I sat with straining ears. Then suddenly another sound became audible—a very gentle, soothing sound, like that of a small jet of steam escaping continually from a kettle. The instant that we heard it, Holmes sprang from the bed, struck a match, and lashed furiously with his cane at the bell-pull.

"You see it, Watson?" he yelled. "You see it?"

But I saw nothing. At the moment when Holmes struck the light I heard a low, clear whistle, but the sudden glare flashing into my weary eyes made it impossible for me to tell what it was at which my friend lashed so savagely. I could, however, see that his face was deadly pale and filled with horror and loathing. He had ceased to strike and was gazing up at the ventilator when suddenly there broke from the silence of the night the most horrible cry to which I have ever listened. It swelled up louder and louder, a hoarse yell of pain and fear and anger all mingled in the one dreadful shriek. They say that away down in the village, and even in the distant parsonage, that cry raised the sleepers from their beds. It struck cold to our hearts, and I stood gazing at Holmes, and he at me, until the last echoes of it had died away into the silence from which it rose.

"What can it mean?" I gasped.

"It means that it is all over," Holmes answered. "And perhaps, after all, it is for the best. Take your pistol, and we will enter Dr. Roylott's room."

With a grave face he lit the lamp and led the way down the corridor. Twice he struck at the chamber door without any reply from within. Then he turned the handle and entered, I at his heels, with the cocked pistol in my hand.

It was a singular sight which met our eyes. On the table stood a dark-lantern with the shutter half open, throwing a brilliant beam of light upon the iron safe, the door of which was ajar. Beside this table, on the wooden chair, sat Dr. Grimesby Roylott clad in a long grey dressing-gown, his bare ankles protruding beneath, and his feet thrust into red heelless Turkish slippers. Across his lap lay the short stock with the long lash which we had noticed during the day. His chin was cocked upward and his eyes were fixed in a dreadful, rigid stare at the corner of the ceiling. Round his brow he had a peculiar yellow band, with brownish speckles, which seemed to be bound tightly round his head. As we entered he made neither sound nor motion.

"The band! the speckled band!" whispered Holmes.

I took a step forward. In an instant his strange headgear began to move, and there reared itself from among his hair the squat diamond-shaped head and puffed neck of a loathsome serpent.

"It is a swamp adder!" cried Holmes; "the deadliest snake in India. He has died within ten seconds of being bitten. Violence does, in truth, recoil upon the violent, and the schemer falls into the pit which he digs for another. Let us thrust this creature back into its den, and we can then remove Miss Stoner to some place of shelter and let the county police know what has happened."

As he spoke he drew the dog-whip swiftly from the dead man's lap, and throwing the noose round the reptile's neck he drew it from its horrid perch and, carrying it at arm's length, threw it into the iron safe, which he closed upon it.

Such are the true facts of the death of Dr. Grimesby Roylott, of Stoke Moran. It is not necessary that I should prolong a narrative which has already run to too great a length by telling how we broke the sad news to the terrified girl, how we conveyed her by the morning train to the care of her good aunt at Harrow, of how the slow process of official inquiry came to the conclusion that the doctor met his fate while indiscreetly playing with a dangerous pet. The little which I had yet to learn of the case was told me by Sherlock Holmes as we travelled back next day.

"I had," said he, "come to an entirely erroneous conclusion which shows, my dear Watson, how dangerous it always is to reason from insufficient data. The presence of the gipsies, and the use of the word 'band,' which was used by the poor girl, no doubt, to explain the appearance which she had caught a hurried glimpse of by the light of her match, were sufficient to put me upon an entirely wrong scent. I can only claim the merit that I instantly reconsidered my position when, however, it became clear to me that whatever danger threatened an occupant of the room could not come either from the window or the door. My attention was speedily drawn, as I have already remarked to you, to this ventilator, and to the bell-rope which hung down to the bed. The discovery that this was a dummy, and that the bed was clamped to the floor, instantly gave rise to the suspicion that the rope was there as a bridge for something passing through the hole and coming to the bed. The idea of a snake instantly occurred to me, and when I coupled it with my knowledge that the doctor was furnished with a supply of creatures from India, I felt that I was probably on the right track. The idea of using a form of poison which could not possibly be discovered by any chemical test was just such a one as would occur to a clever and ruthless man who had had an Eastern training. The rapidity with which such a poison would take effect would also, from his point of view, be an advantage. It would be a sharp-eyed coroner, indeed, who could distinguish the two little dark punctures which would show where the poison fangs had done their work. Then I thought of the whistle. Of course he must recall the snake before the morning light revealed it to the victim. He had trained it, probably by the use of the milk which we saw, to return to him when summoned. He would put it through this ventilator at the hour that he thought best, with the certainty that it would crawl down the rope and land on the bed. It might or might not bite the occupant, perhaps she might escape every night for a week, but sooner or later she must fall a victim.

"I had come to these conclusions before ever I had entered his room. An inspection of his chair showed me that he had been in the habit of standing on it, which of course would be necessary in order that he should reach the ventilator. The sight of the safe, the saucer of milk, and the loop of whipcord were enough to finally dispel any doubts which may have remained. The metallic clang heard by Miss Stoner was obviously caused by her stepfather hastily closing the door of his safe upon its terrible occupant. Having once made up my mind, you know the steps which I took in order to put the matter to the proof. I heard the creature hiss as I have no doubt that you did also, and I instantly lit the light and attacked it."

"With the result of driving it through the ventilator."

"And also with the result of causing it to turn upon its master at the other side. Some of the blows of my cane came home and roused its snakish temper, so that it flew upon the first person it saw. In this way I am no doubt indirectly responsible for Dr. Grimesby Roylott's death, and I cannot say that it is likely to weigh very heavily upon my conscience."

The Stranger's Latchkey

R. Austen Freeman

The Stranger's Latchkey

The contrariety of human nature is a subject that has given a surprising amount of occupation to makers of proverbs and to those moral philosophers who make it their province to discover and expound the glaringly obvious; and especially have they been concerned to enlarge upon that form of perverseness which engenders dislike of things offered under compulsion, and arouses desire of them as soon as their attainment becomes difficult or impossible. They assure us that a man who has had a given thing within his reach and put it by, will, as soon as it is beyond his reach, find it the one thing necessary and desirable; even as the domestic cat which has turned disdainfully from the preferred saucer, may presently be seen with her head jammed hard in the milk-jug, or, secretly and with horrible relish, slaking her thirst at the scullery sink.

To this peculiarity of the human mind was due, no doubt, the fact that no sooner had I abandoned the clinical side of my profession in favour of the legal, and taken up my abode in the chambers of my friend Thorndyke, the famous medico-legal expert, to act as his assistant or junior, than my former mode of life—that of a locum tenens, or minder of other men's practices—which had, when I was following it, seemed intolerably irksome, now appeared to possess many desirable features; and I found myself occasionally hankering to sit once more by the bedside, to puzzle out the perplexing train of symptoms, and to wield that power—the greatest, after all, possessed by man—the power to banish suffering and ward off the approach of death itself.

Hence it was that on a certain morning of the long vacation I found myself installed at The Larches, Burling, in full charge of the practice of my old friend Dr. Hanshaw, who was taking a fishing holiday in Norway. I was not left desolate, however, for Mrs. Hanshaw remained at her post, and the roomy, old-fashioned house accommodated three visitors in addition. One of these was Dr. Hanshaw's sister, a Mrs. Haldean, the widow of a wealthy Manchester cotton factor; the second was her niece by marriage, Miss Lucy Haldean, a very handsome and charming girl of twenty-three; while the third was no less a person than Master Fred, the only child of Mrs. Haldean, and a strapping boy of six.

"It is quite like old times—and very pleasant old times, too—to see you sitting at our breakfast-table, Dr. Jervis." With these gracious words and a friendly smile, Mrs. Hanshaw handed me my tea-cup.

I bowed. "The highest pleasure of the altruist," I replied, "is in contemplating the good fortune of others."

Mrs. Haldean laughed. "Thank you," she said. "You are quite unchanged, I perceive. Still as suave and as—shall I say oleaginous?"

"No, please don't!" I exclaimed in a tone of alarm.

"Then I won't. But what does Dr. Thorndyke say to this backsliding on your part? How does he regard this relapse from medical jurisprudence to common general practice?"

"Thorndyke," said I, "is unmoved by any catastrophe; and he not only regards the 'Decline and Fall-off of the Medical Jurist' with philosophic calm, but he even favours the relapse, as you call it. He thinks it may be useful to me to study the application of medico-legal methods to general practice."

"That sounds rather unpleasant—for the patients, I mean," remarked Miss Haldean.

"Very," agreed her aunt. "Most cold-blooded. What sort of man is Dr. Thorndyke? I feel quite curious about him. Is he at all human, for instance?"

"He is entirely human," I replied; "the accepted tests of humanity being, as I understand, the habitual adoption of the erect posture in locomotion, and the relative position of the end of the thumb—"

"I don't mean that," interrupted Mrs. Haldean. "I mean human in things that matter."

"I think those things matter," I rejoined. "Consider, Mrs. Haldean, what would happen if my learned colleague were to be seen in wig and gown, walking towards the Law Courts in any posture other than the erect. It would be a public scandal."

"Don't talk to him, Mabel," said Mrs. Hanshaw; "he is incorrigible. What are you doing with yourself this morning, Lucy?"

Miss Haldean (who had hastily set down her cup to laugh at my imaginary picture of Dr. Thorndyke in the character of a quadruped) considered a moment.

"I think I shall sketch that group of birches at the edge of Bradham Wood," she said.

"Then, in that case," said I, "I can carry your traps for you, for I have to see a patient in Bradham."

"He is making the most of his time," remarked Mrs. Haldean maliciously to my hostess. "He knows that when Mr. Winter arrives he will retire into the extreme background."

Douglas Winter, whose arrival was expected in the course of the week, was Miss Haldean's fiancé. Their engagement had been somewhat protracted, and was likely to be more so, unless one of them received some unexpected accession of means; for Douglas was a subaltern in the Royal Engineers, living, with great difficulty, on his pay, while Lucy Haldean subsisted on an almost invisible allowance left her by an uncle.

I was about to reply to Mrs. Haldean when a patient was announced, and, as I had finished my breakfast, I made my excuses and left the table.

Half an hour later, when I started along the road to the village of Bradham, I had two companions. Master Freddy had joined the party, and he disputed with me the privilege of carrying the "traps," with the result that a compromise was effected, by which he carried the camp-stool, leaving me in possession of the easel, the bag, and a large bound sketching-block.

"Where are you going to work this morning?" I asked, when we had trudged on some distance.

"Just off the road to the left there, at the edge of the wood. Not very far from the house of the mysterious stranger." She glanced at me mischievously as she made this reply, and chuckled with delight when I rose at the bait.

"What house do you mean?" I inquired.

"Ha!" she exclaimed, "the investigator of mysteries is aroused. He saith, 'Ha! ha!' amidst the trumpets; he smelleth the battle afar off."

"Explain instantly," I commanded, "or I drop your sketch-block into the very next puddle."

"You terrify me," said she. "But I will explain, only there isn't any mystery except to the bucolic mind. The house is called Lavender Cottage, and it stands alone in the fields behind the wood. A fortnight ago it was let furnished to a stranger named Whitelock, who has taken it for the purpose of studying the botany of the district; and the only really mysterious thing about him is that no one has seen him. All arrangements with the house-agent were made by letter, and, as far as I can make out, none of the local tradespeople supply him, so he must get his things from a distance—even his bread, which really is rather odd. Now say I am an inquisitive, gossiping country bumpkin."

"I was going to," I answered, "but it is no use now."

She relieved me of her sketching appliances with pretended indignation, and crossed into the meadow, leaving me to pursue my way alone; and when I presently looked back, she was setting up her easel and stool, gravely assisted by Freddy.

My "round," though not a long one, took up more time than I had anticipated, and it was already past the luncheon hour when I passed the place where I had left Miss Haldean. She was gone, as

I had expected, and I hurried homewards, anxious to be as nearly punctual as possible. When I entered the dining-room, I found Mrs. Haldean and our hostess seated at the table, and both looked up at me expectantly.

"Have you seen Lucy?" the former inquired.

"No," I answered. "Hasn't she come back? I expected to find her here. She had left the wood when I passed just now."

Mrs. Haldean knitted her brows anxiously. "It is very strange," she said, "and very thoughtless of her. Freddy will be famished."

I hurried over my lunch, for two fresh messages had come in from outlying hamlets, effectually dispelling my visions of a quiet afternoon; and as the minutes passed without bringing any signs of the absentees, Mrs. Haldean became more and more restless and anxious. At length her suspense became unbearable; she rose suddenly, announcing her intention of cycling up the road to look for the defaulters, but as she was moving towards the door, it burst open, and Lucy Haldean staggered into the room.

Her appearance filled us with alarm. She was deadly pale, breathless, and wild-eyed; her dress was draggled and torn, and she trembled from head to foot.

"Good God, Lucy!" gasped Mrs. Haldean. "What has happened? And where is Freddy?" she added in a sterner tone.

"He is lost!" replied Miss Haldean in a faint voice, and with a catch in her breath. "He strayed away while I was painting. I have searched the wood through, and called to him, and looked in all the meadows. Oh! where can he have gone?" Her sketching "kit," with which she was loaded, slipped from her grasp and rattled on to the floor, and she buried her face in her hands and sobbed hysterically.

"And you have dared to come back without him?" exclaimed Mrs. Haldean.

"I was getting exhausted. I came back for help," was the faint reply.

"Of course she was exhausted," said Mrs. Hanshaw. "Come, Lucy: come, Mabel; don't make mountains out of molehills. The little man is safe enough. We shall find him presently, or he will come home by himself. Come and have some food, Lucy."

Miss Haldean shook her head. "I can't, Mrs. Hanshaw—really I can't," she said; and, seeing that she was in a state of utter exhaustion, I poured out a glass of wine and made her drink it.

Mrs. Haldean darted from the room, and returned immediately, putting on her hat. "You have got to come with me and show me where you lost him," she said.

"She can't do that, you know," I said rather brusquely. "She will have to lie down for the present. But I know the place, and will cycle up with you."

"Very well," replied Mrs. Haldean, "that will do. What time was it," she asked, turning to her niece, "when you lost the child? and which way—"

She paused abruptly, and I looked at her in surprise. She had suddenly turned ashen and ghastly; her face had set like a mask of stone, with parted lips and staring eyes that were fixed in horror on her niece.

There was a deathly silence for a few seconds. Then, in a terrible voice, she demanded: "What is that on your dress, Lucy?" And, after a pause, her voice rose into a shriek. "What have you done to my boy?"

I glanced in astonishment at the dazed and terrified girl, and then I saw what her aunt had seen—a good-sized blood-stain halfway down the front of her skirt, and another smaller one on her right sleeve. The girl herself looked down at the sinister patch of red and then up at her aunt. "It looks like—like blood," she stammered. "Yes, it is—I think—of course it is. He struck his nose—and it bled—"

"Come," interrupted Mrs. Haldean, "let us go," and she rushed from the room, leaving me to follow.

I lifted Miss Haldean, who was half fainting with fatigue and agitation, on to the sofa, and, whispering a few words of encouragement into her ear, turned to Mrs. Hanshaw.

"I can't stay with Mrs. Haldean," I said. "There are two visits to be made at Rebworth. Will you send the dogcart up the road with somebody to take my place?"

"Yes," she answered. "I will send Giles, or come myself if Lucy is fit to be left."

I ran to the stables for my bicycle, and as I pedalled out into the road I could see Mrs. Haldean already far ahead, driving her machine at frantic speed. I followed at a rapid pace, but it was not until we approached the commencement of the wood, when she slowed down somewhat, that I overtook her.

"This is the place," I said, as we reached the spot where I had parted from Miss Haldean. We dismounted and wheeled our bicycles through the gate, and laying them down beside the hedge, crossed the meadow and entered the wood.

It was a terrible experience, and one that I shall never forget—the white-faced, distracted woman, tramping in her flimsy house-shoes over the rough ground, bursting through the bushes, regardless of the thorny branches that dragged at skin and hair and dainty clothing, and sending forth from time to time a tremulous cry, so dreadfully pathetic in its mingling of terror and coaxing softness, that a lump rose in my throat, and I could barely keep my self-control.

"Freddy! Freddy-boy! Mummy's here, darling!" The wailing cry sounded through the leafy solitude; but no answer came save the whirr of wings or the chatter of startled birds. But even more shocking than that terrible cry—more disturbing and eloquent with dreadful suggestion—was the way in which she peered, furtively, but with fearful expectation, among the roots of the bushes, or halted to gaze upon every molehill and hummock, every depression or disturbance of the ground.

So we stumbled on for a while, with never a word spoken, until we came to a beaten track or footpath leading across the wood. Here I paused to examine the footprints, of which several were visible in the soft earth, though none seemed very recent; but, proceeding a little way down the track, I perceived, crossing it, a set of fresh imprints, which I recognized at once as Miss Haldean's. She was wearing, as I knew, a pair of brown golf-boots, with rubber pads in the leather soles, and the prints made by them were unmistakable.

"Miss Haldean crossed the path here," I said, pointing to the footprints.

"Don't speak of her before me!" exclaimed Mrs. Haldean; but she gazed eagerly at the footprints, nevertheless, and immediately plunged into the wood to follow the tracks.

"You are very unjust to your niece, Mrs. Haldean," I ventured to protest.

She halted, and faced me with an angry frown.

"You don't understand!" she exclaimed. "You don't know, perhaps, that if my poor child is really dead, Lucy Haldean will be a rich woman, and may marry to-morrow if she chooses?"

"I did not know that," I answered, "but if I had, I should have said the same."

"Of course you would," she retorted bitterly. "A pretty face can muddle any man's judgment."

She turned away abruptly to resume her pursuit, and I followed in silence. The trail which we were following zigzagged through the thickest part of the wood, but its devious windings eventually brought us out on to an open space on the farther side. Here we at once perceived traces of another kind. A litter of dirty rags, pieces of paper, scraps of stale bread, bones and feathers, with hoof-marks, wheel ruts, and the ashes of a large wood fire, pointed clearly to a gipsy encampment recently broken up. I laid my hand on the heap of ashes, and found it still warm, and on scattering it with my foot a layer of glowing cinders appeared at the bottom.

"These people have only been gone an hour or two," I said. "It would be well to have them followed without delay."

A gleam of hope shone on the drawn, white face as the bereaved mother caught eagerly at my suggestion.

"Yes," she exclaimed breathlessly; "she may have bribed them to take him away. Let us see which way they went."

We followed the wheel tracks down to the road, and found that they turned towards London. At the same time I perceived the dogcart in the distance, with Mrs. Hanshaw standing beside it; and, as the coachman observed me, he whipped up his horse and approached.

"I shall have to go," I said, "but Mrs. Hanshaw will help you to continue the search."

"And you will make inquiries about the gipsies, won't you?" she said.

I promised to do so, and as the dogcart now came up, I climbed to the seat, and drove off briskly up the London Road.

The extent of a country doctor's round is always an unknown quantity. On the present occasion I picked up three additional patients, and as one of them was a case of incipient pleurisy, which required to have the chest strapped, and another was a neglected dislocation of the shoulder, a great deal of time was taken up. Moreover, the gipsies, whom I ran to earth on Rebworth Common, delayed me considerably, though I had to leave the rural constable to carry out the actual search, and, as a result, the clock of Burling Church was striking six as I drove through the village on my way home.

I got down at the front gate, leaving the coachman to take the dogcart round, and walked up the drive; and my astonishment may be imagined when, on turning the corner, I came suddenly upon the inspector of the local police in earnest conversation with no less a person than John Thorndyke.

"What on earth has brought you here?" I exclaimed, my surprise getting the better of my manners.

"The ultimate motive-force," he replied, "was an impulsive lady named Mrs. Haldean. She telegraphed for me—in your name."

"She oughtn't to have done that," I said.

"Perhaps not. But the ethics of an agitated woman are not worth discussing, and she has done something much worse—she has applied to the local J.P. (a retired Major-General), and our gallant and unlearned friend has issued a warrant for the arrest of Lucy Haldean on the charge of murder."

"But there has been no murder!" I exclaimed.

"That," said Thorndyke, "is a legal subtlety that he does not appreciate. He has learned his law in the orderly-room, where the qualifications to practise are an irritable temper and a loud voice. However, the practical point is, inspector, that the warrant is irregular. You can't arrest people for hypothetical crimes."

The officer drew a deep breath of relief. He knew all about the irregularity, and now joyfully took refuge behind Thorndyke's great reputation.

When he had departed—with a brief note from my colleague to the General—Thorndyke slipped his arm through mine, and we strolled towards the house.

"This is a grim business, Jervis," said he. "That boy has got to be found for everybody's sake. Can you come with me when you have had some food?"

"Of course I can. I have been saving myself all the afternoon with a view to continuing the search."

"Good," said Thorndyke. "Then come in and feed."

A nondescript meal, half tea and half dinner, was already prepared, and Mrs. Hanshaw, grave but self-possessed, presided at the table.

"Mabel is still out with Giles, searching for the boy," she said. "You have heard what she has done!"

I nodded.

"It was dreadful of her," continued Mrs. Hanshaw, "but she is half mad, poor thing. You might run up and say a few kind words to poor Lucy while I make the tea."

I went up at once and knocked at Miss Haldean's door, and, being bidden to enter, found her lying on the sofa, red-eyed and pale, the very ghost of the merry, laughing girl who had gone out with me in the morning. I drew up a chair, and sat down by her side, and as I took the hand she held out to me, she said:

"It is good of you to come and see a miserable wretch like me. And Jane has been so sweet to me, Dr. Jervis; but Aunt Mabel thinks I have killed Freddy—you know she does—and it was really my fault that he was lost. I shall never forgive myself!"

She burst into a passion of sobbing, and I proceeded to chide her gently.

"You are a silly little woman," I said, "to take this nonsense to heart as you are doing. Your aunt is not responsible just now, as you must know; but when we bring the boy home she shall make you a handsome apology. I will see to that."

She pressed my hand gratefully, and as the bell now rang for tea, I bade her have courage and went downstairs.

"You need not trouble about the practice," said Mrs. Hanshaw, as I concluded my lightning repast, and Thorndyke went off to get our bicycles. "Dr. Symons has heard of our trouble, and has called to say that he will take anything that turns up; so we shall expect you when we see you."

"How do you like Thorndyke?" I asked.

"He is quite charming," she replied enthusiastically; "so tactful and kind, and so handsome, too. You didn't tell us that. But here he is. Good-bye, and good luck."

She pressed my hand, and I went out into the drive, where Thorndyke and the coachman were standing with three bicycles.

"I see you have brought your outfit," I said as we turned into the road; for Thorndyke's machine bore a large canvas-covered case strapped on to a strong bracket.

"Yes; there are many things that we may want on a quest of this kind. How did you find Miss Haldean?"

"Very miserable, poor girl. By the way, have you heard anything about her pecuniary interest in the child's death?"

"Yes," said Thorndyke. "It appears that the late Mr. Haldean used up all his brains on his business, and had none left for the making of his will—as often happens. He left almost the whole of his property—about eighty thousand pounds—to his son, the widow to have a life-interest in it. He also left to his late brother's daughter, Lucy, fifty pounds a year, and to his surviving brother Percy, who seems to have been a good-for-nothing, a hundred a year for life. But—and here is the utter folly of the thing—if the son should die, the property was to be equally divided between the brother and the niece, with the exception of five hundred a year for life to the widow. It was an insane arrangement."

"Quite," I agreed, "and a very dangerous one for Lucy Haldean, as things are at present."

"Very; especially if anything should have happened to the child."

"What are you going to do now?" I inquired, seeing that Thorndyke rode on as if with a definite purpose.

"There is a footpath through the wood," he replied. "I want to examine that. And there is a house behind the wood which I should like to see."

"The house of the mysterious stranger," I suggested.

"Precisely. Mysterious and solitary strangers invite inquiry."

We drew up at the entrance to the footpath, leaving Willett the coachman in charge of the three machines, and proceeded up the narrow track. As we went, Thorndyke looked back at the prints of our feet, and nodded approvingly.

"This soft loam," he remarked, "yields beautifully clear impressions, and yesterday's rain has made it perfect."

We had not gone far when we perceived a set of footprints which I recognized, as did Thorndyke also, for he remarked: "Miss Haldean—running, and alone." Presently we met them again, crossing in the opposite direction, together with the prints of small shoes with very high heels. "Mrs. Haldean on the track of her niece," was Thorndyke's comment; and a minute later we encountered them both again, accompanied by my own footprints.

"The boy does not seem to have crossed the path at all," I remarked as we walked on, keeping off the track itself to avoid confusing the footprints.

"We shall know when we have examined the whole length," replied Thorndyke, plodding on with his eyes on the ground. "Ha! here is something new," he added, stopping short and stooping down eagerly—"a man with a thick stick—a smallish man, rather lame. Notice the difference between the two feet, and the peculiar way in which he uses his stick. Yes, Jervis, there is a great deal to interest us in these footprints. Do you notice anything very suggestive about them?"

"Nothing but what you have mentioned," I replied. "What do you mean?"

"Well, first there is the very singular character of the prints themselves, which we will consider presently. You observe that this man came down the path, and at this point turned off into the wood; then he returned from the wood and went up the path again. The imposition of the prints makes that clear. But now look at the two sets of prints, and compare them. Do you notice any difference?"

"The returning footprints seem more distinct—better impressions."

"Yes; they are noticeably deeper. But there is something else." He produced a spring tape from his pocket, and took half a dozen measurements. "You see," he said, "the first set of footprints have a stride of twenty-one inches from heel to heel—a short stride; but he is a smallish man, and lame; the returning ones have a stride of only nineteen and a half inches; hence the returning footprints are deeper than the others, and the steps are shorter. What do you make of that?"

"It would suggest that he was carrying a burden when he returned," I replied.

"Yes; and a heavy one, to make that difference in the depth. I think I will get you to go and fetch Willett and the bicycles."

I strode off down the path to the entrance, and, taking possession of Thorndyke's machine, with its precious case of instruments, bade Willett follow with the other two.

When I returned, my colleague was standing with his hands behind him, gazing with intense preoccupation at the footprints. He looked up sharply as we approached, and called out to us to keep off the path if possible.

"Stay here with the machines, Willett," said he. "You and I, Jervis, must go and see where our friend went to when he left the path, and what was the burden that he picked up."

We struck off into the wood, where last year's dead leaves made the footprints almost indistinguishable, and followed the faint double track for a long distance between the dense clumps of bushes. Suddenly my eye caught, beside the double trail, a third row of tracks, smaller in size and closer together. Thorndyke had seen them, too, and already his measuring-tape was in his hand.

"Eleven and a half inches to the stride," said he. "That will be the boy, Jervis. But the light is getting weak. We must press on quickly, or we shall lose it."

Some fifty yards farther on, the man's tracks ceased abruptly, but the small ones continued alone; and we followed them as rapidly as we could in the fading light.

"There can be no reasonable doubt that these are the child's tracks," said Thorndyke; "but I should like to find a definite footprint to make the identification absolutely certain."

A few seconds later he halted with an exclamation, and stooped on one knee. A little heap of fresh earth from the surface-burrow of a mole had been thrown up over the dead leaves; and fairly planted on it was the clean and sharp impression of a diminutive foot, with a rubber heel showing a central star. Thorndyke drew from his pocket a tiny shoe, and pressed it on the soft earth beside the footprint; and when he raised it the second impression was identical with the first.

"The boy had two pairs of shoes exactly alike," he said, "so I borrowed one of the duplicate pair."

He turned, and began to retrace his steps rapidly, following our own fresh tracks, and stopping only once to point out the place where the unknown man had picked the child up. When we regained the path we proceeded without delay until we emerged from the wood within a hundred yards of the cottage.

"I see Mrs. Haldean has been here with Giles," remarked Thorndyke, as he pushed open the garden-gate. "I wonder if they saw anybody."

He advanced to the door, and having first rapped with his knuckles and then kicked at it vigorously, tried the handle.

"Locked," he observed, "but I see the key is in the lock, so we can get in if we want to. Let us try the back."

The back door was locked, too, but the key had been removed.

"He came out this way, evidently," said Thorndyke, "though he went in at the front, as I suppose you noticed. Let us see where he went."

The back garden was a small, fenced patch of ground, with an earth path leading down to the back gate. A little way beyond the gate was a small barn or outhouse.

"We are in luck," Thorndyke remarked, with a glance at the path. "Yesterday's rain has cleared away all old footprints, and prepared the surface for new ones. You see there are three sets of excellent impressions—two leading away from the house, and one set towards it. Now, you notice that both of the sets leading *from* the house are characterized by deep impressions and short steps, while the set leading *to* the house has lighter impressions and longer steps. The obvious inference is that he went down the path with a heavy burden, came back empty-handed, and went down again—and finally—with another heavy burden. You observe, too, that he walked with his stick on each occasion."

By this time we had reached the bottom of the garden. Opening the gate, we followed the tracks towards the outhouse, which stood beside a cart-track; but as we came round the corner we both stopped short and looked at one another. On the soft earth were the very distinct impressions of the tyres of a motor-car leading from the wide door of the outhouse. Finding that the door was unfastened, Thorndyke opened it, and looked in, to satisfy himself that the place was empty. Then he fell to studying the tracks.

"The course of events is pretty plain," he observed. "First the fellow brought down his luggage, started the engine, and got the car out—you can see where it stood, both by the little pool of oil, and by the widening and blurring of the wheel-tracks from the vibration of the free engine; then he went back and fetched the boy—carried him pick-a-back, I should say, judging by the depth of the toe-marks in the last set of footprints. That was a tactical mistake. He should have taken the boy straight into the shed."

He pointed as he spoke to one of the footprints beside the wheel-tracks, from the toe of which projected a small segment of the print of a little rubber heel.

We now made our way back to the house, where we found Willett pensively rapping at the front door with a cycle-spanner. Thorndyke took a last glance, with his hand in his pocket, at an open window above, and then, to the coachman's intense delight, brought forth what looked uncommonly like a small bunch of skeleton keys. One of these he inserted into the keyhole, and as he gave it a turn, the lock clicked, and the door stood open.

The little sitting-room, which we now entered, was furnished with the barest necessaries. Its centre was occupied by an oilcloth-covered table, on which I observed with surprise a dismembered "Bee" clock (the works of which had been taken apart with a tin-opener that lay beside them) and a box-wood bird-call. At these objects Thorndyke glanced and nodded, as though they fitted into some theory that he had formed; examined carefully the oilcloth around the litter of wheels and pinions, and then proceeded on a tour of inspection round the room, peering inquisitively into the kitchen and store-cupboard.

"Nothing very distinctive or personal here," he remarked. "Let us go upstairs."

There were three bedrooms on the upper floor, of which two were evidently disused, though the windows were wide open. The third bedroom showed manifest traces of occupation, though it was as bare as the others, for the water still stood in the wash-hand basin, and the bed was unmade. To the latter Thorndyke advanced, and, having turned back the bedclothes, examined the interior attentively, especially at the foot and the pillow. The latter was soiled—not to say grimy—though the rest of the bed-linen was quite clean.

"Hair-dye," remarked Thorndyke, noting my glance at it; then he turned and looked out of the open window. "Can you see the place where Miss Haldean was sitting to sketch?" he asked.

"Yes," I replied; "there is the place well in view, and you can see right up the road. I had no idea this house stood so high. From the three upper windows you can see all over the country excepting through the wood."

"Yes," Thorndyke rejoined, "and he has probably been in the habit of keeping watch up here with a telescope or a pair of field-glasses.

Well, there is not much of interest in this room. He kept his effects in a cabin trunk which stood there under the window. He shaved this morning. He has a white beard, to judge by the stubble on the shaving-paper, and that is all. Wait, though. There is a key hanging on that nail. He must have overlooked that, for it evidently does not belong to this house. It is an ordinary town latchkey."

He took the key down, and having laid a sheet of notepaper, from his pocket, on the dressing-table, produced a pin, with which he began carefully to probe the interior of the key-barrel. Presently there came forth, with much coaxing, a large ball of grey fluff, which Thorndyke folded up in the paper with infinite care.

"I suppose we mustn't take away the key," he said, "but I think we will take a wax mould of it."

He hurried downstairs, and, unstrapping the case from his bicycle, brought it in and placed it on the table. As it was now getting dark, he detached the powerful acetylene lamp from his machine, and, having lighted it, proceeded to open the mysterious case. First he took from it a small insufflator, or powder-blower, with which he blew a cloud of light yellow powder over the table around the remains of the clock. The powder settled on the table in an even coating, but when he blew at it smartly with his breath, it cleared off, leaving, however, a number of smeary impressions which stood out in strong yellow against the black oilcloth. To one of these impressions he pointed significantly. It was the print of a child's hand.

He next produced a small, portable microscope and some glass slides and cover-slips, and having opened the paper and tipped the ball of fluff from the key-barrel on to a slide, set to work with a pair of mounted needles to tease it out into its component parts. Then he turned the light of the lamp on to the microscope mirror and proceeded to examine the specimen.

"A curious and instructive assortment this, Jervis," he remarked, with his eye at the microscope: "woollen fibres—no cotton or linen;

he is careful of his health to have woollen pockets—and two hairs; very curious ones, too. Just look at them, and observe the root bulbs."

I applied my eye to the microscope, and saw, among other things, two hairs—originally white, but encrusted with a black, opaque, glistening stain. The root bulbs, I noticed, were shrivelled and atrophied.

"But how on earth," I exclaimed, "did the hairs get into his pocket?"

"I think the hairs themselves answer that question," he replied, "when considered with the other curios. The stain is obviously lead sulphide; but what else do you see?"

"I see some particles of metal—a white metal apparently—and a number of fragments of woody fibre and starch granules, but I don't recognize the starch. It is not wheat-starch, nor rice, nor potato. Do you make out what it is?"

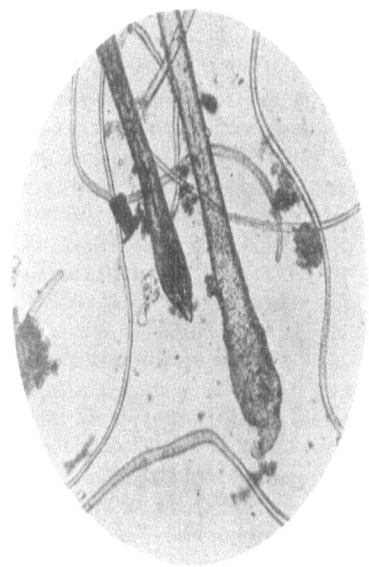

FLUFF FROM KEY-BARREL, MAGNIFIED 77 DIAMETERS.

Thorndyke chuckled. "Experientia does it," said he. "You will have, Jervis, to study the minute properties of dust and dirt. Their evidential value is immense. Let us have another look at that starch; it is all alike, I suppose."

It was; and Thorndyke had just ascertained the fact when the door burst open and Mrs. Haldean entered the room, followed by Mrs. Hanshaw and the police inspector. The former lady regarded my colleague with a glance of extreme disfavour.

"We heard that you had come here, sir," said she, "and we supposed you were engaged in searching for my poor child. But it seems we were mistaken, since we find you here amusing yourselves fiddling with these nonsensical instruments."

"Perhaps, Mabel," said Mrs. Hanshaw stiffly, "it would be wiser, and infinitely more polite, to ask if Dr. Thorndyke has any news for us."

"That is undoubtedly so, madam," agreed the inspector, who had apparently suffered also from Mrs. Haldean's impulsiveness.

"Then perhaps," the latter lady suggested, "you will inform us if you have discovered anything."

"I will tell you." replied Thorndyke, "all that we know. The child was abducted by the man who occupied this house, and who appears to have watched him from an upper window, probably through a glass. This man lured the child into the wood by blowing this bird-call; he met him in the wood, and induced him—by some promises, no doubt—to come with him. He picked the child up and carried him—on his back, I think—up to the house, and brought him in through the front door, which he locked after him. He gave the boy this clock and the bird-call to amuse him while he went upstairs and packed his trunk. He took the trunk out through the back door and down the garden to the shed there, in which he had a motor-car. He got the car out and came back for the boy, whom he carried down to the car, locking the back door after him. Then he drove away."

"You know he has gone," cried Mrs. Haldean, "and yet you stay here playing with these ridiculous toys. Why are you not following him?"

"We have just finished ascertaining the facts," Thorndyke replied calmly, "and should by now be on the road if you had not come."

Here the inspector interposed anxiously. "Of course, sir, you can't give any description of the man. You have no clue to his identity, I suppose?"

"We have only his footprints," Thorndyke answered, "and this fluff which I raked out of the barrel of his latchkey, and have just been examining. From these data I conclude that he is a rather short and thin man, and somewhat lame. He walks with the aid of a thick stick, which has a knob, not a crook, at the top, and which he carries in his left hand. I think that his left leg has been amputated above the knee, and that he wears an artificial limb. He is elderly, he shaves his beard, has white hair dyed a greyish black, is partly bald, and probably combs a wisp of hair over the bald place; he takes snuff, and carries a leaden comb in his pocket."

As Thorndyke's description proceeded, the inspector's mouth gradually opened wider and wider, until he appeared the very type and symbol of astonishment. But its effect on Mrs. Haldean was much more remarkable. Rising from her chair, she leaned on the table and stared at Thorndyke with an expression of awe—even of terror; and as he finished she sank back into her chair, with her hands clasped, and turned to Mrs. Hanshaw.

"Jane!" she gasped, "it is Percy—my brother-in-law! He has described him exactly, even to his stick and his pocket-comb. But I thought he was in Chicago."

"If that is so," said Thorndyke, hastily repacking his case, "we had better start at once."

"We have the dogcart in the road," said Mrs. Hanshaw.

"Thank you," replied Thorndyke. "We will ride on our bicycles, and the inspector can borrow Willett's. We go out at the back by the cart-track, which joins the road farther on."

"Then we will follow in the dogcart," said Mrs. Haldean. "Come, Jane."

The two ladies departed down the path, while we made ready our bicycles and lit our lamps.

"With your permission, inspector," said Thorndyke, "we will take the key with us."

"It's hardly legal, sir," objected the officer. "We have no authority."

"It is quite illegal," answered Thorndyke; "but it is necessary; and necessity—like your military J.P.—knows no law."

The inspector grinned and went out, regarding me with a quivering eyelid as Thorndyke locked the door with his skeleton key. As we turned into the road, I saw the light of the dogcart behind us, and we pushed forward at a swift pace, picking up the trail easily on the soft, moist road.

"What beats me," said the inspector confidentially, as we rode along, "is how he knew the man was bald. Was it the footprints or the latchkey? And that comb, too, that was a regular knock-out."

These points were, by now, pretty clear to me. I had seen the hairs with their atrophied bulbs—such as one finds at the margin of a bald patch; and the comb was used, evidently, for the double purpose of keeping the bald patch covered and blackening the sulphur-charged hair. But the knobbed stick and the artificial limb puzzled me so completely that I presently overtook Thorndyke to demand an explanation.

"The stick," said he, "is perfectly simple. The ferrule of a knobbed stick wears evenly all round; that of a crooked stick wears on one side—the side opposite the crook. The impressions showed that the ferrule of this one was evenly convex; therefore it had no crook. The other matter is more complicated. To begin with, an artificial foot makes a very characteristic impression, owing to its purely passive elasticity, as I will show you to-morrow. But an artificial leg fitted below the knee is quite secure, whereas one fitted above the knee— that is, with an artificial knee-joint worked by a spring—is much less reliable. Now, this man had an artificial foot, and he evidently distrusted his knee-joint, as is shown by his steadying it with his stick on the same side. If he had merely had a weak leg, he would have used the stick with his right hand—with the natural swing of the arm, in fact—unless he had been very lame, which he evidently was not. Still, it was only a question of probability, though the probability was very great. Of course, you understand that those particles of woody fibre and starch granules were disintegrated snuff-grains."

This explanation, like the others, was quite simple when one had heard it, though it gave me material for much thought as we pedalled on along the dark road, with Thorndyke's light flickering in front, and the dogcart pattering in our wake. But there was ample time for reflection; for our pace rather precluded conversation, and we rode on, mile after mile, until my legs ached with fatigue. On and on we went through village after village, now losing the trail in some frequented street, but picking it up again unfailingly as we emerged on to the country road, until at last, in the paved High Street of the little town of Horsefield, we lost it for good. We rode on through the town out on to the country road; but although there were several tracks of motors, Thorndyke shook his head at them all. "I have been studying those tyres until I know them by heart," he said. "No; either he is in the town, or he has left it by a side road."

There was nothing for it but to put up the horse and the machines at the hotel, while we walked round to reconnoitre; and this we did, tramping up one street and down another, with eyes bent on the ground, fruitlessly searching for a trace of the missing car.

Suddenly, at the door of a blacksmith's shop, Thorndyke halted. The shop had been kept open late for the shoeing of a carriage horse, which was just being led away, and the smith had come to the door for a breath of air. Thorndyke accosted him genially.

"Good-evening. You are just the man I wanted to see. I have mislaid the address of a friend of mine, who, I think, called on you this afternoon—a lame gentleman who walks with a stick. I expect he wanted you to pick a lock or make him a key."

"Oh, I remember him!" said the man. "Yes, he had lost his latchkey, and wanted the lock picked before he could get into his house. Had to leave his motor-car outside while he came here. But I took some keys round with me, and fitted one to his latch."

He then directed us to a house at the end of a street close by, and, having thanked him, we went off in high spirits.

"How did you know he had been there?" I asked.

"I didn't; but there was the mark of a stick and part of a left foot on the soft earth inside the doorway, and the thing was inherently probable, so I risked a false shot."

The house stood alone at the far end of a straggling street, and was enclosed by a high wall, in which, on the side facing the street, was a door and a wide carriage-gate. Advancing to the former, Thorndyke took from his pocket the purloined key, and tried it in the lock. It fitted perfectly, and when he had turned it and pushed open the door, we entered a small courtyard. Crossing this, we came to the front door of the house, the latch of which fortunately fitted the same key; and this having been opened by Thorndyke, we trooped into the hall. Immediately we heard the sound of an opening door above, and a reedy, nasal voice sang out:

"Hello, there! Who's that below?"

The voice was followed by the appearance of a head projecting over the baluster rail.

"You are Mr. Percy Haldean, I think," said the inspector.

At the mention of this name, the head was withdrawn, and a quick tread was heard, accompanied by the tapping of a stick on the floor. We started to ascend the stairs, the inspector leading, as the authorized official; but we had only gone up a few steps, when a fierce, wiry little man danced out on to the landing, with a thick stick in one hand and a very large revolver in the other.

"Move another step, either of you," he shouted, pointing the weapon at the inspector, "and I let fly; and mind you, when I shoot I hit."

THE STRANGER IS RUN TO EARTH.

He looked as if he meant it, and we accordingly halted with remarkable suddenness, while the inspector proceeded to parley.

"Now, what's the good of this, Mr. Haldean?" said he. "The game's up, and you know it."

"You clear out of my house, and clear out sharp," was the inhospitable rejoinder, "or you'll give me the trouble of burying you in the garden."

I looked round to consult with Thorndyke, when, to my amazement, I found that he had vanished—apparently through the open hall-door. I was admiring his discretion when the inspector endeavoured to reopen negotiations, but was cut short abruptly.

"I am going to count fifty," said Mr. Haldean, "and if you aren't gone then, I shall shoot."

He began to count deliberately, and the inspector looked round at me in complete bewilderment. The flight of stairs was a long one, and well lighted by gas, so that to rush it was an impossibility. Suddenly my heart gave a bound and I held my breath, for out of an open door behind our quarry, a figure emerged slowly and noiselessly on to the landing. It was Thorndyke, shoeless, and in his shirt-sleeves.

Slowly and with cat-like stealthiness, he crept across the landing until he was within a yard of the unconscious fugitive, and still the nasal voice droned on, monotonously counting out the allotted seconds.

"Forty-one, forty-two, forty-three—"

There was a lightning-like movement—a shout—a flash—a bang—a shower of falling plaster, and then the revolver came clattering down the stairs. The inspector and I rushed up, and in a moment the sharp click of the handcuffs told Mr. Percy Haldean that the game was really up.

Five minutes later Freddy-boy, half asleep, but wholly cheerful, was borne on Thorndyke's shoulders into the private sitting-room of the Black Horse Hotel. A shriek of joy saluted his entrance, and a shower of maternal kisses brought him to the verge of suffocation.

Finally, the impulsive Mrs. Haldean, turning suddenly to Thorndyke, seized both his hands, and for a moment I hoped that she was going to kiss him, too. But he was spared, and I have not yet recovered from the disappointment.

The Sign of the Broken Sword

G. K. Chesterton

The Sign of the Broken Sword

The thousand arms of the forest were grey, and its million fingers silver. In a sky of dark green-blue-like slate the stars were bleak and brilliant like splintered ice. All that thickly wooded and sparsely tenanted countryside was stiff with a bitter and brittle frost. The black hollows between the trunks of the trees looked like bottomless, black caverns of that Scandinavian hell, a hell of incalculable cold. Even the square stone tower of the church looked northern to the point of heathenry, as if it were some barbaric tower among the sea rocks of Iceland. It was a queer night for anyone to explore a churchyard. But, on the other hand, perhaps it was worth exploring.

It rose abruptly out of the ashen wastes of forest in a sort of hump or shoulder of green turf that looked grey in the starlight. Most of the graves were on a slant, and the path leading up to the church was as steep as a staircase. On the top of the hill, in the one flat and prominent place, was the monument for which the place was famous. It contrasted strangely with the featureless graves all round, for it was the work of one of the greatest sculptors of modern Europe; and yet his fame was at once forgotten in the fame of the man whose image he had made. It showed, by touches of the small silver pencil of starlight, the massive metal figure of a soldier recumbent, the strong hands sealed in an everlasting worship, the great head pillowed upon a gun. The venerable face was bearded, or rather whiskered, in the old, heavy Colonel Newcome fashion. The uniform, though suggested with the few strokes of simplicity, was that of modern war. By his right side lay a sword, of which the tip was broken off; on the left side lay a Bible. On glowing summer afternoons wagonettes came full of Americans and cultured suburbans to see the sepulchre; but even then they felt the vast forest land with its one dumpy dome of churchyard and church as a place oddly dumb and neglected. In this freezing darkness of mid-winter one would think he might be left alone with the stars. Nevertheless, in the stillness of those stiff woods a wooden gate creaked, and two dim figures dressed in black climbed up the little path to the tomb.

So faint was that frigid starlight that nothing could have been traced about them except that while they both wore black, one man was enormously big, and the other (perhaps by contrast) almost startlingly small. They went up to the great graven tomb of the historic warrior, and stood for a few minutes staring at it. There was no human, perhaps no living, thing for a wide circle; and a morbid fancy might well have wondered if they were human themselves. In any case, the beginning of their conversation might have seemed strange. After the first silence the small man said to the other:

"Where does a wise man hide a pebble?"

And the tall man answered in a low voice: "On the beach."

The small man nodded, and after a short silence said: "Where does a wise man hide a leaf?"

And the other answered: "In the forest."

There was another stillness, and then the tall man resumed: "Do you mean that when a wise man has to hide a real diamond he has been known to hide it among sham ones?"

"No, no," said the little man with a laugh, "we will let bygones be bygones."

He stamped his cold feet for a second or two, and then said: "I'm not thinking of that at all, but of something else; something rather peculiar. Just strike a match, will you?"

The big man fumbled in his pocket, and soon a scratch and a flare painted gold the whole flat side of the monument. On it was cut in black letters the well-known words which so many Americans had reverently read: "Sacred to the Memory of General Sir Arthur St. Clare, Hero and Martyr, who Always Vanquished his Enemies and Always Spared Them, and Was Treacherously Slain by Them At Last. May God in Whom he Trusted both Reward and Revenge him."

The match burnt the big man's fingers, blackened, and dropped. He was about to strike another, but his small companion stopped him. "That's all right, Flambeau, old man; I saw what I wanted. Or, rather, I didn't see what I didn't want. And now we must walk a mile and a half along the road to the next inn, and I will try to tell you all about it. For Heaven knows a man should have a fire and ale when he dares tell such a story."

They descended the precipitous path, they relatched the rusty gate, and set off at a stamping, ringing walk down the frozen forest road. They had gone a full quarter of a mile before the smaller man spoke again. He said: "Yes; the wise man hides a pebble on the beach. But what does he do if there is no beach? Do you know anything of that great St. Clare trouble?"

"I know nothing about English generals, Father Brown," answered the large man, laughing, "though a little about English policemen. I only know that you have dragged me a precious long dance to all the shrines of this fellow, whoever he is. One would think he got buried in six different places. I've seen a memorial to General St. Clare in Westminster Abbey. I've seen a ramping equestrian statue of General St. Clare on the Embankment. I've seen a medallion of St. Clare in the street he was born in, and another in the street he lived in; and now you drag me after dark to his coffin in the village churchyard. I am beginning to be a bit tired of his magnificent personality, especially as I don't in the least know who he was. What are you hunting for in all these crypts and effigies?"

"I am only looking for one word," said Father Brown. "A word that isn't there."

"Well," asked Flambeau; "are you going to tell me anything about it?"

"I must divide it into two parts," remarked the priest. "First there is what everybody knows; and then there is what I know. Now, what everybody knows is short and plain enough. It is also entirely wrong."

"Right you are," said the big man called Flambeau cheerfully. "Let's begin at the wrong end. Let's begin with what everybody knows, which isn't true."

"If not wholly untrue, it is at least very inadequate," continued Brown; "for in point of fact, all that the public knows amounts precisely to this: The public knows that Arthur St. Clare was a great and successful English general. It knows that after splendid yet careful campaigns both in India and Africa he was in command against Brazil when the great Brazilian patriot Olivier issued his ultimatum. It knows that on that occasion St. Clare with a very small force attacked Olivier with a very large one, and was captured after heroic resistance. And it knows that after his capture, and to the abhorrence of the civilised world, St. Clare was hanged on the nearest tree. He was found swinging there after the Brazilians had retired, with his broken sword hung round his neck."

"And that popular story is untrue?" suggested Flambeau.

"No," said his friend quietly, "that story is quite true, so far as it goes."

"Well, I think it goes far enough!" said Flambeau; "but if the popular story is true, what is the mystery?"

They had passed many hundreds of grey and ghostly trees before the little priest answered. Then he bit his finger reflectively and said: "Why, the mystery is a mystery of psychology. Or, rather, it is a mystery of two psychologies. In that Brazilian business two of the most famous men of modern history acted flat against their characters. Mind you, Olivier and St. Clare were both heroes—the old thing, and no mistake; it was like the fight between Hector and Achilles. Now, what would you say to an affair in which Achilles was timid and Hector was treacherous?"

"Go on," said the large man impatiently as the other bit his finger again.

"Sir Arthur St. Clare was a soldier of the old religious type— the type that saved us during the Mutiny," continued Brown. "He was always more for duty than for dash; and with all his personal courage was decidedly a prudent commander, particularly indignant at any needless waste of soldiers. Yet in this last battle he attempted something that a baby could see was absurd. One need not be a strategist to see it was as wild as wind; just as one need not be a strategist to keep out of the way of a motor-bus. Well, that is the first mystery; what had become of the English general's head? The second riddle is, what had become of the Brazilian general's heart? President Olivier might be called a visionary or a nuisance; but even his enemies admitted that he was magnanimous to the point of knight errantry. Almost every other prisoner he had ever captured had been set free or even loaded with benefits. Men who had really wronged him came away touched by his simplicity and sweetness. Why the deuce should he diabolically revenge himself only once in his life; and that for the one particular blow that could not have hurt him? Well, there you have it. One of the wisest men in the world acted like an idiot for no reason. One of the best men in the world acted like a fiend for no reason. That's the long and the short of it; and I leave it to you, my boy."

"No, you don't," said the other with a snort. "I leave it to you; and you jolly well tell me all about it."

"Well," resumed Father Brown, "it's not fair to say that the public impression is just what I've said, without adding that two things have happened since. I can't say they threw a new light; for nobody can make sense of them. But they threw a new kind of darkness; they threw the darkness in new directions. The first was this. The family physician of the St. Clares quarrelled with that family, and began publishing a violent series of articles, in which he said that the late general was a religious maniac; but as far as the tale went, this seemed to mean little more than a religious man.

"Anyhow, the story fizzled out. Everyone knew, of course, that St. Clare had some of the eccentricities of puritan piety. The second incident was much more arresting. In the luckless and unsupported regiment which made that rash attempt at the Black River there was a certain Captain Keith, who was at that time engaged to St. Clare's daughter, and who afterwards married her. He was one of those who were captured by Olivier, and, like all the rest except the general, appears to have been bounteously treated and promptly set free. Some twenty years afterwards this man, then Lieutenant-Colonel Keith, published a sort of autobiography called 'A British Officer in Burmah and Brazil.' In the place where the reader looks eagerly for some account of the mystery of St. Clare's disaster may be found the following words: 'Everywhere else in this book I have narrated things exactly as they occurred, holding as I do the old-fashioned opinion that the glory of England is old enough to take care of itself. The exception I shall make is in this matter of the defeat by the Black River; and my reasons, though private, are honourable and compelling. I will, however, add this in justice to the memories of two distinguished men. General St. Clare has been accused of incapacity on this occasion; I can at least testify that this action, properly understood, was one of the most brilliant and sagacious of his life. President Olivier by similar report is charged with savage injustice. I think it due to the honour of an enemy to say that he acted on this occasion with even more than his characteristic good feeling. To put the matter popularly, I can assure my countrymen that St. Clare was by no means such a fool nor Olivier such a brute as he looked. This is all I have to say; nor shall any earthly consideration induce me to add a word to it.'"

A large frozen moon like a lustrous snowball began to show

through the tangle of twigs in front of them, and by its light the narrator had been able to refresh his memory of Captain Keith's text from a scrap of printed paper. As he folded it up and put it back in his pocket Flambeau threw up his hand with a French gesture.

"Wait a bit, wait a bit," he cried excitedly. "I believe I can guess it at the first go."

He strode on, breathing hard, his black head and bull neck forward, like a man winning a walking race. The little priest, amused and interested, had some trouble in trotting beside him. Just before them the trees fell back a little to left and right, and the road swept downwards across a clear, moonlit valley, till it dived again like a rabbit into the wall of another wood. The entrance to the farther forest looked small and round, like the black hole of a remote railway tunnel. But it was within some hundred yards, and gaped like a cavern before Flambeau spoke again.

"I've got it," he cried at last, slapping his thigh with his great hand. "Four minutes' thinking, and I can tell your whole story myself."

"All right," assented his friend. "You tell it."

Flambeau lifted his head, but lowered his voice. "General Sir Arthur St. Clare," he said, "came of a family in which madness was hereditary; and his whole aim was to keep this from his daughter, and even, if possible, from his future son-in-law. Rightly or wrongly, he thought the final collapse was close, and resolved on suicide. Yet ordinary suicide would blazon the very idea he dreaded. As the campaign approached the clouds came thicker on his brain; and at last in a mad moment he sacrificed his public duty to his private. He rushed rashly into battle, hoping to fall by the first shot. When he found that he had only attained capture and discredit, the sealed bomb in his brain burst, and he broke his own sword and hanged himself."

He stared firmly at the grey facade of forest in front of him, with the one black gap in it, like the mouth of the grave, into which their path plunged. Perhaps something menacing in the road thus suddenly swallowed reinforced his vivid vision of the tragedy, for he shuddered.

"A horrid story," he said.

"A horrid story," repeated the priest with bent head. "But not the real story."

Then he threw back his head with a sort of despair and cried: "Oh, I wish it had been."

The tall Flambeau faced round and stared at him.

"Yours is a clean story," cried Father Brown, deeply moved. "A sweet, pure, honest story, as open and white as that moon. Madness and despair are innocent enough. There are worse things, Flambeau."

Flambeau looked up wildly at the moon thus invoked; and from where he stood one black tree-bough curved across it exactly like a devil's horn.

"Father—father," cried Flambeau with the French gesture and stepping yet more rapidly forward, "do you mean it was worse than that?"

"Worse than that," said Paul like a grave echo. And they plunged into the black cloister of the woodland, which ran by them in a dim tapestry of trunks, like one of the dark corridors in a dream.

They were soon in the most secret entrails of the wood, and felt close about them foliage that they could not see, when the priest said again:

"Where does a wise man hide a leaf? In the forest. But what does he do if there is no forest?"

"Well, well," cried Flambeau irritably, "what does he do?"

"He grows a forest to hide it in," said the priest in an obscure voice. "A fearful sin."

"Look here," cried his friend impatiently, for the dark wood and the dark saying got a little on his nerves; "will you tell me this story or not? What other evidence is there to go on?"

"There are three more bits of evidence," said the other, "that I have dug up in holes and corners; and I will give them in logical rather than chronological order. First of all, of course, our authority for the issue and event of the battle is in Olivier's own dispatches, which are lucid enough. He was entrenched with two or three regiments on the heights that swept down to the Black River, on the other side of which was lower and more marshy ground. Beyond this again was gently rising country, on which was the first English outpost, supported by others which lay, however, considerably in its rear. The British forces as a whole were greatly superior in numbers; but this particular regiment was just far enough from its base to make Olivier consider the project of crossing the river to cut it off. By sunset, however, he had decided to retain his own position, which was a specially strong one. At daybreak next morning he was thunderstruck to see that this stray handful of English, entirely unsupported from their rear, had flung themselves across the river, half by a bridge to the right, and the other half by a ford higher up, and were massed upon the marshy bank below him.

"That they should attempt an attack with such numbers against such a position was incredible enough; but Olivier noticed something yet more extraordinary. For instead of attempting to seize more solid ground, this mad regiment, having put the river in its rear by one wild charge, did nothing more, but stuck there in the mire like flies in treacle. Needless to say, the Brazilians blew great gaps in them with artillery, which they could only return with spirited but lessening rifle fire. Yet they never broke; and Olivier's curt account ends with a strong tribute of admiration for the mystic valour of these imbeciles. 'Our line then advanced finally,' writes Olivier, 'and drove them into the river; we captured General St. Clare himself and several other officers. The colonel and the major had both fallen in the battle. I cannot resist saying that few finer sights can have been seen in history than the last stand of this extraordinary regiment; wounded officers picking up the rifles of dead soldiers, and the general himself facing us on horseback bareheaded and with a broken sword.' On what happened to the general afterwards Olivier is as silent as Captain Keith."

"Well," grunted Flambeau, "get on to the next bit of evidence."

"The next evidence," said Father Brown, "took some time to find, but it will not take long to tell. I found at last in an almshouse down in the Lincolnshire Fens an old soldier who not only was wounded at the Black River, but had actually knelt beside the colonel of the regiment when he died. This latter was a certain Colonel Clancy, a big bull of an Irishman; and it would seem that he died almost as much of rage as of bullets. He, at any rate, was not responsible for that ridiculous raid; it must have been imposed on him by the general. His last edifying words, according to my informant, were these: 'And there goes the damned old donkey with the end of his sword knocked off. I wish it was his head.' You will remark that everyone seems to have noticed this detail about the broken sword blade, though most people regard it somewhat more reverently than did the late Colonel Clancy. And now for the third fragment."

Their path through the woodland began to go upward, and the speaker paused a little for breath before he went on. Then he continued in the same business-like tone:

"Only a month or two ago a certain Brazilian official died in England, having quarrelled with Olivier and left his country. He was a well-known figure both here and on the Continent, a Spaniard named Espado; I knew him myself, a yellow-faced old dandy, with a hooked nose. For various private reasons I had permission to see the documents he had left; he was a Catholic, of course, and I had been with him towards the end. There was nothing of his that lit up any corner of the black St. Clare business, except five or six common exercise books filled with the diary of some English soldier. I can only suppose that it was found by the Brazilians on one of those that fell. Anyhow, it stopped abruptly the night before the battle.

"But the account of that last day in the poor fellow's life was certainly worth reading. I have it on me; but it's too dark to read it here, and I will give you a resume. The first part of that entry is full of jokes, evidently flung about among the men, about somebody called the Vulture. It does not seem as if this person, whoever he was, was one of themselves, nor even an Englishman; neither is he exactly spoken of as one of the enemy. It sounds rather as if he were some local go-between and non-combatant; perhaps a guide or a journalist. He has been closeted with old Colonel Clancy; but is more often seen talking to the major. Indeed, the major is somewhat prominent in this soldier's narrative; a lean, dark-haired man, apparently, of the name of Murray—a north of Ireland man and a Puritan. There are continual jests about the contrast between this Ulsterman's austerity and the conviviality of Colonel Clancy. There is also some joke about the Vulture wearing bright-coloured clothes.

"But all these levities are scattered by what may well be called the note of a bugle. Behind the English camp and almost parallel to the river ran one of the few great roads of that district. Westward the road curved round towards the river, which it crossed by the bridge before mentioned. To the east the road swept backwards into the wilds, and some two miles along it was the next English outpost. From this direction there came along the road that evening a glitter and clatter of light cavalry, in which even the simple diarist could recognise with astonishment the general with his staff. He rode the great white horse which you have seen so often in illustrated papers and Academy pictures; and you may be sure that the salute they gave him was not merely ceremonial. He, at least, wasted no time on ceremony, but, springing from the saddle immediately, mixed with the group of officers, and fell into emphatic though confidential speech. What struck our friend the diarist most was his special disposition to discuss matters with Major Murray; but, indeed, such a selection, so long as it was not marked, was in no way unnatural. The two men were made for sympathy; they were men who 'read their Bibles'; they were both the old Evangelical type of officer. However this may be, it is certain that when the general mounted again he was still talking earnestly to Murray; and that as he walked his horse slowly down the road towards the river, the tall Ulsterman still walked by his bridle rein in earnest debate. The soldiers watched the two until they vanished behind a clump of trees where the road turned towards the river. The colonel had gone back to his tent, and the men to their pickets; the man with the diary lingered for another four minutes, and saw a marvellous sight.

"The great white horse which had marched slowly down the road, as it had marched in so many processions, flew back, galloping up the road towards them as if it were mad to win a race. At first they thought it had run away with the man on its back; but they soon saw that the general, a fine rider, was himself urging it to full speed. Horse and man swept up to them like a whirlwind; and then, reining up the reeling charger, the general turned on them a face like flame, and called for the colonel like the trumpet that wakes the dead.

"I conceive that all the earthquake events of that catastrophe tumbled on top of each other rather like lumber in the minds of men such as our friend with the diary. With the dazed excitement of a dream, they found themselves falling—literally falling—into their ranks, and learned that an attack was to be led at once across the river. The general and the major, it was said, had found out something at the bridge, and there was only just time to strike for life. The major had gone back at once to call up the reserve along the road behind; it was doubtful if even with that prompt appeal help could reach them in time. But they must pass the stream that night, and seize the heights by morning. It is with the very stir and throb of that romantic nocturnal march that the diary suddenly ends."

Father Brown had mounted ahead; for the woodland path grew

smaller, steeper, and more twisted, till they felt as if they were ascending a winding staircase. The priest's voice came from above out of the darkness.

"There was one other little and enormous thing. When the general urged them to their chivalric charge he half drew his sword from the scabbard; and then, as if ashamed of such melodrama, thrust it back again. The sword again, you see."

A half-light broke through the network of boughs above them, flinging the ghost of a net about their feet; for they were mounting again to the faint luminosity of the naked night. Flambeau felt truth all round him as an atmosphere, but not as an idea. He answered with bewildered brain: "Well, what's the matter with the sword? Officers generally have swords, don't they?"

"They are not often mentioned in modern war," said the other dispassionately; "but in this affair one falls over the blessed sword everywhere."

"Well, what is there in that?" growled Flambeau; "it was a twopence coloured sort of incident; the old man's blade breaking in his last battle. Anyone might bet the papers would get hold of it, as they have. On all these tombs and things it's shown broken at the point. I hope you haven't dragged me through this Polar expedition merely because two men with an eye for a picture saw St. Clare's broken sword."

"No," cried Father Brown, with a sharp voice like a pistol shot; "but who saw his unbroken sword?"

"What do you mean?" cried the other, and stood still under the stars. They had come abruptly out of the grey gates of the wood.

"I say, who saw his unbroken sword?" repeated Father Brown obstinately. "Not the writer of the diary, anyhow; the general sheathed it in time."

Flambeau looked about him in the moonlight, as a man struck blind might look in the sun; and his friend went on, for the first time with eagerness:

"Flambeau," he cried, "I cannot prove it, even after hunting through the tombs. But I am sure of it. Let me add just one more tiny fact that tips the whole thing over. The colonel, by a strange chance, was one of the first struck by a bullet. He was struck long before the troops came to close quarters. But he saw St. Clare's sword broken. Why was it broken? How was it broken? My friend, it was broken before the battle."

"Oh!" said his friend, with a sort of forlorn jocularity; "and pray where is the other piece?"

"I can tell you," said the priest promptly. "In the northeast corner of the cemetery of the Protestant Cathedral at Belfast."

"Indeed?" inquired the other. "Have you looked for it?"

"I couldn't," replied Brown, with frank regret. "There's a great marble monument on top of it; a monument to the heroic Major Murray, who fell fighting gloriously at the famous Battle of the Black River."

Flambeau seemed suddenly galvanised into existence. "You mean," he cried hoarsely, "that General St. Clare hated Murray, and murdered him on the field of battle because—"

"You are still full of good and pure thoughts," said the other. "It was worse than that."

"Well," said the large man, "my stock of evil imagination is used up."

The priest seemed really doubtful where to begin, and at last he said again:

"Where would a wise man hide a leaf? In the forest."

The other did not answer.

"If there were no forest, he would make a forest. And if he wished to hide a dead leaf, he would make a dead forest."

There was still no reply, and the priest added still more mildly and quietly:

"And if a man had to hide a dead body, he would make a field of dead bodies to hide it in."

Flambeau began to stamp forward with an intolerance of delay in time or space; but Father Brown went on as if he were continuing the last sentence:

"Sir Arthur St. Clare, as I have already said, was a man who read his Bible. That was what was the matter with him. When will people understand that it is useless for a man to read his Bible unless he also reads everybody else's Bible? A printer reads a Bible for misprints. A Mormon reads his Bible, and finds polygamy; a Christian Scientist reads his, and finds we have no arms and legs. St. Clare was an old Anglo-Indian Protestant soldier. Now, just think what that might mean; and, for Heaven's sake, don't cant about it. It might mean a man physically formidable living under a tropic sun in an Oriental society, and soaking himself without sense or guidance in an Oriental Book. Of course, he read the Old Testament rather than the New. Of course, he found in the Old Testament anything that he wanted—lust, tyranny, treason. Oh, I dare say he was honest, as you call it. But what is the good of a man being honest in his worship of dishonesty?

"In each of the hot and secret countries to which the man went he kept a harem, he tortured witnesses, he amassed shameful gold; but certainly he would have said with steady eyes that he did it to the glory of the Lord. My own theology is sufficiently expressed by asking which Lord? Anyhow, there is this about such evil, that it opens door after door in hell, and always into smaller and smaller chambers. This is the real case against crime, that a man does not become wilder and wilder, but only meaner and meaner. St. Clare was soon suffocated by difficulties of bribery and blackmail; and needed more and more cash. And by the time of the Battle of the Black River he had fallen from world to world to that place which Dante makes the lowest floor of the universe."

"What do you mean?" asked his friend again.

"I mean that," retorted the cleric, and suddenly pointed at a puddle sealed with ice that shone in the moon. "Do you remember whom Dante put in the last circle of ice?"

"The traitors," said Flambeau, and shuddered. As he looked around at the inhuman landscape of trees, with taunting and almost obscene outlines, he could almost fancy he was Dante, and the priest with the rivulet of a voice was, indeed, a Virgil leading him through a land of eternal sins.

The voice went on: "Olivier, as you know, was quixotic, and would not permit a secret service and spies. The thing, however, was done, like many other things, behind his back. It was managed by my old friend Espado; he was the bright-clad fop, whose hook nose got him called the Vulture. Posing as a sort of philanthropist at the front, he felt his way through the English Army, and at last got his fingers on its one corrupt man—please God!—and that man at the top. St. Clare was in foul need of money, and mountains of it. The discredited family doctor was threatening those extraordinary exposures that afterwards began and were broken off; tales of monstrous and prehistoric things in Park Lane; things done by an English Evangelist that smelt like human sacrifice and hordes of slaves. Money was wanted, too, for his daughter's dowry; for to him the fame of wealth was as sweet as wealth itself. He snapped the last thread, whispered the word to Brazil, and wealth poured in from the enemies of England. But another man had talked to Espado the Vulture as well as he. Somehow the dark, grim young major from Ulster had guessed the hideous truth; and when they walked slowly together down that road towards the bridge Murray was telling the general that he must resign instantly, or be court-martialled and shot. The general temporised with him till they came to the fringe of tropic trees by the bridge; and there by the singing river and the sunlit palms (for I can see the picture) the general drew his sabre and plunged it through the body of the major."

The wintry road curved over a ridge in cutting frost, with cruel black shapes of bush and thicket; but Flambeau fancied that he saw beyond it faintly the edge of an aureole that was not starlight and moonlight, but some fire such as is made by men. He watched it as the tale drew to its close.

"St. Clare was a hell-hound, but he was a hound of breed. Never, I'll swear, was he so lucid and so strong as when poor Murray lay a cold lump at his feet. Never in all his triumphs, as Captain Keith said truly, was the great man so great as he was in this last world-despised defeat. He looked coolly at his weapon to wipe off the blood; he saw the point he had planted between his victim's shoulders had broken off in the body. He saw quite calmly, as through a club windowpane, all that must follow. He saw that men must find the unaccountable corpse; must extract the unaccountable sword-point; must notice the unaccountable broken sword—or absence of sword. He had killed, but not silenced. But his imperious intellect rose against the facer; there was one way yet. He could make the corpse less unaccountable. He could create a hill of corpses to cover this one. In twenty minutes eight hundred English soldiers were marching down to their death."

The warmer glow behind the black winter wood grew richer and brighter, and Flambeau strode on to reach it. Father Brown also quickened his stride; but he seemed merely absorbed in his tale.

"Such was the valour of that English thousand, and such the genius of their commander, that if they had at once attacked the hill, even their mad march might have met some luck. But the evil mind that played with them like pawns had other aims and reasons. They must remain in the marshes by the bridge at least till British corpses should be a common sight there. Then for the last grand scene; the silver-haired soldier-saint would give up his shattered sword to save further slaughter. Oh, it was well organised for an impromptu. But I think (I cannot prove), I think that it was while they stuck there in the bloody mire that someone doubted—and someone guessed."

He was mute a moment, and then said: "There is a voice from nowhere that tells me the man who guessed was the lover... the man to wed the old man's child."

"But what about Olivier and the hanging?" asked Flambeau.

"Olivier, partly from chivalry, partly from policy, seldom encumbered his march with captives," explained the narrator. "He released everybody in most cases. He released everybody in this case."

"Everybody but the general," said the tall man.

"Everybody," said the priest.

Flambeau knit his black brows. "I don't grasp it all yet," he said.

"There is another picture, Flambeau," said Brown in his more mystical undertone. "I can't prove it; but I can do more—I can see it. There is a camp breaking up on the bare, torrid hills at morning, and Brazilian uniforms massed in blocks and columns to march. There is the red shirt and long black beard of Olivier, which blows as he stands, his broad-brimmed hat in his hand. He is saying farewell to the great enemy he is setting free—the simple, snow-headed English veteran, who thanks him in the name of his men. The English remnant stand behind at attention; beside them are stores and vehicles for the retreat. The drums roll; the Brazilians are moving; the English are still like statues. So they abide till the last hum and flash of the enemy have faded from the tropic horizon. Then they alter their postures all at once, like dead men coming to life; they turn their fifty faces upon the general—faces not to be forgotten."

Flambeau gave a great jump. "Ah," he cried, "you don't mean—"

"Yes," said Father Brown in a deep, moving voice. "It was an English hand that put the rope round St. Clare's neck; I believe the hand that put the ring on his daughter's finger. They were English hands that dragged him up to the tree of shame; the hands of men that had adored him and followed him to victory. And they were English souls (God pardon and endure us all!) who stared at him swinging in that foreign sun on the green gallows of palm, and prayed in their hatred that he might drop off it into hell."

As the two topped the ridge there burst on them the strong scarlet light of a red-curtained English inn. It stood sideways in the road, as if standing aside in the amplitude of hospitality. Its three doors stood open with invitation; and even where they stood they could hear the hum and laughter of humanity happy for a night.

"I need not tell you more," said Father Brown. "They tried him in the wilderness and destroyed him; and then, for the honour of England and of his daughter, they took an oath to seal up for ever the story of the traitor's purse and the assassin's sword blade. Perhaps—Heaven help them—they tried to forget it. Let us try to forget it, anyhow; here is our inn."

"With all my heart," said Flambeau, and was just striding into the bright, noisy bar when he stepped back and almost fell on the road.

"Look there, in the devil's name!" he cried, and pointed rigidly at the square wooden sign that overhung the road. It showed dimly the crude shape of a sabre hilt and a shortened blade; and was inscribed in false archaic lettering, "The Sign of the Broken Sword."

"Were you not prepared?" asked Father Brown gently. "He is the god of this country; half the inns and parks and streets are named after him and his story."

"I thought we had done with the leper," cried Flambeau, and spat on the road.

"You will never have done with him in England," said the priest, looking down, "while brass is strong and stone abides. His marble statues will erect the souls of proud, innocent boys for centuries, his village tomb will smell of loyalty as of lilies. Millions who never knew him shall love him like a father—this man whom the last few that knew him dealt with like dung. He shall be a saint; and the truth shall never be told of him, because I have made up my mind at last.

There is so much good and evil in breaking secrets, that I put my conduct to a test. All these newspapers will perish; the anti-Brazil boom is already over; Olivier is already honoured everywhere. But I told myself that if anywhere, by name, in metal or marble that will endure like the pyramids, Colonel Clancy, or Captain Keith, or President Olivier, or any innocent man was wrongly blamed, then I would speak. If it were only that St. Clare was wrongly praised, I would be silent. And I will."

They plunged into the red-curtained tavern, which was not only cosy, but even luxurious inside. On a table stood a silver model of the tomb of St. Clare, the silver head bowed, the silver sword broken. On the walls were coloured photographs of the same scene, and of the system of wagonettes that took tourists to see it. They sat down on the comfortable padded benches.

"Come, it's cold," cried Father Brown; "let's have some wine or beer."

"Or brandy," said Flambeau.

The Hammer of God

G. K. Chesterton

The Hammer of God

The little village of Bohun Beacon was perched on a hill so steep that the tall spire of its church seemed only like the peak of a small mountain. At the foot of the church stood a smithy, generally red with fires and always littered with hammers and scraps of iron; opposite to this, over a rude cross of cobbled paths, was "The Blue Boar," the only inn of the place. It was upon this crossway, in the lifting of a leaden and silver daybreak, that two brothers met in the street and spoke; though one was beginning the day and the other finishing it. The Rev. and Hon. Wilfred Bohun was very devout, and was making his way to some austere exercises of prayer or contemplation at dawn. Colonel the Hon. Norman Bohun, his elder brother, was by no means devout, and was sitting in evening dress on the bench outside "The Blue Boar," drinking what the philosophic observer was free to regard either as his last glass on Tuesday or his first on Wednesday. The colonel was not particular.

The Bohuns were one of the very few aristocratic families really dating from the Middle Ages, and their pennon had actually seen Palestine. But it is a great mistake to suppose that such houses stand high in chivalric tradition. Few except the poor preserve traditions. Aristocrats live not in traditions but in fashions. The Bohuns had been Mohocks under Queen Anne and Mashers under Queen Victoria. But like more than one of the really ancient houses, they had rotted in the last two centuries into mere drunkards and dandy degenerates, till there had even come a whisper of insanity. Certainly there was something hardly human about the colonel's wolfish pursuit of pleasure, and his chronic resolution not to go home till morning had a touch of the hideous clarity of insomnia. He was a tall, fine animal, elderly, but with hair still startlingly yellow. He would have looked merely blonde and leonine, but his blue eyes were sunk so deep in his face that they looked black. They were a little too close together. He had very long yellow moustaches; on each side of them a fold or furrow from nostril to jaw, so that a sneer seemed cut into his face. Over his evening clothes he wore a curious pale yellow coat that looked more like a very light dressing gown than an overcoat, and on the back of his head was stuck an extraordinary broad-brimmed hat of a bright green colour, evidently some oriental curiosity caught up at random. He was proud of appearing in such incongruous attires— proud of the fact that he always made them look congruous.

His brother the curate had also the yellow hair and the elegance, but he was buttoned up to the chin in black, and his face was clean-shaven, cultivated, and a little nervous. He seemed to live for nothing but his religion; but there were some who said (notably the blacksmith, who was a Presbyterian) that it was a love of Gothic architecture rather than of God, and that his haunting of the church like a ghost was only another and purer turn of the almost morbid thirst for beauty which sent his brother raging after women and wine. This charge was doubtful, while the man's practical piety was indubitable. Indeed, the charge was mostly an ignorant misunderstanding of the love of solitude and secret prayer, and was founded on his being often found kneeling, not before the altar, but in peculiar places, in the crypts or gallery, or even in the belfry. He was at the moment about to enter the church through the yard of the smithy, but stopped and frowned a little as he saw his brother's cavernous eyes staring in the same direction. On the hypothesis that the colonel was interested in the church he did not waste any speculations. There only remained the blacksmith's shop, and though the blacksmith was a Puritan and none of his people, Wilfred Bohun had heard some scandals about a beautiful and rather celebrated wife. He flung a suspicious look across the shed, and the colonel stood up laughing to speak to him.

"Good morning, Wilfred," he said. "Like a good landlord I am watching sleeplessly over my people. I am going to call on the blacksmith."

Wilfred looked at the ground, and said: "The blacksmith is out. He is over at Greenford."

"I know," answered the other with silent laughter; "that is why I am calling on him."

"Norman," said the cleric, with his eye on a pebble in the road, "are you ever afraid of thunderbolts?"

"What do you mean?" asked the colonel. "Is your hobby meteorology?"

"I mean," said Wilfred, without looking up, "do you ever think that God might strike you in the street?"

"I beg your pardon," said the colonel; "I see your hobby is folk-lore."

"I know your hobby is blasphemy," retorted the religious man, stung in the one live place of his nature. "But if you do not fear God, you have good reason to fear man."

The elder raised his eyebrows politely. "Fear man?" he said.

"Barnes the blacksmith is the biggest and strongest man for forty miles round," said the clergyman sternly. "I know you are no coward or weakling, but he could throw you over the wall."

This struck home, being true, and the lowering line by mouth and nostril darkened and deepened. For a moment he stood with the heavy sneer on his face. But in an instant Colonel Bohun had recovered his own cruel good humour and laughed, showing two dog-like front teeth under his yellow moustache. "In that case, my dear Wilfred," he said quite carelessly, "it was wise for the last of the Bohuns to come out partially in armour."

And he took off the queer round hat covered with green, showing that it was lined within with steel. Wilfred recognised it indeed as a light Japanese or Chinese helmet torn down from a trophy that hung in the old family hall.

"It was the first hat to hand," explained his brother airily; "always the nearest hat—and the nearest woman."

"The blacksmith is away at Greenford," said Wilfred quietly; "the time of his return is unsettled."

And with that he turned and went into the church with bowed head, crossing himself like one who wishes to be quit of an unclean spirit. He was anxious to forget such grossness in the cool twilight of his tall Gothic cloisters; but on that morning it was fated that his still round of religious exercises should be everywhere arrested by small shocks. As he entered the church, hitherto always empty at that hour, a kneeling figure rose hastily to its feet and came towards the full daylight of the doorway. When the curate saw it he stood still with surprise. For the early worshipper was none other than the village idiot, a nephew of the blacksmith, one who neither would nor could care for the church or for anything else. He was always called "Mad Joe," and seemed to have no other name; he was a dark, strong, slouching lad, with a heavy white face, dark straight hair, and a mouth always open. As he passed the priest, his moon-calf countenance gave no hint of what he had been doing or thinking of. He had never been known to pray before. What sort of prayers was he saying now? Extraordinary prayers surely.

Wilfred Bohun stood rooted to the spot long enough to see the idiot go out into the sunshine, and even to see his dissolute brother hail him with a sort of avuncular jocularity. The last thing he saw was the colonel throwing pennies at the open mouth of Joe, with the serious appearance of trying to hit it.

This ugly sunlit picture of the stupidity and cruelty of the earth sent the ascetic finally to his prayers for purification and new thoughts. He went up to a pew in the gallery, which brought him under a coloured window which he loved and always quieted his spirit; a blue window with an angel carrying lilies. There he began to think less about the half-wit, with his livid face and mouth like a fish. He began to think less of his evil brother, pacing like a lean lion in his horrible hunger. He sank deeper and deeper into those cold and sweet colours of silver blossoms and sapphire sky.

In this place half an hour afterwards he was found by Gibbs, the village cobbler, who had been sent for him in some haste. He got to his feet with promptitude, for he knew that no small matter would have brought Gibbs into such a place at all. The cobbler was, as in many villages, an atheist, and his appearance in church was a shade more extraordinary than Mad Joe's. It was a morning of theological enigmas.

"What is it?" asked Wilfred Bohun rather stiffly, but putting out a trembling hand for his hat.

The atheist spoke in a tone that, coming from him, was quite startlingly respectful, and even, as it were, huskily sympathetic.

"You must excuse me, sir," he said in a hoarse whisper, "but we didn't think it right not to let you know at once. I'm afraid a rather dreadful thing has happened, sir. I'm afraid your brother—"

Wilfred clenched his frail hands. "What devilry has he done now?" he cried in voluntary passion.

"Why, sir," said the cobbler, coughing, "I'm afraid he's done nothing, and won't do anything. I'm afraid he's done for. You had really better come down, sir."

The curate followed the cobbler down a short winding stair which brought them out at an entrance rather higher than the street. Bohun saw the tragedy in one glance, flat underneath him like a plan. In the yard of the smithy were standing five or six men mostly in black, one in an inspector's uniform. They included the doctor, the Presbyterian minister, and the priest from the Roman Catholic chapel, to which the blacksmith's wife belonged. The latter was speaking to her, indeed, very rapidly, in an undertone, as she, a magnificent woman with red-gold hair, was sobbing blindly on a bench. Between these two groups, and just clear of the main heap of hammers, lay a man in evening dress, spread-eagled and flat on his face. From the height above Wilfred could have sworn to every item of his costume and appearance, down to the Bohun rings upon his fingers; but the skull was only a hideous splash, like a star of blackness and blood.

Wilfred Bohun gave but one glance, and ran down the steps into the yard. The doctor, who was the family physician, saluted him, but he scarcely took any notice. He could only stammer out: "My brother is dead. What does it mean? What is this horrible mystery?" There was an unhappy silence; and then the cobbler, the most outspoken man present, answered: "Plenty of horror, sir," he said; "but not much mystery."

"What do you mean?" asked Wilfred, with a white face.

"It's plain enough," answered Gibbs. "There is only one man for forty miles round that could have struck such a blow as that, and he's the man that had most reason to."

"We must not prejudge anything," put in the doctor, a tall, black-bearded man, rather nervously; "but it is competent for me to corroborate what Mr. Gibbs says about the nature of the blow, sir; it is an incredible blow. Mr. Gibbs says that only one man in this district could have done it. I should have said myself that nobody could have done it."

A shudder of superstition went through the slight figure of the curate. "I can hardly understand," he said.

"Mr. Bohun," said the doctor in a low voice, "metaphors literally fail me. It is inadequate to say that the skull was smashed to bits like an eggshell. Fragments of bone were driven into the body and the ground like bullets into a mud wall. It was the hand of a giant."

He was silent a moment, looking grimly through his glasses; then he added: "The thing has one advantage—that it clears most people of suspicion at one stroke. If you or I or any normally made man in the country were accused of this crime, we should be acquitted as an infant would be acquitted of stealing the Nelson column."

"That's what I say," repeated the cobbler obstinately; "there's only one man that could have done it, and he's the man that would have done it. Where's Simeon Barnes, the blacksmith?"

"He's over at Greenford," faltered the curate.

"More likely over in France," muttered the cobbler.

"No; he is in neither of those places," said a small and colourless voice, which came from the little Roman priest who had joined the group. "As a matter of fact, he is coming up the road at this moment."

The little priest was not an interesting man to look at, having stubbly brown hair and a round and stolid face. But if he had been as splendid as Apollo no one would have looked at him at that moment. Everyone turned round and peered at the pathway which wound across the plain below, along which was indeed walking, at his own huge stride and with a hammer on his shoulder, Simeon the smith. He was a bony and gigantic man, with deep, dark, sinister eyes and a dark chin beard. He was walking and talking quietly with two other men; and though he was never specially cheerful, he seemed quite at his ease.

"My God!" cried the atheistic cobbler, "and there's the hammer he did it with."

"No," said the inspector, a sensible-looking man with a sandy moustache, speaking for the first time. "There's the hammer he did it with over there by the church wall. We have left it and the body exactly as they are."

All glanced round and the short priest went across and looked down in silence at the tool where it lay. It was one of the smallest and the lightest of the hammers, and would not have caught the eye among the rest; but on the iron edge of it were blood and yellow hair.

After a silence the short priest spoke without looking up, and there was a new note in his dull voice. "Mr. Gibbs was hardly right," he said, "in saying that there is no mystery. There is at least the mystery of why so big a man should attempt so big a blow with so little a hammer."

"Oh, never mind that," cried Gibbs, in a fever. "What are we to do with Simeon Barnes?"

"Leave him alone," said the priest quietly. "He is coming here of himself. I know those two men with him. They are very good fellows from Greenford, and they have come over about the Presbyterian chapel."

Even as he spoke the tall smith swung round the corner of the church, and strode into his own yard. Then he stood there quite still, and the hammer fell from his hand. The inspector, who had preserved impenetrable propriety, immediately went up to him.

"I won't ask you, Mr. Barnes," he said, "whether you know anything about what has happened here. You are not bound to say. I hope you don't know, and that you will be able to prove it. But I must go through the form of arresting you in the King's name for the murder of Colonel Norman Bohun."

"You are not bound to say anything," said the cobbler in officious excitement. "They've got to prove everything. They haven't proved yet that it is Colonel Bohun, with the head all smashed up like that."

"That won't wash," said the doctor aside to the priest. "That's out of the detective stories. I was the colonel's medical man, and I knew his body better than he did. He had very fine hands, but quite peculiar ones. The second and third fingers were the same length. Oh, that's the colonel right enough."

As he glanced at the brained corpse upon the ground the iron eyes of the motionless blacksmith followed them and rested there also.

"Is Colonel Bohun dead?" said the smith quite calmly. "Then he's damned."

"Don't say anything! Oh, don't say anything," cried the atheist cobbler, dancing about in an ecstasy of admiration of the English legal system. For no man is such a legalist as the good Secularist.

The blacksmith turned on him over his shoulder the august face of a fanatic.

"It's well for you infidels to dodge like foxes because the world's law favours you," he said; "but God guards His own in His pocket, as you shall see this day."

Then he pointed to the colonel and said: "When did this dog die in his sins?"

"Moderate your language," said the doctor.

"Moderate the Bible's language, and I'll moderate mine. When did he die?"

"I saw him alive at six o'clock this morning," stammered Wilfred Bohun.

"God is good," said the smith. "Mr. Inspector, I have not the slightest objection to being arrested. It is you who may object to arresting me. I don't mind leaving the court without a stain on my character. You do mind perhaps leaving the court with a bad set-back in your career."

The solid inspector for the first time looked at the blacksmith with a lively eye; as did everybody else, except the short, strange priest, who was still looking down at the little hammer that had dealt the dreadful blow.

"There are two men standing outside this shop," went on the blacksmith with ponderous lucidity, "good tradesmen in Greenford whom you all know, who will swear that they saw me from before midnight till daybreak and long after in the committee room of our Revival Mission, which sits all night, we save souls so fast. In Greenford itself twenty people could swear to me for all that time. If I were a heathen, Mr. Inspector, I would let you walk on to your downfall. But as a Christian man I feel bound to give you your chance, and ask you whether you will hear my alibi now or in court."

The inspector seemed for the first time disturbed, and said, "Of course I should be glad to clear you altogether now."

The smith walked out of his yard with the same long and easy stride, and returned to his two friends from Greenford, who were indeed friends of nearly everyone present. Each of them said a few words which no one ever thought of disbelieving. When they had spoken, the innocence of Simeon stood up as solid as the great church above them.

One of those silences struck the group which are more strange and insufferable than any speech. Madly, in order to make conversation, the curate said to the Catholic priest:

"You seem very much interested in that hammer, Father Brown."

"Yes, I am," said Father Brown; "why is it such a small hammer?"

The doctor swung round on him.

"By George, that's true," he cried; "who would use a little hammer with ten larger hammers lying about?"

Then he lowered his voice in the curate's ear and said: "Only the kind of person that can't lift a large hammer. It is not a question of force or courage between the sexes. It's a question of lifting power in the shoulders. A bold woman could commit ten murders with a light hammer and never turn a hair. She could not kill a beetle with a heavy one."

Wilfred Bohun was staring at him with a sort of hypnotised horror, while Father Brown listened with his head a little on one side, really interested and attentive. The doctor went on with more hissing emphasis:

"Why do these idiots always assume that the only person who hates the wife's lover is the wife's husband? Nine times out of ten the person who most hates the wife's lover is the wife. Who knows what insolence or treachery he had shown her—look there!"

He made a momentary gesture towards the red-haired woman on the bench. She had lifted her head at last and the tears were drying on her splendid face. But the eyes were fixed on the corpse with an electric glare that had in it something of idiocy.

The Rev. Wilfred Bohun made a limp gesture as if waving away all desire to know; but Father Brown, dusting off his sleeve some ashes blown from the furnace, spoke in his indifferent way.

"You are like so many doctors," he said; "your mental science is really suggestive. It is your physical science that is utterly impossible. I agree that the woman wants to kill the co-respondent much more than the petitioner does. And I agree that a woman will always pick up a small hammer instead of a big one. But the difficulty is one of physical impossibility. No woman ever born could have smashed a man's skull out flat like that." Then he added reflectively, after a pause: "These people haven't grasped the whole of it. The man was actually wearing an iron helmet, and the blow scattered it like broken glass. Look at that woman. Look at her arms."

Silence held them all up again, and then the doctor said rather sulkily: "Well, I may be wrong; there are objections to everything. But I stick to the main point. No man but an idiot would pick up that little hammer if he could use a big hammer."

With that the lean and quivering hands of Wilfred Bohun went up to his head and seemed to clutch his scanty yellow hair. After an instant they dropped, and he cried: "That was the word I wanted; you have said the word."

Then he continued, mastering his discomposure: "The words you said were, 'No man but an idiot would pick up the small hammer.'"

"Yes," said the doctor. "Well?"

"Well," said the curate, "no man but an idiot did." The rest stared at him with eyes arrested and riveted, and he went on in a febrile and feminine agitation.

"I am a priest," he cried unsteadily, "and a priest should be no shedder of blood. I—I mean that he should bring no one to the gallows. And I thank God that I see the criminal clearly now— because he is a criminal who cannot be brought to the gallows."

"You will not denounce him?" inquired the doctor.

"He would not be hanged if I did denounce him," answered Wilfred with a wild but curiously happy smile. "When I went into the church this morning I found a madman praying there—that poor Joe, who has been wrong all his life. God knows what he prayed; but with such strange folk it is not incredible to suppose that their prayers are all upside down. Very likely a lunatic would pray before killing a man. When I last saw poor Joe he was with my brother. My brother was mocking him."

"By Jove!" cried the doctor, "this is talking at last. But how do you explain—"

The Rev. Wilfred was almost trembling with the excitement of his own glimpse of the truth. "Don't you see; don't you see," he cried feverishly; "that is the only theory that covers both the queer things, that answers both the riddles. The two riddles are the little hammer and the big blow. The smith might have struck the big blow, but would not have chosen the little hammer. His wife would have chosen the little hammer, but she could not have struck the big blow. But the madman might have done both. As for the little hammer— why, he was mad and might have picked up anything. And for the big blow, have you never heard, doctor, that a maniac in his paroxysm may have the strength of ten men?"

The doctor drew a deep breath and then said, "By golly, I believe you've got it."

Father Brown had fixed his eyes on the speaker so long and steadily as to prove that his large grey, ox-like eyes were not quite so insignificant as the rest of his face. When silence had fallen he said with marked respect: "Mr. Bohun, yours is the only theory yet propounded which holds water every way and is essentially unassailable. I think, therefore, that you deserve to be told, on my positive knowledge, that it is not the true one." And with that the old little man walked away and stared again at the hammer.

"That fellow seems to know more than he ought to," whispered the doctor peevishly to Wilfred. "Those popish priests are deucedly sly."

"No, no," said Bohun, with a sort of wild fatigue. "It was the lunatic. It was the lunatic."

The group of the two clerics and the doctor had fallen away from the more official group containing the inspector and the man he had arrested. Now, however, that their own party had broken up, they heard voices from the others. The priest looked up quietly and then looked down again as he heard the blacksmith say in a loud voice:

"I hope I've convinced you, Mr. Inspector. I'm a strong man, as you say, but I couldn't have flung my hammer bang here from Greenford. My hammer hasn't got wings that it should come flying half a mile over hedges and fields."

The inspector laughed amicably and said: "No, I think you can be considered out of it, though it's one of the rummiest coincidences I ever saw. I can only ask you to give us all the assistance you can in finding a man as big and strong as yourself. By George! you might be useful, if only to hold him! I suppose you yourself have no guess at the man?"

"I may have a guess," said the pale smith, "but it is not at a man." Then, seeing the scared eyes turn towards his wife on the bench, he put his huge hand on her shoulder and said: "Nor a woman either."

"What do you mean?" asked the inspector jocularly. "You don't think cows use hammers, do you?"

"I think no thing of flesh held that hammer," said the blacksmith in a stifled voice; "mortally speaking, I think the man died alone."

Wilfred made a sudden forward movement and peered at him with burning eyes.

"Do you mean to say, Barnes," came the sharp voice of the cobbler, "that the hammer jumped up of itself and knocked the man down?"

"Oh, you gentlemen may stare and snigger," cried Simeon; "you clergymen who tell us on Sunday in what a stillness the Lord smote Sennacherib. I believe that One who walks invisible in every house defended the honour of mine, and laid the defiler dead before the door of it. I believe the force in that blow was just the force there is in earthquakes, and no force less."

Wilfred said, with a voice utterly undescribable: "I told Norman myself to beware of the thunderbolt."

"That agent is outside my jurisdiction," said the inspector with a slight smile.

"You are not outside His," answered the smith; "see you to it," and, turning his broad back, he went into the house.

The shaken Wilfred was led away by Father Brown, who had an easy and friendly way with him. "Let us get out of this horrid place, Mr. Bohun," he said. "May I look inside your church? I hear it's one of the oldest in England. We take some interest, you know," he added with a comical grimace, "in old English churches."

Wilfred Bohun did not smile, for humour was never his strong point. But he nodded rather eagerly, being only too ready to explain the Gothic splendours to someone more likely to be sympathetic than the Presbyterian blacksmith or the atheist cobbler.

"By all means," he said; "let us go in at this side." And he led the way into the high side entrance at the top of the flight of steps. Father Brown was mounting the first step to follow him when he felt a hand on his shoulder, and turned to behold the dark, thin figure of the doctor, his face darker yet with suspicion.

"Sir," said the physician harshly, "you appear to know some secrets in this black business. May I ask if you are going to keep them to yourself?"

"Why, doctor," answered the priest, smiling quite pleasantly, "there is one very good reason why a man of my trade should keep things to himself when he is not sure of them, and that is that it is so constantly his duty to keep them to himself when he is sure of them. But if you think I have been discourteously reticent with you or anyone, I will go to the extreme limit of my custom. I will give you two very large hints."

"Well, sir?" said the doctor gloomily.

"First," said Father Brown quietly, "the thing is quite in your own province. It is a matter of physical science. The blacksmith is mistaken, not perhaps in saying that the blow was divine, but certainly in saying that it came by a miracle. It was no miracle, doctor, except in so far as man is himself a miracle, with his strange and wicked and yet half-heroic heart. The force that smashed that skull was a force well known to scientists—one of the most frequently debated of the laws of nature."

The doctor, who was looking at him with frowning intentness, only said: "And the other hint?"

"The other hint is this," said the priest. "Do you remember the blacksmith, though he believes in miracles, talking scornfully of the impossible fairy tale that his hammer had wings and flew half a mile across country?"

"Yes," said the doctor, "I remember that."

"Well," added Father Brown, with a broad smile, "that fairy tale was the nearest thing to the real truth that has been said today." And with that he turned his back and stumped up the steps after the curate.

The Reverend Wilfred, who had been waiting for him, pale and impatient, as if this little delay were the last straw for his nerves, led him immediately to his favourite corner of the church, that part of the gallery closest to the carved roof and lit by the wonderful window with the angel. The little Latin priest explored and admired everything exhaustively, talking cheerfully but in a low voice all the time. When in the course of his investigation he found the side exit and the winding stair down which Wilfred had rushed to find his brother dead, Father Brown ran not down but up, with the agility of a monkey, and his clear voice came from an outer platform above.

"Come up here, Mr. Bohun," he called. "The air will do you good."

Bohun followed him, and came out on a kind of stone gallery or balcony outside the building, from which one could see the illimitable plain in which their small hill stood, wooded away to the purple horizon and dotted with villages and farms. Clear and square, but quite small beneath them, was the blacksmith's yard, where the inspector still stood taking notes and the corpse still lay like a smashed fly.

"Might be the map of the world, mightn't it?" said Father Brown.

"Yes," said Bohun very gravely, and nodded his head.

Immediately beneath and about them the lines of the Gothic building plunged outwards into the void with a sickening swiftness akin to suicide. There is that element of Titan energy in the architecture of the Middle Ages that, from whatever aspect it be seen, it always seems to be rushing away, like the strong back of some maddened horse. This church was hewn out of ancient and silent stone, bearded with old fungoids and stained with the nests of birds. And yet, when they saw it from below, it sprang like a fountain at the stars; and when they saw it, as now, from above, it poured like a cataract into a voiceless pit. For these two men on the tower were left alone with the most terrible aspect of Gothic; the monstrous foreshortening and disproportion, the dizzy perspectives, the glimpses of great things small and small things great; a topsy-turvydom of stone in the mid-air. Details of stone, enormous by their proximity, were relieved against a pattern of fields and farms, pygmy in their distance. A carved bird or beast at a corner seemed like some vast walking or flying dragon wasting the pastures and villages below. The whole atmosphere was dizzy and dangerous, as if men were upheld in air amid the gyrating wings of colossal genii; and the whole of that old church, as tall and rich as a cathedral, seemed to sit upon the sunlit country like a cloudburst.

"I think there is something rather dangerous about standing on these high places even to pray," said Father Brown. "Heights were made to be looked at, not to be looked from."

"Do you mean that one may fall over," asked Wilfred.

"I mean that one's soul may fall if one's body doesn't," said the other priest.

"I scarcely understand you," remarked Bohun indistinctly.

"Look at that blacksmith, for instance," went on Father Brown calmly; "a good man, but not a Christian—hard, imperious, unforgiving. Well, his Scotch religion was made up by men who prayed on hills and high crags, and learnt to look down on the world more than to look up at heaven. Humility is the mother of giants. One sees great things from the valley; only small things from the peak."

"But he—he didn't do it," said Bohun tremulously.

"No," said the other in an odd voice; "we know he didn't do it."

After a moment he resumed, looking tranquilly out over the plain with his pale grey eyes. "I knew a man," he said, "who began by worshipping with others before the altar, but who grew fond of high and lonely places to pray from, corners or niches in the belfry or the spire. And once in one of those dizzy places, where the whole world seemed to turn under him like a wheel, his brain turned also, and he fancied he was God. So that, though he was a good man, he committed a great crime."

Wilfred's face was turned away, but his bony hands turned blue and white as they tightened on the parapet of stone.

"He thought it was given to him to judge the world and strike down the sinner. He would never have had such a thought if he had been kneeling with other men upon a floor. But he saw all men walking about like insects. He saw one especially strutting just below him, insolent and evident by a bright green hat—a poisonous insect."

Rooks cawed round the corners of the belfry; but there was no other sound till Father Brown went on.

"This also tempted him, that he had in his hand one of the most awful engines of nature; I mean gravitation, that mad and quickening rush by which all earth's creatures fly back to her heart when released. See, the inspector is strutting just below us in the smithy. If I were to toss a pebble over this parapet it would be something like a bullet by the time it struck him. If I were to drop a hammer—even a small hammer—"

Wilfred Bohun threw one leg over the parapet, and Father Brown had him in a minute by the collar.

"Not by that door," he said quite gently; "that door leads to hell."

Bohun staggered back against the wall, and stared at him with frightful eyes.

"How do you know all this?" he cried. "Are you a devil?"

"I am a man," answered Father Brown gravely; "and therefore have all devils in my heart. Listen to me," he said after a short pause. "I know what you did—at least, I can guess the great part of it. When you left your brother you were racked with no unrighteous rage, to the extent even that you snatched up a small hammer, half inclined to kill him with his foulness on his mouth. Recoiling, you thrust it under your buttoned coat instead, and rushed into the church. You pray wildly in many places, under the angel window, upon the platform above, and a higher platform still, from which you could see the colonel's Eastern hat like the back of a green beetle crawling about. Then something snapped in your soul, and you let God's thunderbolt fall."

Wilfred put a weak hand to his head, and asked in a low voice: "How did you know that his hat looked like a green beetle?"

"Oh, that," said the other with the shadow of a smile, "that was common sense. But hear me further. I say I know all this; but no one else shall know it. The next step is for you; I shall take no more steps; I will seal this with the seal of confession. If you ask me why, there are many reasons, and only one that concerns you. I leave things to you because you have not yet gone very far wrong, as assassins go. You did not help to fix the crime on the smith when it was easy; or on his wife, when that was easy. You tried to fix it on the imbecile because you knew that he could not suffer. That was one of the gleams that it is my business to find in assassins. And now come down into the village, and go your own way as free as the wind; for I have said my last word."

They went down the winding stairs in utter silence, and came out into the sunlight by the smithy. Wilfred Bohun carefully unlatched the wooden gate of the yard, and going up to the inspector, said: "I wish to give myself up; I have killed my brother."

The Coin of Dionysius

Ernest Bramah

The Coin of Dionysius

It was eight o'clock at night and raining, scarcely a time when a business so limited in its clientele as that of a coin dealer could hope to attract any customer, but a light was still showing in the small shop that bore over its window the name of Baxter, and in the even smaller office at the back the proprietor himself sat reading the latest *Pall Mall*. His enterprise seemed to be justified, for presently the door bell gave its announcement, and throwing down his paper Mr. Baxter went forward.

As a matter of fact the dealer had been expecting someone and his manner as he passed into the shop was unmistakably suggestive of a caller of importance. But at the first glance towards his visitor the excess of deference melted out of his bearing, leaving the urbane, self-possessed shopman in the presence of the casual customer.

"Mr. Baxter, I think?" said the latter. He had laid aside his dripping umbrella and was unbuttoning overcoat and coat to reach an inner pocket. "You hardly remember me, I suppose? Mr. Carlyle—two years ago I took up a case for you—"

"To be sure. Mr. Carlyle, the private detective—"

"Inquiry agent," corrected Mr. Carlyle precisely.

"Well," smiled Mr. Baxter, "for that matter I am a coin dealer and not an antiquarian or a numismatist. Is there anything in that way that I can do for you?"

"Yes," replied his visitor; "it is my turn to consult you." He had taken a small wash-leather bag from the inner pocket and now turned something carefully out upon the counter. "What can you tell me about that?"

The dealer gave the coin a moment's scrutiny.

"There is no question about this," he replied. "It is a Sicilian tetradrachm of Dionysius."

"Yes, I know that—I have it on the label out of the cabinet. I can tell you further that it's supposed to be one that Lord Seastoke gave two hundred and fifty pounds for at the Brice sale in '94."

"It seems to me that you can tell me more about it than I can tell you," remarked Mr. Baxter. "What is it that you really want to know?"

"I want to know," replied Mr. Carlyle, "whether it is genuine or not."

"Has any doubt been cast upon it?"

"Certain circumstances raised a suspicion—that is all."

The dealer took another look at the tetradrachm through his magnifying glass, holding it by the edge with the careful touch of an expert. Then he shook his head slowly in a confession of ignorance.

"Of course I could make a guess—"

"No, don't," interrupted Mr. Carlyle hastily. "An arrest hangs on it and nothing short of certainty is any good to me."

"Is that so, Mr. Carlyle?" said Mr. Baxter, with increased interest. "Well, to be quite candid, the thing is out of my line. Now if it was a rare Saxon penny or a doubtful noble I'd stake my reputation on my opinion, but I do very little in the classical series."

Mr. Carlyle did not attempt to conceal his disappointment as he returned the coin to the bag and replaced the bag in the inner pocket.

"I had been relying on you," he grumbled reproachfully. "Where on earth am I to go now?"

"There is always the British Museum."

"Ah, to be sure, thanks. But will anyone who can tell me be there now?"

"Now? No fear!" replied Mr. Baxter. "Go round in the morning—"

"But I must know to-night," explained the visitor, reduced to despair again. "To-morrow will be too late for the purpose."

Mr. Baxter did not hold out much encouragement in the

circumstances.

"You can scarcely expect to find anyone at business now," he remarked. "I should have been gone these two hours myself only I happened to have an appointment with an American millionaire who fixed his own time." Something indistinguishable from a wink slid off Mr. Baxter's right eye. "Offmunson he's called, and a bright young pedigree-hunter has traced his descent from Offa, King of Mercia. So he—quite naturally—wants a set of Offas as a sort of collateral proof."

"Very interesting," murmured Mr. Carlyle, fidgeting with his watch. "I should love an hour's chat with you about your millionaire customers—some other time. Just now—look here, Baxter, can't you give me a line of introduction to some dealer in this sort of thing who happens to live in town? You must know dozens of experts."

"Why, bless my soul, Mr. Carlyle, I don't know a man of them away from his business," said Mr. Baxter, staring. "They may live in Park Lane or they may live in Petticoat Lane for all I know. Besides, there aren't so many experts as you seem to imagine. And the two best will very likely quarrel over it. You've had to do with 'expert witnesses,' I suppose?"

"I don't want a witness; there will be no need to give evidence. All I want is an absolutely authoritative pronouncement that I can act on. Is there no one who can really say whether the thing is genuine or not?"

Mr. Baxter's meaning silence became cynical in its implication as he continued to look at his visitor across the counter. Then he relaxed.

"Stay a bit; there is a man—an amateur—I remember hearing wonderful things about some time ago. They say he really does know."

"There you are," explained Mr. Carlyle, much relieved. "There always is someone. Who is he?"

"Funny name," replied Baxter. "Something Wynn or Wynn something." He craned his neck to catch sight of an important motor-car that was drawing to the kerb before his window. "Wynn Carrados! You'll excuse me now, Mr. Carlyle, won't you? This looks like Mr. Offmunson."

Mr. Carlyle hastily scribbled the name down on his cuff.

"Wynn Carrados, right. Where does he live?"

"Haven't the remotest idea," replied Baxter, referring the arrangement of his tie to the judgment of the wall mirror. "I have never seen the man myself. Now, Mr. Carlyle, I'm sorry I can't do any more for you. You won't mind, will you?"

Mr. Carlyle could not pretend to misunderstand. He enjoyed the distinction of holding open the door for the transatlantic representative of the line of Offa as he went out, and then made his way through the muddy streets back to his office. There was only one way of tracing a private individual at such short notice—through the pages of the directories, and the gentleman did not flatter himself by a very high estimate of his chances.

Fortune favoured him, however. He very soon discovered a Wynn Carrados living at Richmond, and, better still, further search failed to unearth another. There was, apparently, only one householder at all events of that name in the neighbourhood of London. He jotted down the address and set out for Richmond.

The house was some distance from the station, Mr. Carlyle learned. He took a taxicab and drove, dismissing the vehicle at the gate. He prided himself on his power of observation and the accuracy of his deductions which resulted from it-a detail of his business. "It's nothing more than using one's eyes and putting two and two together," he would modestly declare, when he wished to be deprecatory rather than impressive. By the time he had reached the front door of "The Turrets" he had formed some opinion of the position and tastes of the people who lived there.

A man-servant admitted Mr. Carlyle and took his card—his private card, with the bare request for an interview that would not detain Mr. Carrados for ten minutes. Luck still favoured him; Mr. Carrados was at home and would see him at once. The servant, the hall through which they passed, and the room into which he was shown, all contributed something to the deductions which the quietly observant gentleman, was half unconsciously recording.

"Mr. Carlyle," announced the servant.

The room was a library or study. The only occupant, a man of about Carlyle's own age, had been using a typewriter up to the moment of his visitor's entrance. He now turned and stood up with an expression of formal courtesy.

"It's very good of you to see me at this hour," apologised Mr. Carlyle.

The conventional expression of Mr. Carrados's face changed a little.

"Surelymymanhasgotyournamewrong?"heexplained."Isn'titLouis Calling?"

Mr. Carlyle stopped short and his agreeable smile gave place to a sudden flash of anger or annoyance.

"No sir," he replied stiffly. "My name is on the card which you have before you."

"I beg your pardon," said Mr. Carrados, with perfect good-humour. "I hadn't seen it. But I used to know a Calling some years ago—at St. Michael's."

"St. Michael's!" Mr. Carlyle's features underwent another change, no less instant and sweeping than before. "St. Michael's! Wynn Carrados? Good heavens! it isn't Max Wynn—old 'Winning' Wynn"?

"A little older and a little fatter—yes," replied Carrados. "I have changed my name you see."

"Extraordinary thing meeting like this," said his visitor, dropping into a chair and staring hard at Mr. Carrados. "I have changed more than my name. How did you recognize me?"

"The voice," replied Carrados. "It took me back to that little smoke-dried attic den of yours where we—"

"My God!" exclaimed Carlyle bitterly, "don't remind me of what we were going to do in those days." He looked round the well-furnished, handsome room and recalled the other signs of wealth that he had noticed. "At all events, you seem fairly comfortable, Wynn."

"I am alternately envied and pitied," replied Carrados, with a placid tolerance of circumstance that seemed characteristic of him. "Still, as you say, I am fairly comfortable."

"Envied, I can understand. But why are you pitied?"

"Because I am blind," was the tranquil reply.

"Blind!" exclaimed Mr. Carlyle, using his own eyes superlatively. "Do you mean—literally blind?"

"Literally…. I was riding along a bridle-path through a wood about a dozen years ago with a friend. He was in front. At one point a twig sprang back—you know how easily a thing like that happens. It just flicked my eye—nothing to think twice about."

"And that blinded you?"

"Yes, ultimately. It's called amaurosis."

"I can scarcely believe it. You seem so sure and self-reliant. Your eyes are full of expression—only a little quieter than they used to be. I believe you were typing when I came….Aren't you having me?"

"You miss the dog and the stick?" smiled Carrados. "No; it's a fact."

"What an awful affliction for you, Max. You were always such an impulsive, reckless sort of fellow—never quiet. You must miss such a fearful lot."

"Has anyone else recognized you?" asked Carrados quietly.

"Ah, that was the voice, you said," replied Carlyle.

"Yes; but other people heard the voice as well. Only I had no blundering, self-confident eyes to be hoodwinked."

"That's a rum way of putting it," said Carlyle. "Are your ears never hoodwinked, may I ask?"

"Not now. Nor my fingers. Nor any of my other senses that have to look out for themselves."

"Well, well," murmured Mr. Carlyle, cut short in his sympathetic emotions. "I'm glad you take it so well. Of course, if you find it an advantage to be blind, old man——" He stopped and reddened. "I beg your pardon," he concluded stiffly.

"Not an advantage perhaps," replied the other thoughtfully. "Still it has compensations that one might not think of. A new world to explore, new experiences, new powers awakening; strange new perceptions; life in the fourth dimension. But why do you beg my pardon, Louis?"

"I am an ex-solicitor, struck off in connexion with the falsifying of a trust account, Mr. Carrados," replied Carlyle, rising.

"Sit down, Louis," said Carrados suavely. His face, even his incredibly living eyes, beamed placid good-nature. "The chair on which you will sit, the roof above you, all the comfortable surroundings to which you have so amiably alluded, are the direct result of falsifying a trust account. But do I call you 'Mr. Carlyle' in consequence? Certainly not, Louis."

"I did not falsify the account," cried Carlyle hotly. He sat down however, and added more quietly: "But why do I tell you all this? I have never spoken of it before."

"Blindness invites confidence," replied Carrados. "We are out of the running—human rivalry ceases to exist. Besides, why shouldn't you? In my case the account *was* falsified."

"Of course that's all bunkum, Max" commented Carlyle. "Still, I appreciate your motive."

"Practically everything I possess was left to me by an American cousin, on the condition that I took the name of Carrados. He made his fortune by an ingenious conspiracy of doctoring the crop reports and unloading favourably in consequence. And I need hardly remind you that the receiver is equally guilty with the thief."

"But twice as safe. I know something of that, Max … Have you any idea what my business is?"

"You shall tell me," replied Carrados.

"I run a private inquiry agency. When I lost my profession I had to do something for a living. This occurred. I dropped my name, changed my appearance and opened an office. I knew the legal side down to the ground and I got a retired Scotland Yard man to organize the outside work."

"Excellent!" cried Carrados. "Do you unearth many murders?"

"No," admitted Mr. Carlyle; "our business lies mostly on the conventional lines among divorce and defalcation."

"That's a pity," remarked Carrados. "Do you know, Louis, I always had a secret ambition to be a detective myself. I have even thought lately that I might still be able to do something at it if the chance came my way. That makes you smile?"

"Well, certainly, the idea——"

"Yes, the idea of a blind detective—the blind tracking the alert—"

"Of course, as you say, certain facilities are no doubt quickened," Mr. Carlyle hastened to add considerately, "but, seriously, with the exception of an artist, I don't suppose there is any man who is more utterly dependent on his eyes."

Whatever opinion Carrados might have held privately, his genial exterior did not betray a shadow of dissent. For a full minute he continued to smoke as though he derived an actual visual enjoyment from the blue sprays that travelled and dispersed across the room. He had already placed before his visitor a box containing cigars of a brand which that gentleman keenly appreciated but generally regarded as unattainable, and the matter-of-fact ease and certainty with which the blind man had brought the box and put it before him had sent a questioning flicker through Carlyle's mind.

"You used to be rather fond of art yourself, Louis," he remarked presently. "Give me your opinion of my latest purchase—the bronze lion on the cabinet there." Then, as Carlyle's gaze went about the room, he added quickly: "No, not that cabinet—the one on your left."

Carlyle shot a sharp glance at his host as he got up, but Carrados's expression was merely benignly complacent. Then he strolled across to the figure.

"Very nice," he admitted. "Late Flemish, isn't it?"

"No, It is a copy of Vidal's 'Roaring Lion.'"

"Vidal?"

"A French artist." The voice became indescribably flat. "He, also, had the misfortune to be blind, by the way."

"You old humbug, Max!" shrieked Carlyle, "you've been thinking that out for the last five minutes." Then the unfortunate man bit his lip and turned his back towards his host.

"Do you remember how we used to pile it up on that obtuse ass Sanders, and then roast him?" asked Carrados, ignoring the half-smothered exclamation with which the other man had recalled himself.

"Yes," replied Carlyle quietly. "This is very good," he continued, addressing himself to the bronze again. "How ever did he do it?"

"With his hands."

"Naturally. But, I mean, how did he study his model?"

"Also with his hands. He called it 'seeing near.'"

"Even with a lion—handled it?"

"In such cases he required the services of a keeper, who brought the animal to bay while Vidal exercised his own particular gifts ... You don't feel inclined to put me on the track of a mystery, Louis?"

Unable to regard this request as anything but one of old Max's unquenchable pleasantries, Mr. Carlyle was on the point of making a suitable reply when a sudden thought caused him to smile knowingly. Up to that point, he had, indeed, completely forgotten the object of his visit. Now that he remembered the doubtful Dionysius and Baxter's recommendation he immediately assumed that some mistake had been made. Either Max was not the Wynn Carrados he had been seeking or else the dealer had been misinformed; for although his host was wonderfully expert in the face of his misfortune, it was inconceivable that he could decide the genuineness of a coin without seeing it. The opportunity seemed a good one of getting even with Carrados by taking him at his word.

"Yes," he accordingly replied, with crisp deliberation, as he re-crossed the room; "yes, I will, Max. Here is the clue to what seems to be a rather remarkable fraud." He put the tetradrachm into his host's hand. "What do you make of it?"

For a few seconds Carrados handled the piece with the delicate manipulation of his finger-tips while Carlyle looked on with a self-appreciative grin. Then with equal gravity the blind man weighed the coin in the balance of his hand. Finally he touched it with his tongue.

"Well?" demanded the other.

"Of course I have not much to go on, and if I was more fully in your confidence I might come to another conclusion——"

"Yes, yes," interposed Carlyle, with amused encouragement.

"Then I should advise you to arrest the parlourmaid, Nina Brun, communicate with the police authorities of Padua for particulars of the career of Helene Brunesi, and suggest to Lord Seastoke that he should return to London to see what further depredations have been made in his cabinet."

Mr. Carlyle's groping hand sought and found a chair, on to which he dropped blankly. His eyes were unable to detach themselves for a single moment from the very ordinary spectacle of Mr. Carrados's mildly benevolent face, while the sterilized ghost of his now forgotten amusement still lingered about his features.

"Good heavens!" he managed to articulate, "how do you know?"

"Isn't that what you wanted of me?" asked Carrados suavely.

"Don't humbug, Max," said Carlyle severely. "This is no joke." An undefined mistrust of his own powers suddenly possessed him in the presence of this mystery. "How do you come to know of Nina Brun and Lord Seastoke?"

"You are a detective, Louis," replied Carrados. "How does one know these things? By using one's eyes and putting two and two together."

Carlyle groaned and flung out an arm petulantly.

"Is it all bunkum, Max? Do you really see all the time—though that doesn't go very far towards explaining it."

"Like Vidal, I see very well—at close quarters," replied Carrados, lightly running a forefinger along the inscription on the tetradrachm. "For longer range I keep another pair of eyes. Would you like to test them?"

Mr. Carlyle's assent was not very gracious; it was, in fact, faintly sulky. He was suffering the annoyance of feeling distinctly unimpressive in his own department; but he was also curious.

"The bell is just behind you, if you don't mind," said his host. "Parkinson will appear. You might take note of him while he is in."

The man who had admitted Mr. Carlyle proved to be Parkinson.

"This gentleman is Mr. Carlyle, Parkinson," explained Carrados the moment the man entered. "You will remember him for the future?"

Parkinson's apologetic eye swept the visitor from head to foot, but so lightly and swiftly that it conveyed to that gentleman the comparison of being very deftly dusted.

"I will endeavour to do so, sir," replied Parkinson, turning again to his master.

"I shall be at home to Mr. Carlyle whenever he calls. That is all."

"Very well, sir."

"Now, Louis," remarked Mr. Carrados briskly, when the door had closed again, "you have had a good opportunity of studying Parkinson. What is he like?"

"In what way?"

"I mean as a matter of description. I am a blind man—I haven't seen my servant for twelve years—what idea can you give me of him? I asked you to notice."

"I know you did, but your Parkinson is the sort of man who has very little about him to describe. He is the embodiment of the ordinary. His height is about average——"

"Five feet nine," murmured Carrados. "Slightly above the mean."

"Scarcely noticeably so. Clean-shaven. Medium brown hair. No particularly marked features. Dark eyes. Good teeth."

"False," interposed Carrados. "The teeth—not the statement."

"Possibly," admitted Mr. Carlyle. "I am not a dental expert and I had no opportunity of examining Mr. Parkinson's mouth in detail. But what is the drift of all this?"

"His clothes?"

"Oh, just the ordinary evening dress of a valet. There is not much room for variety in that."

"You noticed, in fact, nothing special by which Parkinson could be identified?"

"Well, he wore an unusually broad gold ring on the little finger of the left hand."

"But that is removable. And yet Parkinson has an ineradicable mole—a small one, I admit—on his chin. And you a human sleuth-hound. Oh, Louis!"

"At all events," retorted Carlyle, writhing a little under this good-humoured satire, although it was easy enough to see in it Carrados's affectionate intention—"at all events, I dare say I can give as good a description of Parkinson as he can give of me."

"That is what we are going to test. Ring the bell again."

"Seriously?"

"Quite. I am trying my eyes against yours. If I can't give you fifty out of a hundred I'll renounce my private detectorial ambition for ever."

"It isn't quite the same," objected Carlyle, but he rang the bell.

"Come in and close the door, Parkinson," said Carrados when the man appeared. "Don't look at Mr. Carlyle again—in fact, you had better stand with your back towards him, he won't mind. Now describe to me his appearance as you observed it."

Parkinson tendered his respectful apologies to Mr. Carlyle for the liberty he was compelled to take, by the deferential quality of his voice.

"Mr. Carlyle, sir, wears patent leather boots of about size seven and very little used. There are five buttons, but on the left boot one button—the third up—is missing, leaving loose threads and not the more usual metal fastener. Mr. Carlyle's trousers, sir, are of a dark material, a dark grey line of about a quarter of an inch width on a darker ground. The bottoms are turned permanently up and are, just now, a little muddy, if I may say so."

"Very muddy," interposed Mr. Carlyle generously. "It is a wet night, Parkinson."

"Yes, sir; very unpleasant weather. If you will allow me, sir, I will brush you in the hall. The mud is dry now, I notice. Then, sir," continued Parkinson, reverting to the business in hand, "there are dark green cashmere hose. A curb-pattern key-chain passes into the left-hand trouser pocket."

From the visitor's nether garments the photographic-eyed Parkinson proceeded to higher ground, and with increasing wonder Mr. Carlyle listened to the faithful catalogue of his possessions. His fetter-and-link albert of gold and platinum was minutely described.

His spotted blue ascot, with its gentlemanly pearl scarfpin, was set forth, and the fact that the buttonhole in the left lapel of his morning coat showed signs of use was duly noted. What Parkinson saw he recorded, but he made no deductions. A handkerchief carried in the cuff of the right sleeve was simply that to him and not an indication that Mr. Carlyle was, indeed, left-handed.

But a more delicate part of Parkinson's undertaking remained. He approached it with a double cough.

"As regards Mr. Carlyle's personal appearance, sir—"

"No, enough!" cried the gentleman concerned hastily. "I am more than satisfied. You are a keen observer, Parkinson."

"I have trained myself to suit my master's requirements, sir," replied the man. He looked towards Mr. Carrados, received a nod and withdrew.

Mr. Carlyle was the first to speak.

"That man of yours would be worth five pounds a week to me, Max," he remarked thoughtfully. "But, of course—"

"I don't think that he would take it," replied Carrados, in a voice of equally detached speculation. "He suits me very well. But you have the chance of using his services—indirectly."

"You still mean that—seriously?"

"I notice in you a chronic disinclination to take me seriously, Louis. It is really—to an Englishman—almost painful. Is there something inherently comic about me or the atmosphere of The Turrets?"

"No, my friend," replied Mr. Carlyle, "but there is something essentially prosperous. That is what points to the improbable. Now what is it?"

"It might be merely a whim, but it is more than that," replied Carrados. "It is, well, partly vanity, partly *ennui*, partly"—certainly there was something more nearly tragic in his voice than comic now—"partly hope."

Mr. Carlyle was too tactful to pursue the subject.

"Those are three tolerable motives," he acquiesced. "I'll do anything you want, Max, on one condition."

"Agreed. And it is?"

"That you tell me how you knew so much of this affair." He tapped the silver coin which lay on the table near them. "I am not easily flabbergasted," he added.

"You won't believe that there is nothing to explain—that it was purely second-sight?"

"No," replied Carlyle tersely: "I won't."

"You are quite right. And yet the thing is very simple."

"They always are—when you know," soliloquised the other. "That's what makes them so confoundedly difficult when you don't."

"Here is this one then. In Padua, which seems to be regaining its old reputation as the birthplace of spurious antiques, by the way, there lives an ingenious craftsman named Pietro Stelli. This simple soul, who possesses a talent not inferior to that of Cavino at his best, has for many years turned his hand to the not unprofitable occupation of forging rare Greek and Roman coins. As a collector and student of certain Greek colonials and a specialist in forgeries I have been familiar with Stelli's workmanship for years. Latterly he seems to have come under the influence of an international crook called—at the moment—Dompierre, who soon saw a way of utilizing Stelli's genius on a royal scale. Helene Brunesi, who in private life is—and really is, I believe—Madame Dompierre, readily lent her services to the enterprise."

"Quite so," nodded Mr. Carlyle, as his host paused.

"You see the whole sequence, of course?"

"Not exactly—not in detail," confessed Mr. Carlyle.

"Dompierre's idea was to gain access to some of the most celebrated cabinets of Europe and substitute Stelli's fabrications for the genuine coins. The princely collection of rarities that he would thus amass might be difficult to dispose of safely, but I have no doubt that he had matured his plans. Helene, in the person of Nina Brun, an Anglicised French parlourmaid—a part which she fills to perfection—was to obtain wax impressions of the most valuable pieces and to make the exchange when the counterfeits reached her. In this way it was obviously hoped that the fraud would not come to light until long after the real coins had been sold, and I gather that she has already done her work successfully in general houses. Then, impressed by her excellent references and capable manner, my housekeeper engaged her, and for a few weeks she went about her duties here. It was fatal to this detail of the scheme, however, that I have the misfortune to be blind. I am told that Helene has so innocently angelic a face as to disarm suspicion, but I was incapable of being impressed and that good material was thrown away. But one morning my material fingers—which, of course, knew nothing of Helene's angelic face—discovered an unfamiliar touch about the surface of my favourite Euclideas, and, although there was doubtless nothing to be seen, my critical sense of smell reported that wax had been recently pressed against it. I began to make discreet inquiries and in the meantime my cabinets went to the local bank for safety. Helene countered by receiving a telegram from Angiers, calling her to the death-bed of her aged mother. The aged mother succumbed; duty compelled Helene to remain at the side of her stricken patriarchal father, and doubtless The Turrets was written off the syndicate's operations as a bad debt."

"Very interesting," admitted Mr. Carlyle; "but at the risk of seeming obtuse"—his manner had become delicately chastened—"I must say that I fail to trace the inevitable connexion between Nina Brun and this particular forgery—assuming that it is a forgery."

"Set your mind at rest about that, Louis," replied Carrados. "It is a forgery, and it is a forgery that none but Pietro Stelli could have achieved. That is the essential connexion. Of course, there are accessories. A private detective coming urgently to see me with a notable tetradrachm in his pocket, which he announces to be the clue to a remarkable fraud—well, really, Louis, one scarcely needs to be blind to see through that."

"And Lord Seastoke? I suppose you happened to discover that Nina Brun had gone there?"

"No, I cannot claim to have discovered that, or I should certainly have warned him at once when I found out—only recently—about the gang. As a matter of fact, the last information I had of Lord Seastoke was a line in yesterday's *Morning Post* to the effect that he was still at Cairo. But many of these pieces—" He brushed his finger almost lovingly across the vivid chariot race that embellished the reverse of the coin, and broke off to remark: "You really ought to take up the subject, Louis. You have no idea how useful it might prove to you some day."

"I really think I must," replied Carlyle grimly. "Two hundred and fifty pounds the original of this cost, I believe."

"Cheap, too; it would make five hundred pounds in New York to-day. As I was saying, many are literally unique. This gem by Kimon is—here is his signature, you see; Peter is particularly good at lettering—and as I handled the genuine tetradrachm about two years ago, when Lord Seastoke exhibited it at a meeting of our society in Albemarle Street, there is nothing at all wonderful in my being able to fix the locale of your mystery. Indeed, I feel that I ought to apologize for it all being so simple."

"I think," remarked Mr. Carlyle, critically examining the loose threads on his left boot, "that the apology on that head would be more appropriate from me."

Sheer Melodrama

Edgar Wallace

Sheer Melodrama

IT was Mr. Reeder who planned the raid on Tommy Fenalow's snide shop and worked out all the details except the composition of the raiding force. Tommy had a depot at Golders Green whither trusted agents came, purchasing Treasury notes for £7 10s. per hundred, or £70 a thousand. Only experts could tell the difference between Tommy's currency and that authorised by and printed for H.M. Treasury. They were the right shades of brown and green, the numbers were of issued series, the paper was exact. They were printed in Germany at £3 a thousand, and Tommy made thousands per cent. profit.

Mr. Reeder discovered all about Tommy's depot in his spare time, and reported the matter to his chief, the Director of Public Prosecutions. From Whitehall to Scotland Yard is two minutes' walk, and in just that time the information got across.

'Take Inspector Greyash with you and superintend the raid,' were his instructions.

He left the inspector to make all the arrangements, and amongst those who learnt of the projected coup was a certain detective officer who made more money from questionable associations than he did from Government. This officer 'blew' the raid to Tommy, and when Mr. Reeder and his bold men arrived at Golders Green, there was Tommy and three friends playing a quiet game of auction bridge, and the only Treasury notes discoverable were veritable old masters.

'It is a pity,' sighed J. G. when they reached the street; 'a great pity. Of course I hadn't the least idea that Detective-Constable Wilshore was in our party. He is--er--not quite loyal.'

'Wilshore?' asked the officer, aghast. 'Do you mean he "blew" the raid to Tommy?'

Mr. Reeder scratched his nose and said gently, that he thought so.

'He has quite a big income from various sources--by the way, he banks with the Midland and Derbyshire, and his account is in his wife's maiden name. I tell you this in case--er--it may be useful.'

It was useful enough to secure the summary ejection of the unfaithful Wilshore from the force, but it was not sufficiently useful to catch Tommy, whose parting words were:

'You're clever, Reeder; but you've got to be lucky to catch me!'

Tommy was in the habit of repeating this scrap of conversation to such as were interested. It was an encounter of which he was justifiably proud, for few dealers in 'slush' and 'snide' have ever come up against Mr. J. G. and got away with it.

'It's worth a thousand pounds to me--ten thousand! I'd pay that money to make J. G. look sick, anyway, the old dog! I guess the Yard will think twice before it tries to shop me again, and that's the real kick in the raid. J. G.'s name is Jonah at head-quarters, and if I can do anything to help, it will be mud!'

To a certain Ras Lal Punjabi, an honoured (and paying) guest, Mr. Fenalow told this story, with curious results.

A good wine tastes best in its own country, and a man may drink sherry by the cask in Jerez de la Frontena and take no ill, whereas if he attempted so much as a bottle in Fleet Street, he would suffer cruelly. So also does the cigarette of Egypt preserve its finest bouquet for such as smoke it in the lounge of a Cairo hotel.

Crime is yet another quantity which does not bear transplanting. The American safe-blower may flourish in France just so long as he acquires by diligent study, and confines himself to, the Continental method. It is possible for the European thief to gain a fair livelihood in oriental countries, but there is no more tragic sight in the world than the Eastern mind endeavouring to adapt itself to the complexities of European roguery.

Ras Lal Punjabi enjoyed a reputation in Indian police circles as the cleverest native criminal India had ever produced. Beyond a short term in Poona Jail, Ras Lal had never seen the interior of a prison, and such was his fame in native circles that, during this short period of incarceration, prayers for his deliverance were offered at certain temples, and it was agreed that he would never have been convicted at all but for some pretty hard swearing on the part of the police commissioner sahib--and anyway, all sahibs hang together, and it was a European judge who sent him down.

He was a general practitioner of crime, with a leaning towards specialisation in jewel thefts. A man of excellent and even gentlemanly appearance, with black and shiny hair parted at the side and curling up over one brow in an inky wave, he spoke English, Hindustani and Tamil very well indeed, had a sketchy knowledge of the law (on his visiting cards was the inscription 'Failed LL.B.') and a very full acquaintance with the science of precious stones.

During Mr. Ras Las Punjabi's brief rest in Poona, the police commissioner sahib, whose unromantic name was Smith, married a not very good-looking girl with a lot of money. Smith Sahib knew that beauty was only skin deep and that she had a kind heart, which is notoriously preferable to the garniture of coronets. It was honestly a love match. Her father owned jute mills in Calcutta, and on festive occasions, such as the Governor-General's ball, she carried several lakhs of rupees on her person; but even rich people are loved for themselves alone.

Ras Lal owed his imprisonment to an unsuccessful attempt he had made upon two strings of pearls the property of the lady in question, and when he learnt, on his return to freedom, that Smith Sahib had married the resplendent girl and had gone to England, he very naturally attributed the hatred and bitterness of Smith Sahib to purely personal causes, and swore vengeance.

Now in India the business of every man is the business of his servants. The preliminary inquiries, over which an English or

American jewel thief would spend a small fortune, can be made at the cost of a few annas. When Ras Lal came to England he found that he had overlooked this very important fact.

Smith, sahib and memsahib, were out of town; they were, in fact, on the high seas en route for New York when Ras Lal was arrested on the conventional charge of 'being a suspected person.' Ras had shadowed the Smiths' butler, and, having induced him to drink, had offered him immense sums to reveal the place, receptacle, drawer, safe, box or casket wherein 'Mrs. Commissioner Smith's' jewels were kept. His excuse for asking, namely, that he had had a wager with his brother that the jewels were kept under the Memsahib's bed, showed a lamentable lack of inventive power. The butler, an honest man, though a drinker of beer, informed the police. Ras Lal and his friend and assistant Ram were arrested, brought before a magistrate, and would have been discharged but for the fact that Mr. J. G. Reeder saw the record of the case and was able to supply from his own files very important particulars of the dark man's past. Therefore Mr. Ras Lal was sent down to hard labour for six months, but, what was more maddening, the story of his ignominious failure was, he guessed, broadcast throughout India.

This was the thought which distracted him in his lonely cell at Wormwood Scrubbs. What would India think of him?--he would be the scorn of the bazaars, 'the mocking point of third-rate mediocrities,' to use his own expression. And automatically he switched his hate from Smith Sahib to one Mr. J. G. Reeder. And his hate was very real, more real because of the insignificance and unimportance of this Reeder Sahib, whom he likened to an ancient cow, a sneaking weasel, and other things less translatable. And in the six months of his durance he planned desperate and earnest acts of reprisal.

Released from prison, he decided that the moment was not ripe for a return to India. He wished to make a close study of Mr. J. G.

Reeder and his habits, and, being a man with plenty of money, he could afford the time, and, as it happened, could mix business with pleasure.

Mr. Tommy Fenalow found means of getting in touch with the gentleman from the Orient whilst he was in Wormwood Scrubbs, and the handsome limousine that met Ras Lal at the gates of the Scrubbs when he came out of jail was both hired and occupied by Tommy, a keen business man, who had been offered by his German printer a new line of one-hundred-rupee notes that might easily develop into a most profitable side-line.

'You come along and lodge at my expense, boy,' said the sympathetic Tommy, who was very short, very stout, and had eyes that bulged like a pug dog's. 'You've been badly treated by old Reeder, and I'm going to tell you a way of getting back on him, with no risk and a ninety per cent profit. Listen, a friend of mine--'

It was never Tommy who had snide for sale: invariably the hawker of forged notes was a mysterious 'friend.'

So Ras was lodged in a service flat which formed part of a block owned by Mr. Fenalow, who was a very rich man indeed. Some weeks after this, Tommy crossed St. James's Street to intercept his old enemy.

'Good morning, Mr. Reeder.'

Mr. J. G. Reeder stopped and turned back.

'Good morning, Mr. Fenalow,' he said, with that benevolent solicitude which goes so well with a frock coat and square-toed shoes. 'I am glad to see that you are out again, and I do trust that you will now find a more--er--legitimate outlet for your undoubted talents.'

Tommy went angrily red.

'I haven't been in "stir" and you know it, Reeder! It wasn't for want of trying on your part. But you've got to be something more than clever to catch me--you've got to be lucky! Not that there's anything to catch me over--I've never done a crook thing in my life, as you well know.'

He was so annoyed that the lighter exchanges of humour he had planned slipped from his memory.

He had an appointment with Ras Lal, and the interview was entirely satisfactory. Mr. Ras Lal made his way that night to an uncomfortably situated rendezvous and there met his new friend.

'This is the last place in the world old man Reeder would dream of searching,' said Tommy enthusiastically, 'and if he did he would find nothing. Before he could get into the building, the stuff would be put out of sight.'

'It is a habitation of extreme convenience,' said Ras Lal.

'It is yours, boy,' replied Tommy magnificently. 'I only keep this place to get-in and put-out. The stuff's not here for an hour and the rest of the time the store's empty. As I say, old man Reeder has gotta be something more than clever--he's gotta be lucky!'

At parting he handed his client a key, and with that necessary instrument tendered a few words of advice and warning.

'Never come here till late. The police patrol passes the end of the road at ten, one o'clock and four. When are you leaving for India?'

'On the twenty-third,' said Ras, 'by which time I shall have uttered a few reprisals on that cad Reeder.'

'I shouldn't like to be in his shoes,' said Tommy, who could afford to be sycophantic, for he had in his pocket two hundred pounds' worth of real money which Ras had paid in advance for a vaster quantity of money which was not so real.

It was a few days after this that Ras Lal went to the Orpheum Theatre, and it was no coincidence that he went there on the same night that Mr. Reeder escorted a pretty lady to the same place of amusement.

When Mr. J. G. Reeder went to the theatre (and his going at all was contingent upon his receiving a complimentary ticket) he invariably chose a melodrama, and preferably a Drury Lane melodrama, where to the thrill of the actors' speeches was added the amazing action of wrecked railway trains, hair-raising shipwrecks and terrific horse-races in which the favourite won by a nose. Such things may seem wildly improbable to blasé dramatic critics--especially favourites winning--but Mr. Reeder saw actuality in all such presentations.

Once he was inveigled into sitting through a roaring farce, and was the only man in the house who did not laugh. He was, indeed, such a depressing influence that the leading lady sent a passionate request to the manager that 'the miserable-looking old man in the middle of the front row' should have his money returned and be requested to leave the theatre. Which, as Mr. Reeder had come in on a free ticket, placed the manager in a very awkward predicament.

Invariably he went unaccompanied, for he had no friends, and fifty-two years had come and gone without bringing to his life romance or the melting tenderness begot of dreams. In some manner Mr. Reeder had become acquainted with a girl who was like no other girl with whom he had been brought into contact. Her name was Belman, Margaret Belman, and he had saved her life, though this fact did not occur to him as frequently as the recollection that he had imperilled that life before he had saved it. And he had a haunting sense of guilt for quite another reason.

He was thinking of her one day--he spent his life thinking about people, though the majority of these were less respectable than Miss Margaret Belman. He supposed that she would marry the very good-looking young man who met her street car at the corner of the Embankment every morning and returned with her to the Lewisham High Road every night. It would be a very nice wedding, with hired motor-cars, and the vicar himself performing the ceremony, and a wedding breakfast provided by the local caterer, following which bride and bridegroom would be photographed on the lawn surrounded by their jovial but unprepossessing relatives. And after this, one specially hired car would take them to Eastbourne for an expensive honeymoon. And after that all the humdrum and scrapings of life, rising through villadom to a little car of their own and Saturday afternoon tennis parties.

Mr. Reeder sighed deeply. How much more satisfactory was the stage drama, where all the trouble begins in the first act and is satisfactorily settled in the last. He fingered absently the two slips of green paper that had come to him that morning. Row A, seats 17 and 18. They had been sent by a manager who was under some obligation to him. The theatre was the Orpheum, home of transpontine drama, and the play was 'The Fires of Vengeance.' It looked like being a pleasant evening.

He took an envelope from the rack, addressed it to the box office, and had begun to write the accompanying letter returning the surplus voucher, when an idea occurred to him. He owed Miss Margaret Belman something, and the debt was on his conscience. He had once, for reasons of expediency, described her as his wife. This preposterous claim had been made to appease a mad woman, it is true, but it had been made. She was now holding a good position--a secretaryship at one of the political head-quarters, for which post she had to thank Mr. J. G. Reeder, if she only knew it.

He took up the 'phone and called her number, and, after the normal delay, heard her voice.

'Er--Miss Belman,' Mr. Reeder coughed, 'I have--er--two tickets for a theatre tonight. I wonder if you would care to go?'

Her astonishment was almost audible.

'That is very nice of you, Mr. Reeder. I should love to come with you.'

Mr. J. G. Reeder turned pale.

'What I mean is, I have two tickets--I thought perhaps that your--er--your--er--that somebody else would like to go--what I mean was--'

He heard a gentle laugh at the other end of the phone.

'What you mean is that you don't wish to take me,' she said, and for a man of his experience he blundered badly.

'I should esteem it an honour to take you,' he said, in terror that he should offend her, 'but the truth is, I thought--'

'I will meet you at the theatre--which is it? Orpheum--how lovely! At eight o'clock.'

Mr. Reeder put down the instrument, feeling limp and moist. It is the truth that he had never taken a lady to any kind of social function in his life, and as there grew upon him the tremendous character of this adventure he was overwhelmed and breathless. A murderer waking from dreams of revelry to find himself in the condemned cell suffered no more poignant emotions than Mr. Reeder, torn from the smooth if treacherous currents of life and drawing nearer and nearer to the horrid vortex of unusualness.

'Bless me,' said Mr. Reeder, employing a strictly private expression which was reserved for his own crises.

He employed in his private office a young woman who combined a meticulous exactness in the filing of documents with a complete absence of those attractions which turn men into gods, and in other days set the armies of Perseus moving towards the walls of Troy. She was invariably addressed by Mr. Reeder as 'Miss.' He believed her name to be 'Oliver.' She was in truth a married lady with two children, but her nuptials had been celebrated without his knowledge.

To the top floor of a building in Regent Street Mr. Reeder repaired for instruction and guidance.

'It is not--er--a practice of mine to--er--accompany ladies to the theatre, and I am rather at a loss to know what is expected of me, the more so since the young lady is--er--a stranger to me.'

His frosty-visaged assistant sneered secretly. At Mr. Reeder's time of life, when such natural affections as were not atrophied should in decency be fossilised!

He jotted down her suggestions.

'Chocolates indeed? Where can one procure--? Oh, yes, I remember seeing the attendants sell them. Thank you so much, Miss--er--'

And as he went out, closing the door carefully behind him, she sneered openly.

'They all go wrong at seventy,' she said insultingly.

Margaret hardly knew what to expect when she came into the flamboyant foyer of the Orpheum. What was the evening equivalent to the square-topped derby and the tightly-buttoned frock coat of ancient design which he favoured in the hours of business? She would have passed the somewhat elegantly dressed gentleman in the correct pique waistcoat and the perfectly tied butterfly bow, only he claimed her attention.

'Mr. Reeder!' she gasped.

It was indeed Mr. Reeder: with not so much as a shirt-stud wrong; with a suit of the latest mode, and shoes glossy and V-toed. For Mr. Reeder, like many other men, dressed according to his inclination in business hours, but accepted blindly the instructions of his tailor in the matter of fancy raiment. Mr. J. G. Reeder was never conscious of his clothing, good or bad--he was, however, very conscious of his strange responsibility.

He took her cloak (he had previously purchased programmes and a large box of chocolates, which he carried by its satin ribbon). There was a quarter of an hour to wait before the curtain went up, and Margaret felt it incumbent upon her to offer an explanation.

'You spoke about "somebody" else; do you mean Roy--the man who sometimes meets me at Westminster?'

Mr. Reeder had meant that young man. 'He and I were good friends,' she said, 'no more than that--we aren't very good friends anymore.'

She did not say why. She might have explained in a sentence if she had said that Roy's mother held an exalted opinion of her only son's qualities, physical and mental, and that Roy thoroughly endorsed his mother's judgment, but she did not.

'Ah!' said Mr. Reeder unhappily. Soon after this the orchestra drowned further conversation, for they were sitting in the first row near to the noisiest of the brass and not far removed from the shrillest of the wood-wind. In odd moments, through the thrilling first act, she stole a glance at her companion. She expected to find this man mildly amused or slightly bored by the absurd contrast between the realities which he knew and the theatricalities which were presented on the stage. But whenever she looked, he was absorbed in the action of the play; she could almost feel him tremble when the hero was strapped to a log and thrown into the boiling mountain stream, and when the stage Jove was rescued on the fall of the curtain, she heard, with something like stupefaction, Mr. Reeder's quivering sigh of relief.

'But surely, Mr. Reeder, this bores you?' she protested, when the lights in the auditorium went up.

'This--you mean the play--bore me? Good gracious, no! I think it is very fine, remarkably fine.'

'But it isn't life, surely? The story is so wildly improbable, and the incidents--oh, yes, I'm enjoying it all; please don't look so worried! Only I thought that you, who knew so much about criminology--is that the word?--would be rather amused.'

Mr. Reeder was looking very anxiously at her.

'I'm afraid it is not the kind of play--'

'Oh, but it is--I love melodrama. But doesn't it strike you as being--far-fetched? For instance, that man being chained to a log, and the mother agreeing to her son's death?'

Mr. Reeder rubbed his nose thoughtfully.

'The Bermondsey gang chained Harry Salter to a plank, turned it over and let him down, just opposite Billingsgate Market. I was at the execution of Tod Rowe, and he admitted it on the scaffold. And it was "Lee" Pearson's mother who poisoned him at Teddington to get his insurance money so that she could marry again. I was at the trial and she took her sentence laughing--now what else was there in that act? Oh, yes, I remember: the proprietor of the saw-mill tried to get the young lady to marry him by threatening to send her father to prison. That has been done hundreds of times--only in a worse way. There is really nothing very extravagant about a melodrama except the prices of the seats, and I usually get my tickets free!'

She listened, at first dumbfounded and then with a gurgle of amusement.

'How queer--and yet--well, frankly, I have only met melodrama once in life, and even now I cannot believe it. What happens in the next act?'

Mr. Reeder consulted his programme.

'I rather believe that the young woman in the white dress is captured and removed to the harem of an Eastern potentate,' he said precisely, and this time the girl laughed aloud.

'Have you a parallel for that?' she asked triumphantly, and Mr. Reeder was compelled to admit that he knew no exact parallel, but--

'It is rather a remarkable coincidence,' he said, 'a very remarkable coincidence!'

She looked at her programme, wondering if she had overlooked anything so very remarkable.

'There is at this moment, watching me from the front row of the dress circle--I beg you not to turn your head--one who, if he is not a potentate, is undoubtedly Eastern; there are, in fact, two dark-complexioned gentlemen, but only one may be described as important.'

'But why are they watching you?' she asked in surprise.

'Possibly,' said Mr. Reeder solemnly, 'because I look so remarkable in evening dress.'

One of the dark-complexioned gentlemen turned to his companion at this moment.

'It is the woman he travels with every day; she lives in the same street, and is doubtless more to him than anybody in the world, Ram. See how she laughs in his face and how the old so-and-so looks at her! When men come to his great age they grow silly about women. This thing can be done to-night. I would sooner die than go back to Bombay without accomplishing my design upon this such-and-such and so-forth.'

Ram, his chauffeur, confederate and fellow jail-bird, who was cast in a less heroic mould, and had, moreover, no personal vendetta, suggested in haste that the matter should be thought over.

'I have cogitated every hypothesis to its logical conclusions,' said Ras Lal in English.

'But, master,' said his companion urgently, 'would it not be wise to leave this country and make a fortune with the new money which the fat little man can sell to us?'

'Vengeance is mine,' said Ras Lal in English.

He sat through the next act which, as Mr. Reeder had truly said, depicted the luring of an innocent girl into the hateful clutches of a Turkish pasha and, watching the development of the plot, his own scheme underwent revision. He did not wait to see what happened in the third and fourth acts--there were certain preparations to be made.

'I still think that, whilst the story is awfully thrilling, it is awfully impossible,' said Margaret, as they moved slowly through the crowded vestibule. 'In real life--in civilised countries, I mean--masked men do not suddenly appear from nowhere with pistols and say "Hands up!"--not really, do they, Mr. Reeder?' she coaxed.

Mr. Reeder murmured a reluctant agreement.

'But I have enjoyed it tremendously!' she said with enthusiasm, and looking down into the pink face Mr. Reeder felt a curious sensation which was not entirely pleasure and not wholly pain.

'I am very glad,' he said.

Both the dress-circle and the stalls disgorged into the foyer, and he was looking round for a face he had seen when he arrived. But neither Ras Lal nor his companion in misfortune was visible. Rain was falling dismally, and it was some time before he found a cab.

'Luxury upon luxury,' smiled Margaret, when he took his place by her side. 'You may smoke if you wish.'

Mr. Reeder took a paper packet of cigarettes from his waistcoat pocket, selected a limp cylinder, and lit it.

'No plays are quite like life, my dear young lady,' he said, as he carefully pushed the match through the space between the top of the window and the frame. 'Melodramas appeal most to me because of their idealism.'

She turned and stared at him.

'Idealism?' she repeated incredulously.

He nodded.

'Have you ever noticed that there is nothing sordid about a melodrama? I once saw a classical drama--"Oedipus"--and it made me feel sick. In melodrama even the villains are heroic and the inevitable and unvarying moral is "Truth crushed to earth will rise again"--isn't that idealism? And they are wholesome. There are no sex problems; unpleasant things are never shown in an attractive light--you come away uplifted.'

'If you are young enough,' she smiled.

'One should always be young enough to rejoice in the triumph of virtue,' said Mr. Reeder soberly.

They crossed Westminster Bridge and bore left to the New Kent Road. Through the rain-blurred windows J. G. picked up the familiar landmarks and offered a running commentary upon them in the manner of a guide. Margaret had not realised before that history was made in South London.

'There used to be a gibbet here--this ugly-looking goods station was the London terminus of the first railways--Queen Alexandra drove from there when she came to be married--the thoroughfare on the right after we pass the Canal bridge is curiously named Bird-in-Bush Road--'

A big car had drawn level with the cab, and the driver was shouting something to the cabman. Even the suspicious Mr. Reeder suspected no more than an exchange of offensiveness, till the cab suddenly turned into the road he had been speaking about. The car had fallen behind, but now drew abreast.

'Probably the main road is up,' said J. G., and at that moment the cab slowed and stopped.

He was reaching out for the handle when the door was pulled open violently, and in the uncertain light Mr. Reeder saw a broad-shouldered man standing in the road.

'Alight quickly!'

In the man's hand was a long, black Colt, and his face was covered from chin to forehead by a mask.

'Quickly--and keep your hands erect!'

Mr. Reeder stepped out into the rain and reached to close the door.

'The female also--come, miss!'

'Here--what's the game--you told me the New Cross Road was blocked.' It was the cabman talking.

'Here is a five--keep your mouth shut.'

The masked man thrust a note at the driver.

'I don't want your money--'

'You require my bullet in your bosom perchance, my good fellow?' asked Ras Lal sardonically.

Margaret had followed her escort into the road by this time. The car had stopped just behind the cab. With the muzzle of the pistol stuck into his back, Mr. Reeder walked to the open door and entered. The girl followed, and the masked man jumped after them and closed the door. Instantly the interior was flooded with light.

'This is a considerable surprise to a clever and intelligent police detective?'

Their captor sat on the opposite seat, his pistol on his knees. Through the holes of the black mask a pair of brown eyes gleamed malevolently. But Mr. Reeder's interest was in the girl. The shock had struck the colour from her face, but he observed with thankfulness that her chief emotion was not fear. She was numb with amazement, and was stricken speechless.

The car had circled and was moving swiftly back the way they had come. He felt the rise of the Canal bridge, and then the machine turned abruptly to the right and began the descent of a steep hill. They were running towards Rotherhithe--he had an extraordinary knowledge of London's topography.

The journey was a short one. He felt the car wheels bump over an uneven roadway for a hundred yards, the body rocking uncomfortably, and then with a jar of brakes the machine stopped suddenly.

They were on a narrow muddy lane. On one side rose the arches of a railway aqueduct, on the other an open space bounded by a high fence. Evidently the driver had pulled up short of their destination, for they had to squelch and slide through the thick mud for another fifty yards before they came to a narrow gateway in the fence. Through this they struck a cinder-path leading to a square building, which Mr. Reeder guessed was a small factory of some kind. Their conductor flashed a lamp on the door, and in weatherworn letters the detective read:

'The Storn-Filton Leather Company.'

'Now!' said the man, as he turned a switch. 'Now, my false-swearing and corrupt police official, I have a slight bill to settle with you.'

They were in a dusty lobby, enclosed on three sides by matchboard walls.

'"Account" is the word you want, Ras Lal,' murmured Mr. Reeder.

For a moment the man was taken aback, and then, snatching the mask from his face:

'I am Ras Lal! And you shall repent it! For you and for your young missus this is indeed a cruel night of anxiety!'

Mr. Reeder did not smile at the quaint English. The gun in the man's hand spoke all languages without error, and could be as fatal in the hands of an unconscious humorist as if it were handled by the most savage of purists.

And he was worried about the girl: she had not spoken a word since their capture. The colour had come back to her cheeks, and that was a good sign. There was, too, a light in her eyes which Reeder could not associate with fear.

Ras Lal, taking down a long cord that hung on a nail in the wooden partition, hesitated.

'It is not necessary,' he said, with an elaborate shrug of shoulder; 'the room is sufficiently reconnoitred--you will be innocuous there.'

Flinging open a door, he motioned them to pass through and mount the bare stairs which faced them. At the top was a landing and a large steel door set in the solid brickwork.

Pulling back the iron bolt, he pushed at the door, and it opened with a squeak. It was a large room, and had evidently been used for the storage of something inflammable, for the walls and floor were of rough-faced concrete and above a dusty desk an inscription was painted, 'Danger. Don't smoke in this store.' There were no windows except one some eighteen inches square, the top of which was near the ceiling. In one corner of the room was a heap of grimy paper files, and on the desk a dozen small wooden boxes, one of which had been opened, for the nail-bristling lid was canted up at an angle.

'Make yourself content for half an hour or probably forty minutes,' said Ras Lal, standing in the doorway with his ostentatious revolver. 'At that time I shall come for your female; to-morrow she will be on a ship with me, bound for--ah, who knows where?'

'Shut the door as you go out,' said Mr. J. G. Reeder; 'there is an unpleasant draught.'

Mr. Tommy Fenalow came on foot at two o'clock in the morning and, passing down the muddy lane, his electric torch suddenly revealed car marks. Tommy stopped like a man shot. His knees trembled beneath him and his heart entered his throat at the narrowest end. For a while he was undecided whether it would be better to run or walk away. He had no intention of going forward. And then he heard a voice. It was Ras Lal's assistant, and he nearly swooned with joy. Stumbling forward, he came up to the shivering man.

'Did that fool boss of yours bring the car along here?' he asked in a whisper.

'Yas--Mr. Ras Lal,' said Ram with whom the English language was not a strong point.

'Then he's a fool!' growled Tommy. 'Gosh! he put my heart in my mouth!'

Whilst Ram was getting together sufficient English to explain what had happened, Tommy passed on. He found his client sitting in the lobby, a black cheroot between his teeth, a smile of satisfaction on his dark face.

'Welcome!' he said, as Tommy closed the door. 'We have trapped the weasel.'

'Never mind about the weasel,' said the other impatiently. 'Did you find the rupees?'

Ras Lal shook his head.

'But I left them in the store--ten thousand notes. I thought you'd have got them and skipped before this,' said Mr. Fenalow anxiously.

'I have something more important in the store--come and see my friend.'

He preceded the bewildered Tommy up the stairs, turned on the landing light and threw open the door.

'Behold--' he said, and said no more.

'Why, it is Mr. Fenalow!' said Mr. J. G.

One hand held a packet of almost life-like rupee notes; as for the other hand--

'You oughter known he carried a gun, you dam' black baboon,' hissed Tommy. 'An' to put him in a room where the stuff was, and a telephone!'

He was being driven to the local police station, and for the moment was attached to his companion by links of steel.

'It was a mere jest or a piece of practical joking, as I shall explain to the judge in the morning,' said Ras airily.

Tommy Fenalow's reply was unprintable.

Three o'clock boomed out from St. John's Church as Mr. Reeder accompanied an excited girl to the front door of her boarding-house.

'I can't tell you how I--I've enjoyed tonight,' she said.

Mr. Reeder glanced uneasily at the dark face of the house.

'I hope--er--your friends will not think it remarkable that you should return at such an hour--'

Despite her assurance, he went slowly home with an uneasy feeling that her name had in some way been compromised. And in melodrama, when a heroine's name is compromised, somebody has to marry her.

That was the disturbing thought that kept Mr. Reeder awake all night.

Author Biographies

Ernest Bramah

Ernest Bramah Smith was born was near Manchester in 1868. He was a poor student, and dropped out of the Manchester Grammar School when sixteen years old to go into the farming business. During his late teens, he began to contribute short stories and vignettes to the *Birmingham News*. A few years later, he moved to London's Grub Street - famous for its concentration of impoverished 'hack writers' – and eventually became editor of a number of journals.

Bramah found commercial and critical success with his first novel, *The Wallet of Kai Lung*, in 1900. The character of Kai Lang – a travelling storyteller in China – went on to feature in a number of his works, many of which featured fantasy elements such as dragons and gods, and utilised an idiosyncratic form of Mandarin English. Something of a recluse, Bramah also wrote political science fiction – in fact, his 1907 novel *The Secret of the League* was acknowledged by George Orwell as a forerunner to his famous novel *Nineteen Eighty-Four* – and even tried his hand at detective fiction. At the height of his fame, Bramah's mystery tales, featuring the blind detective Max Carrados, appeared alongside Sir Arthur Conan Doyle's *Sherlock Holmes* stories in the *Strand Magazine,* even occasionally outselling them. Bramah died in 1942, aged 74.

G. K. Chesterton

Gilbert Keith Chesterton was born in London in 1874. He studied at the Slade School of Art, and upon graduating began to work as a freelance journalist. By 1905, he had a regular and popular column with the *Illustrated London News,* and began to write on an array of topics. Over the course of his life, his literary output was incredibly diverse and highly prolific, ranging from philosophy and ontology to art criticism and detective fiction. However, he is probably best-remembered for his Christian apologetics, most notably in *Orthodoxy* (1908) and *The Everlasting Man* (1925). George Bernard Shaw dubbed Chesterton "a man of colossal genius," and of his fiction Argentine author Jorge Luis Borges said "Chesterton knew how to make the most of a detective story." Chesterton died in 1936, aged 62.

Charles Dickens

Charles John Huffam Dickens was born in Landport, Portsmouth in 1812. When he was ten years old, his family settled in Camden Town, a poor neighbourhood of London. A defining moment in the young Dickens' life came only two years later, when his father – the inspiration for the character of Mr Micawber in *David Copperfield* – was imprisoned in the Marshalsea debtor's prison. As a result, Dickens was sent to Warren's blacking factory, where he worked in appalling conditions and gained a first-hand acquaintance with poverty. After three years Dickens resumed his education, but the experience was highly formative for him, and would later be fictionalised in both *David Copperfield* and *Great Expectations*.

Dickens' writing career began in around 1830, when he started to write for the journals *The Mirror of Parliament* and *The True Sun*. Three years later, he became parliamentary journalist for *The Morning Chronicle*, and also began to have some successes with his fiction: His first short story, A 'Dinner at Popular Walk', appeared in the *Monthly Magazine* in December of 1833, and his first book, a collection titled *Sketches by Boz*, was published in 1836. However, his real breakthrough came in 1837, with the serialised publication of *Posthumous Papers of the Pickwick Club* – the work was hugely popular, and transformed Dickens into a well-known literary figure.

Over the next few years, at an almost incredible rate, Dickens wrote *Oliver Twist* (1837-39), *Nicholas Nickleby* (1838-39) and *The Old Curiosity Shop* and *Barnaby Rudge* (1840-41). In 1842, he travelled with his wife to the United States and Canada (where he gave lectures denouncing slavery), and in the years following produced his five 'Christmas Books'. During the fifties, after brief spells living in Italy and Switzerland, he continued to write at a seemingly inexhaustible pace, producing some of his best work:

David Copperfield (1849-50), Bleak House (1852-53), Hard Times (1854), Little *Dorrit* (1857), *A Tale of Two Cities* (1859), and *Great Expectations* (1861).

During the latter stages of his life, Dickens turned his focus from writing to giving readings. In 1869, during one such reading, he collapsed, showing symptoms of a mild stroke. He died at home one year later, aged 58. He was buried in the Poets' Corner of Westminster Abbey, where the inscription on his tomb reads: "He was a sympathiser to the poor, the suffering, and the oppressed; and by his death, one of England's greatest writers is lost to the world." Dickens is now regarded as the greatest writer of the Victorian era, and one of the greatest English authors since Shakespeare.

Sir Arthur Conan Doyle

Arthur Conan Doyle was born in Edinburgh, Scotland, in 1859. It was between 1876 and 1881, while studying medicine at the University of Edinburgh, that he began writing short stories, and his first piece was published in *Chambers's Edinburgh Journal* before he was 20. In 1882, Conan Doyle opened an independent medical practice in Southsea, near Portsmouth. It was here, while waiting for patients, that he turned to writing fiction again, composing his first novel, *The Narrative of John Smith*.

In 1887, Conan Doyle's first significant work, *A Study in Scarlet,* appeared in *Beeton's Christmas Annual*. It featured the first appearance of detective Sherlock Holmes, the protagonist who was to eventually make Conan Doyle's reputation. A prolific writer, Conan Doyle continued to produce a range of fictional works over the following years. In 1893, feeling that the character of Sherlock Holmes was distracting him from his historical novels, he had Holmes apparently plunge to his death in the short story 'The Final Problem'. However, eight years later, following a public outcry from his readers, Conan Doyle 'resurrected' the detective in what is now widely regarded as his *magnum opus, The Hound of the Baskervilles.*

Sherlock Holmes went on to feature in fifty-six short stories and four novels, cementing Conan Doyle's reputation as probably the most famous crime writer of all time. Aside from his fiction, Conan Doyle was also a passionate political campaigner – a pamphlet he published in 1902, defending the United Kingdom's much-criticised role in the Boer War, is seen as a major contributor to his receiving of a knighthood in that same year.

In his later years, following the death of his son in World War I, Conan Doyle became deeply interested in spiritualism and psychic phenomena, producing several works on the subjects and engaging in a very public friendship and falling out with the American magician Harry Houdini. He died of a heart attack while living in East Sussex in 1930, aged 71.

R. Austin Freeman

Richard Austin Freeman was born in London in 1862. He first trained as an apothecary and then studied medicine at Middlesex Hospital, qualifying in 1887. He entered the Colonial Service and was sent to Accra (present-day Ghana) on the Gold Coast, but returned in 1891, aged 29, suffering from blackwater fever.

Finding himself unable to secure a permanent medical position, Freeman turned to writing fiction. The first story featuring his well-known protagonist Dr. Thorndyke – a medico-legal forensic investigator – was published in 1907, and although Freeman's early works were seen as simple homages to his contemporary, Sir Arthur Conan Doyle, he quickly developed his own style: The 'inverted detective story', in which the identity of the criminal is shown from the beginning, and the story then describes the detective's attempt to solve the mystery. Freeman's writing was interrupted by the First World War, during which he served as a Captain in the Royal Army Medical Corps, but after the armistice he produced a Thorndyke novel almost every year until his death in 1943.

Amongst Freeman's best-known works are the short stories 'The Red Thumb Mark' (1907), 'The Case of Oscar Brodski' (1912), and the novels *The Mystery of Angelina Frood* (1924), *As a Thief in the Night* (1928), *The Penrose Mystery* (1936), *The Stoneware Monkey* (1938) and *Mr. Polton Explains* (1940). Although overshadowed by other writers of his era, Freeman has undergone something of a critical revival in recent years: Raymond Chandler called him "a wonderful performer" with "no equal in his genre," and in 2008 *The Independent* included him in their 'Forgotten Authors' series, stating that "his 30-odd books are certainly worth rediscovery."

Anna Katharine Green

Anna Katharine Green was born in Brooklyn, New York, USA in 1846. She aspired to be a writer from a young age, and corresponded with Ralph Waldo Emerson during her late teens. When her poetry failed to gain recognition, Green produced her first and best-known novel, *The Leavenworth Case* (1878). Praised by Wilkie Collins, the novel was year's bestseller, establishing Green's reputation.

Green went on to publish around forty books, including *A Strange Disappearance* (1880), *Hand and Ring* (1883), *The Mill Mystery* (1886), *Behind Closed Doors* (1888), *Forsaken Inn* (1890), *Marked "Personal"* (1893), *Miss Hurd: An Enigma* (1894),
The Doctor, His Wife, and the Clock (1895),
The Affair Next Door (1897), *Lost Man's Lane* (1898), *Agatha Webb* (1899), *The Circular Study* (1900), *The Filigree Ball* (1903), *The House in the Mist* (1905), *The Millionaire Baby* (1905), *The Woman in the Alcove* (1906), *The Sword of Damocles* (1909), *The House of the Whispering Pines* (1910), *Initials Only* (1911), *Dark Hollow* (1914), *The Mystery of the Hasty Arrow* (1917), *The Step on the Stair* (1923).

Green wrote at a time when fiction, and especially crime fiction, was dominated by men. However, she is now credited with shaping detective fiction into its classic form, and developing the trope of the recurring detective. Her main character was detective Ebenezer Gryce of the New York Metropolitan Police Force. In three novels, he is assisted by the spinster Amelia Butterworth – the prototype for Miss Marple, Miss Silver and other literary creations. Green also invented the 'girl detective' with the character of Violet Strange, a debutante with a secret life as a sleuth. She died in 1935 in Buffalo, New York, aged 88.

Edgar Allan Poe

Edgar Allan Poe was born in Boston, Massachusetts in 1809. He was left an orphan at a very young age, following the abscondence of his father and subsequent death of his mother, but was taken in by a couple from Richmond, Virginia. After a brief spell living in England and Scotland, Poe enrolled at the newly-established University of Virginia. However, after just one semester, having become estranged from his foster father due to gambling debts, and finding himself unable to fund his studies, he dropped out. In 1827, aged 18, Poe travelled back to Boston, the city of his birth.

By now in severe financial trouble, Poe lied about his age in order to enlist in the army. After spending two years posted to South Carolina, and having failed as an officer's cadet at West Point, Poe left the military by getting deliberately court-martialled. He left for New York in 1831, where he released his third collection of poems, the first two having received almost zero attention. Not long after its publication, in March of 1831, Poe returned to Baltimore.

From 1831 onwards, Poe began in earnest to try and make a living as a writer, and turned from poetry to prose. Despite often finding himself penniless, and frequently having to move city to stay in employment as a critic, during the thirties and forties Poe published a good amount of fiction. Most of his best known short-stories, such as 'The Tell Tale Heart,' 'Ligeia', 'William Wilson' and 'The Fall of the House of Usher', were published between 1835 and 1845. In January 1845, Poe published his poem 'The Raven', which – despite fact that he only received $9 for it – was a great success, turning him overnight into something of a household name.

Poe died in 1849, aged just 40. The circumstances were somewhat odd; he was found wandering the streets of Baltimore at five in the morning, delirious and wearing someone else's clothes, and he repeatedly cried out "Reynolds!" during the hours before his death. The cause of death remains a mystery, with everything from epilepsy to rabies cited. However, whatever the reason behind his unusual passing, Poe's legacy is a formidable one: He is seen today as one of the greatest practitioners of Gothic and detective fiction that ever lived, and popular culture is replete with references to him.

Edgar Wallace

Richard Horatio Edgar Wallace was born in London, England in 1875. He received his early education at St. Peter's School and the Board School, but after a frenetic teens involving a rash engagement and frequently changing employment circumstances, Wallace went into the military. He served in the Royal West Kent Regiment in England and then as part of the Medical Staff Corps stationed in South Africa. However, Wallace disliked army life, finding it too physically testing. Eventually he managed to work his way into the press corps, becoming a war correspondent with the *Daily Mail* in 1898 during the Boer War. It was during this time that Wallace met Rudyard Kipling, a man he greatly admired.

In 1902, Wallace became editor of the *Rand Daily Mail,* earning a handsome salary. However, a dislike of "economising" and a lavish lifestyle saw him constantly in debt. Whilst in the Balkans covering the Russo-Japanese War, Wallace found the inspiration for *The Four Just Men,* published in 1905. This novel is now regarded as the prototype of modern thriller novels. However, by 1908, due to more terrible financial management, Wallace was penniless again, and he and his wife wound up living in a virtual slum in London. A lifeline came in the form of his *Sanders of the River* stories, serialized in a magazine of the day, which (despite being seen to contain pro-imperialist and racist overtones today) were highly popular, and sparked two decades of prolific output from Wallace.

Over the rest of his life, Wallace produced some 173 books and wrote 17 plays. These were largely adventure narratives with elements of crime or mystery, and usually combined a bombastic sensationalism with hammy violence. Arguably his best – and certainly his most successful, sparking as it did a semi-successful stint in Hollywood – work is his 1925 novel *The Gaunt Stranger,* later renamed *The Ringer* for the stage.

Wallace died suddenly in Beverly Hills, California in 1932, aged 57. At the time of his death, he had been earning what would today be considered a multi-million pound salary, yet incredibly, was hugely in debt, with no cash to his name. Sadly, he never got to see his most successful work – the 'gorilla picture' script he had earlier helped pen, which just a year after his death became the 1933 classic, *King Kong*.